THE MEANING OF CHRITMA

Hettie Ashwin

Published by Slipperygrip

Paperback
ISBN: 9782491490348
Pocket Edition
ISBN: 9782491490355

Books by Hettie Ashwin

Humour

(12 ludicrously laugh out loud series)

Literary Licence
The Reluctant Messiah
Mr Tripp buys a lifestyle
Barney's Test
The Truffle War
Fat Bits
Murder! Mayhem! and lesser cuts of meat.
I'd rather glue me nut sack to a bullet train
Nowhere near Anywhere
A Fate worse than Death
Value Added
Soup to Nuts
Aa & Ida's bold adventure

Humorous Memoir

Boat to Baguette
Living it up in France

Thriller

The Crowing of the Beast

Speculative fiction

The Mask of Deceit
Pi - trilogy

Short Stories

After the Rains & other Stories
A shilling on the Bar

Novella series.

A strange kind of Paradise. 1-5

Non fiction

Productive Procrastination

✦

Advertising –
a judicious mixture
of
flattery and threats.

Northrop Frye

✦ CHAPTER 1

Earl Schuler had called it the 'graveyard of bright ideas.' Lois looked at the dusty boxes, the rolled up posters, the ring binders languishing in the dank archives of **Catchpole & Wood Advertising** and wondered, not for the first time, why she had fought for a place at University, put up with more than her fair share of 'the male gaze' and persevered 'in a man's world dearie', to get a degree in marketing when all they wanted her to do was clean up, proofread, and put the kettle on.

She picked up a poster, scaring a resident cockroach and upset a cardboard box. A statue tumbled out to land at her feet. A gold statue. The plaque said;

Earl Schuler
For advertising excellence.
WACK-O

A finger was held high in exultation.

Of course a girl can dream. Lois Mackenzie dreamed of a bit of advertising excellence herself. She only needed to make her mark. She only needed to shine. As she looked around there was fat chance of shining in the dungeon of the archives of **Catchpole & Wood Advertising**.

'Got to start somewhere,' she said to the cockroach and threw herself once again into cleaning and sorting the graveyard of bright ideas.

On the dot of twelve o'clock the door was locked and Lois walked the two flights of stairs to the offices of **CWA,** washed her hands at the small kitchen sink and sat down to contemplate her bright future.

'All done?' Mr Schuler asked.

'Not quite,' Lois said, smiled, then added, 'I'm sorting by years so it will take some time.'

'Right.' Earl Schuler stubbed out his cigarette, nodded and took a bite of his sandwich.

Lois wiped her sweaty hands on her linen skirt and stared at her unappetising ham sandwich. It was curling at the edges and looked like it had been left behind by Burke and Wills on their exploration of the Australian interior. She poked it, and in a brave effort, picked it up to eat before her lunch half hour was over. The ham decided to forgo the rendezvous and slid along the melted butter to end up in her lap.

'Bugger,' she jumped up and hit her knee on her desk, upsetting her, now tepid, fizzy drink. Whisking her papers from the yellow liquid the stapler flew straight and true to her foot.

'Awwww, damn.' She hobbled to her chair and the effort of keeping her figure on one heel of her shoe was too much, it snapped.

'Lois?' Mr Schuler looked over to the growing catastrophe.

'It's alright. I'm alright,' She sat down on her swivel chair to survey the disaster.

'They were cheap,' she held up her heel.

'Too cheap,' Mr Schuler said.

'Poor people pay twice,' Mr Brucholtz added from his corner of the office.

Lois looked at the large grease spot on her skirt. It was the one decent skirt she owned. Now she'd need to fork out her hard earned money for dry cleaning. There was no mention at University on how to eat, pay for dry cleaning and a new pair of shoes on about one pound and six pence, she mused.

'It's so hot in here,' she said, as if that statement would explain all the ills of her life, work and the world in general.

'Hmmm.' Mr Schuler said and undid one more button on his once white shirt.

The office tea-towel was employed to wipe her desk, although the puddle was evaporating to a sticky residue as fast as she tried to clean.

And the office clock ticked down the lunch half-hour. They all looked at it until its large hand reached the thirty minute mark.

'Ah.' Mr Schuler took a deep breath, lit another cigarette and picked up a pencil.

Brucholtz picked up a set square and looked at his drafting board.

And the clock ticked.

⌘

'Did you get a note too?' Lois looked at Earl Schuler who was mopping his brow with an oversized cotton handkerchief.

'Uhuh.' Earl was a man of few words. That particular habit had kept him in the employ of **Catchpole & Wood Advertising** for nigh on twenty-five years.

Lois looked over to Norman Brucholtz in illustration.

Norm nodded, 'Yep.' He then picked up a sheet of cardboard and fanned himself.

'Any ideas,' Lois put the question to her colleagues while picking a loose thread from her shirt sleeve. Her button fell off.

‘Nope.’

‘No.’

Merritt Claremont-Grove came back from the toilet.

‘You get a note Merritt?’ Norm asked.

‘That’s right.’ Merritt pulled a wet paper towel from the back of his neck and wiped his face. ‘Two o’clock, the boardroom, sharp.’

‘You don’t suppose it’s about air conditioning?’

They all knew the idea was a fanciful one. Neither Mr Catchpole nor Mr Wood were known for lashing out on such things as decent toilet paper, new desk blotters or, heaven forbid, air conditioning.

‘Lois, Mackenzie, Mac,’ Norm drawled, ‘I think you’ve gone a little crazy in the heat. ‘Catchpole and Wood,’ Norm stood up and adopted a pose that everyone in the office identified as Mr Wood when he was on his high horse, ‘I say again, Catchpole and Wood do not shilly-shally with trivial pursuits. We deal in peoples’ dreams.’

‘Well I dream of an air-conditioner,’ Lois said.

‘I second that,’ Merritt said and nipped back into the toilet to freshen his paper towel.

✦

The sun beat through the window of the boardroom on the second floor of C&W Advertising and turned the room into a furnace. Alice, Mr Wood’s secretary, stood by the door as the employees filed in.

She nodded, ‘Mr Claremont-Grove.’

She shifted her weight to her other hip, ‘Mr Brucholtz’.

She moved back, ‘Mr Schuler,’ she pointed to the cigarette parked on his lip. ‘Miss Mackenzie.’ Earl pinched the offending cigarette and put it in his shirt pocket for later. Once inside everyone filed around the large table.

‘Oh hell, I must have dropped my pencil.’ Lois scooted out before Alice shut the door.

Mr Wood and Mr Catchpole opened the door dead on two p.m. Probably the first time they had set foot in the building all week, such was their heady schedule of late breakfast, lunch at the club, and drinks with associates at five.

‘Sit down,’ Mr Wood took the seat at the head of the long mahogany table.

‘William,’ Mr Wood motioned to Catchpole to take the seat to his right.

‘And dealer takes two,’ Merritt whispered under his breath. Earl narrowed his eyes at the whipper-snapper. Catchpole nodded to his nephew. Merritt smiled and winked at his relative.

‘I think the gentlemen can remove their coats,’ Mr Wood said in a small gesture of magnanimity.

Lois shot through the door pencil and pad at the ready.

She smiled at Mr Wood.

‘Sit over there and later put the kettle on, there’s a good girl.’

‘I’m...’ Lois began.

‘Now, as you know,’ Wood started.

‘Sir,’ Lois balanced on one heel. Her mother’s words echoed,

‘Lois Mary Mackenzie, it takes nothing to be nice.’ They stuck in her throat. She cleared said throat when Norm uttered an ‘errr.’

Earl coughed and Merritt pulled out a chair and saved the day.

‘Uncle,’ he addressed Catchpole, this is Miss Mackenzie.

‘Who?’

'One of the team.' Merritt ushered Lois to a seat. She sat down and tried to smile, look confident and not grind her teeth.

Wood took a large breath, wiped his forehead with an expensive looking handkerchief and didn't finish until he'd established they were not shilly-shallying, but dealing in peoples' dreams. Norm raised an eyebrow in Lois's direction. She pursed her lips lest a smirk emerge.

They sat and sweated, listening to Mr Wood expound on the state of the Agency, the need for smart thinking, the underhanded dealings of their competitors who saw television as the way forward in these heady days of 1950 and CWA's need to step up to the mark.

'We may be small, but who put the whack in *Wack-O* breakfast cereal?' It was a rhetorical question that the crew had heard many times.

Merritt rolled his eyes so far back he could see the tag on his shirt collar. Earl had a glazed look and Norm had doodled a picture to rival Hieronymus Bosch's garden of delights. Lois sat on the edge of her seat; not in awe and anticipation, but because the plastic chairs made her legs sweat and stick to her nylon slip.

'So, people,' Mr Wood began, looking over to Catchpole for some sort of accolade, 'we have some exciting news.'

'News,' Catchpole said and wiped his face with his handkerchief.

'We have,' Wood began, 'secured,' his eye roamed the room, 'a large account.'

'Account,' Mr Catchpole reiterated and nodded.

Leaning forward Lois asked. 'Who sir?' She leaned a little too far and slid right off the chair hitting her chin on the side of the very expensive mahogany table.

There was a moment of silence, her colleagues naturally rushed to her aid.

'It's alright, I'm alright.' She stood up and plopped herself down in her chair, her chin bruising like a prize fighter.

'Our new campaign is for Shotley's Home Goods.' Theodore Wood gave the staff something he thought was a smile.

'Home Goods,' Catchpole added.

'Shops in every major city.'

'City.'

'Network of affiliates.'

'Affiliates.'

'I thought they were represented by Gilbert & Grave Sir?' Norm said.

'Ah, Gilbert & Grave.' Mr Wood tapped his fingers on the table. The staff looked to Mr Catchpole. He stayed silent on the matter.

'For the moment. But,' and Wood held up one finger, 'we have been fortunate enough to be given an opportunity to display our talents.'

'Talents,' Catchpole came to life again.

'Old man Shotley, a member of my club, has given us their new line.'

'What is it?' Merritt asked, then added, 'sir?'

'I give you...the FRIDGE-O-MATIC' Mr Wood held up a small pamphlet about the Fridge-o-matic.

Catchpole nodded.

'It will be the Christmas line.'

The men at the coal face of advertising gave a silent groan. Merritt went so far as to take a long breath and let it out as a sigh of the damned.

'Christmas,' Catchpole smiled and wiped his brow.

'My secretary will give you the brief.' Mr Wood stood up and looked at his minions.

‘We have an opportunity here. I expect your best. We are dealing with peoples’ dreams.’ He walked out and Catchpole followed hot on his heels.

‘He’s dreaming.’ Merritt said when they had left.

‘Hmmm.’ Earl shook his head.

‘Jesus Christ,’ Norm said, although no-one thought he was talking about the saviour.

‘What’s the problem?’ Lois asked. As she’d only been at CWA for five months, straight out of university, class of 1949, she’d not seen all the cut and thrust of advertising. You can only glean so much by putting the kettle on.

‘Just wait Lois, just wait.’ Norm parked his pencil behind his ear and they followed him out.

‘So, can someone please explain?’ Lois sat down on the edge of Earl’s desk and fiddled with his glass ash tray.

‘Mac, it’s like this,’ Norm began, ‘Christmas is a hard nut to crack.

‘Hard nut to crack,’ here Merritt waved his arms about theatrically. In fact he did everything theatrically and thought himself cut from the same cloth as Noel Coward. Although Merritt was still wet behind the ears at CWA with just two Christmases under his belt, he felt he could contribute something to the conversation, albeit reiteration.

‘So many competing interests at that time of year,’ Earl added.

‘Impossible nut to crack Mac,’ Norm added.

‘I’ve seen more accounts fail at Christmas than I’ve had hot turkey dinners,’ Earl fanned himself with his old calendar. ‘You’ve got more chance of choking on a gall stone than selling a dream to the lacklustre, exhausted, bored and lifeless public.

‘So, it’s not an opportunity...’ Lois started when Norm held up his hands.

‘Nope Lois, definitely not.’

‘Not a chance luvvie,’ Merritt drew in his share of oxygen in the building through his nose and let it out again.

‘The Golden finger,’ Earl gazed off to the distance and thought of a time when he had the go-get-em attitude Lois was busting to get out.

‘But just suppose...’

‘Mac, you’re dreaming.’

‘But Norm. I remember a lecture we had at University. They said everything was an opportunity if you look at it with fresh eyes.’

‘Ah, university.’ The men tisked, smirked and shook their collective heads. ‘It’s not the real world Mac.’ Norm took his pencil from its parking spot behind his ear and sauntered over to his drafting board.

Lois stood up and pursed her lips. If there was one thing Lois Mackenzie was good at, it was digging her heels in, even if she only had one.

⌘

With one hour on the clock before knock-off time, everyone was on wind-down. There was about as much life in the employees as three week old roadkill.

Lois contemplated walking home barefoot, but the footpath would still be boiling hot, the crowds would crucify her toes and she’d look a bit silly. She toyed with idea of sticky tape, then decided she’d nip to the big department store and buy a pair of thongs. She might flip-flop all the way home but it would save her feet for another day.

‘Norm?’ Lois packed away her pens, her thesaurus, her dictionary, her writing pad and sauntered over to the illustrator’s corner.

‘Hmmm?’ Norm put down his pencil, brushed his rubber crumbs on the floor and looked up.

‘I wonder, you know, just wondering, well, I was just thinking, sort of, thinking you know, about the,’

‘Fridge-o-matic?’ Norm leaned on his elbows.

‘That’s it,’ Lois nodded and smiled.

‘And you want to know why we can’t make a go of it?’

‘Well, yes. That’s it.’

‘It’s like this,’ and here Norm turned to Earl and said, ‘A bit of help here Earl.’

Earl Schuler stood up with a crack of his knees and sloped over to the illustrator’s corner.

Earl began,

‘Back in the day when we were fresh, bright and the public were just beginning to be coaxed by advertising, you could sell anything with a promise.’

‘People were practically begging to be told what to buy, it was all so new, exciting, different,’ Norm said.

‘We sold pogo sticks that could lacerate a child’s leg to leave eighteen stitches and scar for life. We sold Lively Liver pills to people who had drunk their liver to oblivion.’

Earl sighed and a wistful look came over his face.

‘This is 1950. No-one want Lively Liver Pill Earl. No-one,’ Norm said. Earls moment dangled like old elastic on a washing line.

‘We sold *Wack-O* breakfast cereal,’ Earl added.

‘that had a plastic toy inside that might choke a three year old,’ Norm said. ‘And the public loved it.’ Norm tapped his pencil on his drafting board.

‘But those days are long gone.’ Earl shook his head and his face resembled someone reading an obituary.

‘The public, those dearies who have a little money in their purse are wary, miserly, and don’t believe a word we say, even if it is the truth,’ Merritt said while he fanned himself with a poster of *Wack-O* cereal. Norm raised an eyebrow at the word, truth. It just didn’t sit well with the cut and thrust of advertising. Merritt was apt to say some dumb things in his short tenure, but mislabelling advertising as the truth just about put the lid on it.

'Saturated by promises.'

'Cynical, lacklustre and exhausted,' Norm finished.

'So Lois, when we get a Christmas account thrown in our face, it is not a gift, it is not manna from heaven, it is a tortuous road to mediocrity or worse, a death knell.' Earl kept fanning himself with 1948.

'How do you excite people about a Fridge-o-matic then?' Lois asked.

'You don't. You give them a glossy pamphlet, a few pictures that show cold jelly and a ham and move on with your life.' Norm put his pencil down and folded his arms.

'He's right,' Earl said. 'I've been in the business too many years to believe in miracles Lois. You will soon see.'

'On the nail,' Merritt said. 'I don't know much, but I know Earl Schuler.' They all waited for the rest of the pronouncement, but Merritt had said all he thought he needed to say. In his three years at CWA he'd yet to make his mark; or tax the ol' grey matter into cognitive thought.

'If you want a crack at it Lois, it's your baby,' Earl Schuler said and raised an eyebrow.

'Me?' Lois looked at her colleagues.

'Why not.' Norm looked at Earl.

'Yup' Earl said and lit yet another cigarette.

'Alrighty then.' Lois breathed in and rubbed her sweaty hands together. 'I'm on it.'

⁂

The clock on the wall showed five o'clock. The place would be empty at 5:01, except Lois fidgeted with her handbag and the three men waited for her.

'I wonder,' she began.

'Hmm?' Earl looked at the clock.

‘I just think a look at the archives might help? You know, just take something home to look at?’

‘The archives?’ Norm ran his fingers through his hair. ‘The graveyard of bright ideas.’

Merritt snorted a laugh. He’d heard of bright ideas, but as yet he hadn’t had one. What he actually did in the office besides swan about and put the rubbish out was anyone’s guess.

‘Yes, just, well, you know, look at old campaigns and such. I saw some old boxes down there.’ Lois shut her purse and the clasp pinched that small bit of skin between thumb and forefinger, making her fling her purse which hit Merritt on the back of the head.

‘Sorry, it hurt. My hand you see. Sorry.’

‘Didn’t get anything vital,’ Merritt said rubbing his head. Now Norm snorted a laugh. Earl looked at the clock. 5:07.

‘Be quick.’ Earl said and perched on Lois’s desk.

‘Look, why don’t you spend the morning down there,’ Norm suggested. ‘Look for inspiration on a good breakfast,’ he stole a glance at the clock. ‘You must know your way around by now.'

‘Alright.’

‘Let’s get out of here,’ Merritt said. It was the only bright idea he’d had all day.

✦ CHAPTER 2

Shoppers threw themselves into the large department store, and revelled in the air conditioning. The doorman had a hard time keeping the door shut as the cold air escaped every time another red-faced potential customer shoved their way inside.

‘Madam,’ Ed said, as a large woman bustled her bustle through the door, shoving Lois out of the way and into Ed.

‘Sorry, I’m sorry,’ Lois righted herself and found her hair had caught on Ed’s lapel badge shaped like a star with the number twenty-five in the centre.

‘Awww,’ she pulled away as Ed grabbed her.

‘Easy does it Miss,’ Ed disentangled Lois and pulled her to one side. She looked at the star on his lapel.

‘Twenty-five years’ service and I’ve never seen anything like this. Madness that’s what it is Miss. Madness.’

It was then he noticed her feet.

‘Oh,’ Lois tried to hide her feet. ‘My heel broke.’

‘Ah.’ Ed looked up to see a woman with a small child get trapped in the door by a man carrying a toy car. ‘Excuse me a sec Miss,’ Ed said and went to sort out the mess.

‘Not even the 1st of December and they are crazy,’ he said. ‘It’s bedlam.’

‘Yes, I see that.’ Lois straightened herself and her hair, which had strayed from its French chignon, and now resembled a sausage with hair on it. Everything she did resulted in chaos, and she tried so hard to go by the book.

‘Ed Milligan Miss.’

Lois Mackenzie.' Lois held out her hand. 'Thanks for the save.'

'My pleasure Miss Mackenzie, my pleasure. Now, what are you chasing?'

'Shoes. Thongs. Something to get me home.'

'Right you are. Second floor, far left corner.'

'Thanks.' Lois smiled and pulled a wayward hair from her eye.

'You mind yourself Miss. The crowds are a little rambunctious this year.'

'I'll do that Ed.' And she sashayed right into the glass door and hit her head.

'Mind yourself Miss.'

'Yes,' Lois refocussed and grabbing the handle walked through the doors into the refrigerated air of Cravens Department Store, the only store with its own credit card, car park and air conditioning on all floors.

⌘

Shopping takes on a whole new meaning when you've been to university and studied the phenomenon of marketing. Lois looked at the signs, the banners and the promises with a critical eye. She tried to imagine the advertising staff who might have sat around and dreamt up a slogan, a colour scheme or a promise of paradise. They were ideas people. They were her kind of people. Go get 'em kind of people. She vaguely thought of her tutor, and his 'sermons' on method equal results. She liked the idea—a lot.

'Can I help you Miss?' A young girl stood in front of Lois and studied her feet.

'Ah, um, my shoe broke. I need something cheap to get me home on the train.'

'Gawd almighty. You need hobnail boots to survive the train.'

'Yes, well you are probably right, but a pair of thongs will do for now.' The young woman put her hair behind her ears and sized up Lois.

'Size six?'

'About that.'

'These are cheap.' A pair of rubber thongs with surfboards painted on them were presented. The shop assistant, Trudy, looked over to her floor supervisor. 'Although Madame might consider a pair of court shoes,' the assistant smirked and whispered, 'at three times the price.' She hoiked her head in her supervisors direction and smiled.

'No, just the thongs thanks.' Lois tried them on. 'These will do.'

'Right you are Miss.' Trudy took the thongs to the counter to be rung up. 'Will Madam be wearing them?'

'You bet I will.' Lois paid and put the thongs on her dirty feet. 'My heel broke and well...'

'Let me see.' Trudy took the cheap court shoe and tisked. 'You got these at Martins.'

'Yes.'

'They're rubbish. Look at the small tacks. No glue. They are a disaster waiting to happen.'

'I know that now.'

'Look, if you want quality, then Simpsons on Gerald Street have the goods.' Lois thought a personal recommendation or 'word of mouth' as her professor would say, worth its weight in gold.

'Shouldn't you be selling Cravens wares?'

'Oh tosh. Cravens don't sell good stuff. Simpsons shoes are for years. It's worth it.'

'Well, thanks Trudy...?

'Simpson.' Trudy smiled and winked.

People jostled on the station platform waiting for the train to open its doors. Lois was squashed between a man reading a newspaper, an old gentleman puffing on a Lucky Strike cigarette with sweaty armpits and a woman who had her Christmas shopping in several string bags all with sharp edges and pokey bits. She prayed for a seat, but when push came to shove the object was to just get on the train, and a seat a welcome bonus. The whistle blew, people pushed, shoved and in the melee someone trod on her thong and she lost it. She was herded into the carriage and stood with the population of Sydney going home. The people sweated, the carriage swayed and no-one spoke as the effort was just too much in the stifling heat. The door was open, but the air that blew in was hot enough to cook a Sunday roast.

At *Cream of Tartar works* stop, Lois shoved her weight to the door and fought to get off. A young man shoved her out the door and she lost her other thong to the railway line.

'Oh bugger.' There was flippin' chaos again just when she thought she'd beaten it into submission.

'Miss,' a mother scowled and grabbed her little cherubs hand to pull him away. The cherub poked his tongue out at Lois. She reciprocated and the mother caught it.

'Disgusting.'

'Aren't they,' Lois pointed to the little child who was squealing for an icy pole when he got home.

By the time she had walked the twenty minutes to Lucknow Close and Flat 4 her mood had lightened bringing a sense of embarrassment at her outburst directed at the mother. The poor woman was probably just a frazzled as she was and the kid not much comfort. She looked at her feet. They were almost black from the dirt, and tender from the stones.

'Frazzled,' she said as she walked. 'Flippin' heat.' It was the probable cause of all her ills.

Flat 4 was on the ground floor surrounded by concrete on all sides and boiled in the sun every day. It had one window with a fly screen which opened onto the frypan of a front yard and a back door that refused to open to get a through draft. Lois hopped over the hot path and stood on tip toe on the small front door mat made of melting point rubber. The key, always a bit troublesome refused to work. She jiggled, she inserted and re-inserted and then a small miracle happened and it clicked. She threw the door open and stepped from the frying pan to the fire.

'Knock knock,' Mrs Provoichkin rattled the screen door. 'Thought I saw you come home.' The old woman wheezed and sucked the life out of her Benson & Hedges fag.

'Lois took a deep breath, the hot air making her gasp.'

'Didn't scare you did I dear?'

'No. No Mrs Provoichkin.'

'Well, I just thought I'd let you know there's been no electricity for about three hours. The radio said there was an 'unpresident demand.'

'Unprecedent?'

'That's right,' Mrs Provoichkin hacked out a cough that sounded like half a lung.

'I don't know why they just don't make some more. Anyway, your fridge might...well you know.' Mrs Provoichkin caught a fly on the wing and threw it out the door.

'Thanks, I'll take a look.' Lois walked from her one room lounge/kitchenette back to the front door and held the handle. She just wanted to eat something and relax.

'So you might want to take a look.'

'I will.' She stood at the door and waited for the old woman to make a move.

'Could be you will want to eat everything up.' And there it was. The old lady was angling for something for free.

‘All I have is a bottle of beer, three tomatoes, a limp lettuce and some mayonnaise.’ Lois looked into the kitchenette and saw her bread curling at the corners.

‘Beer.’

‘Hmm.’

‘Might be warm. No good if it’s warm.’

‘No.’

They stood and looked at one another. A minute went by, then another, all the while Lois heard the old woman breathing while she had her hand on the door.

‘You want the beer Mrs Provoichkin?’

‘Well...only if you are sure,’ the gravel voice said.

‘I’m sure.’ Lois handed over the warm brew. ‘Well thanks for the heads up Mrs Provoichkin. Bye.’

‘Oh, bye dear. Just being neighbourly.’

‘Yes, thanks.’ Lois ushered the wizened old woman out and shut the door. It often occurred to Lois that without her, Mrs. Crisp might just wither away. By her reckoning she’d kept the old Polish woman alive for nigh on a year and a half. Half a loaf of bread here, sliced ham there, and quite a few potatoes.

The sun knocked off for the day leaving behind its heat in the bricks, the roof tiles, the road and every stick of second hand furniture Lois owned. She ate her tomato and found a packet of peanuts behind the bread bin.

The fridge was trying hard to crank itself up to temperature, but it laboured in the heat, so Lois gave up looking for cold air.

Her fan was positioned over the bath and Lois lowered herself into the tepid water to relax. She often did her best thinking in the bath, and now she went over her day. Her tutor said she should relax, not take things too seriously. He described her as intense. She thought it a compliment. He said she should read some books on relaxation. What she found were books on how to succeed.

Those books fuelled her ambitions. They had titles like *The Seven Steps to Success. The Way to the Top via Lists* and *Healthy Competition for a Winner*. Lois ate it up.

Now she made a list on her notepad which she kept beside the bath.

#get Golden finger award

#find slogan for Fridge-o-matic

#

#

#

She tapped her pencil on the hashtags. She could have put down, have fun, get out more, get a life. The last one was accompanied by her mother's voice, even though her mother lived in Queensland around 1000 miles up the coast. Lois contemplated her list. Throughout her formative years her mother always had something to say about every aspect of Lois Mary Mackenzie's life. It was a trying experience—one she tried to forget, or rise above as Amethyst Greenock suggested in *How to overcome...*' apparently Amethyst thought life in general was something to overcome.

Lois agreed with Amethyst and threw herself into reinventing Lois Mary Mackenzie which was another of Miss Amethyst Greenock's gems to overcoming life. She sprang from the ashes of her mother's disappointment to become 'intense', focussed and driven to succeed. Shirley Mackenzie, a product of her era often asked 'why?' Why do all that study and then have a baby~ et al? Lois felt there was more to life than the kitchen sink. It was the *et al* that bothered Lois. She wanted to make something of her life. Although her will to succeed was at odds with her natural instinct to be a people pleaser. Her one foray into love had said she was a pushover for any sob story. He said there was a wide difference in being a doormat and being charitable. Apparently he thought she was the former while angling for a bit of the latter. She fed him for the whole of the second year of university before he dropped out and became a plumber.

While she lay naked on top of her sheets, the fan blowing hot air around in a dilatory manner, Lois took a deep breath and told herself to focus. She then conjured a plan to attack the Fridge-o-matic. The first step would be to study the archives and find out what did and didn't work. CWA might have made its name with Wack-*O* breakfast cereal, it might have had a modicum of success with Lively Liver pills and pogo sticks, but what had it done lately? Norm was working on clip-on ties for young men of the future, Earl was wrestling with Handy rubber gloves ~in all shapes, colours and sizes, and Merritt had found a sandwich place in the city that made sandwiches while you wait. She was working on editing Kwik start shoe polish. Polish in a tube that wet a sponge. No more rags and black fingernails. Earl had passed it on with vague instructions to 'look it over'. It was run of the mill stuff for a student in the top percentile.

She'd cut her teeth on coloured toothbrushes and earned a distinction. Her toothbrush campaign was flawless, so much so, her tutor took it to Wandsley cosmetics and toiletries and passed it off as his own. But, for a people pleaser, nothing was too much trouble, shoe polish or plagiarism, it didn't matter.

'Method.' She turned on her side and tried to sleep. Ed Milligan loomed out of the darkness.

'Such a nice genuine man, a real star.'

Trudy Simpson came by.

'She knew how to instil trust in the consumer.

The cherub stood and whinged for an icy pole.

The metal fan blade began to oscillate and a slight tink, tink, tink could be heard as Lois Mackenzie drifted off, dreaming of rubber glove sandwiches smothered in shoe polish. She also dreamed of a Fridge-o-matic full of icy poles. 95 degrees Fahrenheit at midnight will do that to a frazzled brain.

✦ CHAPTER 3

The chatter on the train station was of the weather. Words like unprecedent, unusual and bloody boiling were heard. *Cream of Tartar works* station collected about a dozen souls ready to trade their daily toil for the promise of wages. Lois knew all the faces and smiled at each person as she waited for the train to take her to the city centre. At this stage, people were fresh, clean and ready for anything. She smoothed down her skirt, adjusted her blouse with the pretty lace collar and re-touched her hair.

The train, stopping at every station, soon became crowded, but the workers were still in top spirits. Their lunch was still fresh, their make-up still performing and their underarms in their suit jackets still smelling like Palmolive soap. People chatted about the week-end, the beach a popular topic.

'Scorcher.'

'They say 100 degrees all week-end.'

'Burnt to a crisp just mowing the lawn.'

'Bondi beach will be packed.'

'What I wouldn't give to have a fridge that worked.'

That last quip got Lois's ears pricked. She looked at the young woman who had a newly minted engagement ring on her finger. This was just the sort of person she needed to pitch her campaign.

'My Billy, asks for something from the ol' fridge every five minutes,' the other woman said. 'He may be three, but his first words were 'fridge mummy'. Anyone would think it was holding the Holy Grail or something.' The women exited at Circular Quay.

The view from the train stop took in the delights of the harbour. Lois squinted at the harsh sunlight and shaded her eyes.

'Hot one eh?' a man said.

'Yes, hot,' Lois replied.

'What I wouldn't do for a cold one,' the fellow added.

'Me too,' a woman said.

The heat, the unrelenting Australian summer practically sucked the will to live right out of. you.

CWA was just two blocks from the train stop, and Lois walked on the shady side of the street with the rest of the population. The sunny side of the street was reserved for people with a death wish, even at this early hour. She jostled along with the workers and then slipped off and into the old foyer of Holland Holdings, now holding a Chiropractor, an accounting firm, a dentist, a job agency and CWA on the second floor. Mr Wood often remarked they had the first floor and twenty staff in their hay days, but 'television killed that in 1949' Mr Wood lamented. Although television was only introduced last year, the death knell rang loud and clear. Lois came at the new beginning of CWA or it might be the end, it was a moot point.

She rode the old lift to the second floor and the first thing to hit was the odour of bodies and stale tobacco from the day before. There was no draft, no open windows, no air.

'Morning Mac,' Norm met her at the door with a cup of tea in his hand.

'Don't they feed you at home?' Lois asked.

'Ah. Four children at the table, wife busy. It's much calmer here.' He saluted with his cup and sauntered over to his illustrator's corner.

'Does your wife get a calm moment?' Lois enquired and smiled.

'Sure does. Every Sunday. My turn to take the chitlins. Breakfast in bed, coffee at ten et al.' Norm waved his hand in the air. Sunday is Gwen's day.' *Ah the et al,* she thought.

'Nice,' Lois said while thinking of the six other days of the week. Perhaps women can't have it all, but one seventh was better than nothing with a good man like Norm.

'Morning Earl,' Lois stood at Earl's desk and looked at his mock-up of rubber gloves.

'Handy & a colour for every task,' he posited to Lois. She screwed her nose up.

'Stink?' Earl asked.

She nodded.

'Why don't you play on keeping your hands young.'

'Ya think?

'Worth a try.' Lois walked to her desk in the corner and went through her routine. Pull out thesaurus, dictionary, pens, pencils. Arrange them on desk. Put handbag away. Take three deep breaths and compose yourself for the day. Her *The Seven Steps to Success* book suggested five deep breaths, but Lois thought three enough. No need to be coaxed into excess. She wasn't your average gullible reader.

✦

'No this is not the Country Womens' Association. This is Catchpole and Wood Advertising.' Alice put down the phone and looked at Lois. 'Happens all the time. If only they called it Wood and Catchpole. I could have told them, but then what do I know.'

'CWA. I never thought.'

'Most people don't.' Alice said. 'Now what can I do for you Miss Mackenzie?'

Alice Lomax handed over the archive keys with a warning, 'don't make it your life's work Miss Mackenzie.'

Lois took the keys and smiled. 'Miss Lomax, Alice,'

'Yes?'

Why did we get the account from Shotley?'

'Look Miss Mackenzie, it's like this. The only reason we got this poison chalice from Grave is that they too know about Christmas. Palm it off on some unsuspecting agency. CWA, sweet as a nut. They don't look bad when it fails. Old man Shotley's faith is renewed in Graves and they carry on raking it in. Wood is so far up 'the Khyber pass' he wouldn't know a poison chalice if he sat on it.'

'Oh.'

'That's about it in a nutshell.' Alice put a new sheet of paper in her typewriter and dinged the carriage bell. 'Take it from me, this has rotten egg written all over it.'

'Oh.'

'I've been here since Wack-*O* Miss Mackenzie, I've seen it all. This will be the last hurrah, if you ask me,' Alice shrugged, 'but no-one ever does.' She rolled her paper on the typewriter and pressed TAB. 'Have you got your CV in order Miss Mackenzie?'

'Surely not?'

'Just in case that's all. Just in case.' Miss Lomax began to type.

Lois descended the stairs to the basement once again. It was dank. It was dark. It was about ten degrees cooler underground and surrounded by cement.

CWA shared the storage space with the dentist on the ground floor, and the chiropractor on first. Here was the evidence of CWA's hay days. Stacked cardboard posters, old pay slips, buff manila folders of bright ideas, ledgers and old office furniture. She looked at her handy-work from the last week. All the ring-binders were numbered in years, the boxes stacked awaiting their fate. She thumbed through the manila folders and marvelled at gingivitis tablets, pencil sharpeners 'to make your point!', socks with *REAL* elastic, and soap on a rope, something, she thought, that obviously didn't catch on. There wasn't much to go on, nothing to give that spark she was looking for or evidence of genius. Wack-*O* breakfast cereal was everywhere, from posters to banners and small badges for lapels, *collect all 6!* Wack-*O* had kept CWA afloat for years it seemed. All the other cereals had quickly jumped on the band wagon and put toys in their boxes, but Wack-*O* was the first. Then she saw it. The statue was in a box with bunting. She reverently picked it up and stood it on a box of wage slips. The Golden Finger pointed to the sky *Earl Schuler. For advertising excellence..* ~

'One day,' she said. 'One day.' The thought of being unemployed by Christmas a world away from her particular daydream.

With an armful of folders she locked the door and ascended into the heat. It was only when she was handing the keys back to Alice that she remembered she'd left her pad and pencil in the archive.

'I'll be back in a tick.'

Descending once again she opened the door to the cool air and a small shaft of light from the hallway hit the Golden Finger projecting itself as a small star in the darkness. It looked inviting. It looked like a sign, a message. If one believed in fate, it might have had that moniker, but Lois Mackenzie was a practical modern sensible young woman. She smiled, picked up her forgotten pad and pencil, took one last look and closed the door.

But fate has a way of creeping up on you and tapping you on the shoulder from behind.

⁂

'Find anything?' Merritt asked as he cleaned his fingernails with a paperclip.

'Not much.' Lois plonked the folders on her desk and sat down.

'You know, I was thinking...' Merritt began.

'That'd be a first,' Norm quipped.

'Well, as it happens I do have big ideas sometimes.'

Earl looked up from his pink rubber gloves. 'This should be good.'

'Well, you see my aunt, well she has a refrigerator.'

'Hmm.' Earl turned on his chair to get the whole story.

'Well my aunt said what a refrigerator needs is,' and here Merritt stopped to gather his inmates full attention, 'what a refrigerator needs is,'

'Yes?' Norm asked.

'A...'

'Hmm?'

'A...'

'Merritt?' Lois frowned and leaned in.

'Um, well I've just lost it. But my Aunt Lydia said something. I'll think of it in a minute. She was certain a refrigerator needed it.

Earl muttered, 'the attention span of a toilet light,' and went back to his rubber gloves.

⁂

Lois pulled up her chair and looked at the old manila folders. They were named with the Newman account, the Hair remover account, the Block and Hart account. She flicked through the folders looking at mock-ups, notes and pointers in margins. The ideas might have been cutting edge at the time, but now they looked like study notes from her university days. *How did the people really swallow all this rubbish*, she thought. It certainly was a golden era when you could sell sand to an Arab or sunglasses to a blind man. She sat back and tapped her pencil on her teeth, then closed her eyes and the vision of the Golden finger came to mind.

It's funny how the brain works. One thing leads to another and then BOOM suddenly you're a genius.

'That's it,' Lois said.

'Hmm?' Earl inquired.

'A miracle. What we need is a miracle.' Lois stood up and accidentally hooked her shoe in her chair strut. The chair crashed to the floor, but not before it tore a ladder in her new pair of stockings.

'A miracle?' Norm asked. 'All that university education and whatdayaget?'

'The miracle of Christmas. The story of Christmas,' Lois said.

'It's been done,' Norm said.

'To death,' Earl added.

'Not like this,' Lois said warming to her epiphany.

'Aren't you sick to death of the cotton wool snow? Aren't you fed up of seeing the winter wonderland and singing about sleighbells. This is Australia for God's sake. It's 100 bloody degrees in the flippin' shade.' She had their attention.

'Only advertising can get the world to think differently,' Lois said.

'What about religion?' Norm asked.

'Pfft.'

'What we need is a new Christmas tradition. An Australian tradition.' Somewhere in Lois's brain the wheels were turning, the pieces were moving. Ed Milligan, Trudy

Simpson, the golden finger in the cool of the basement. It was all moving, slotting into place. And last came the boy with his icy pole. Click!

'Make the star at Christmas a Fridge-o-matic one.'

The men looked at her like she had been standing out in the sun too long.

'Don't you see?' Door opens, kids faces light up as they look at the light in the fridge. The Star of Bethlehem only now it's the guiding light of a Fridge-o-matic at Christmas.'

'Joseph and Mary have a Fridge-o-matic. What better recommendation than that!'

The men looked at her.

'She's got a point you know,' Merritt said.

✦ CHAPTER 4

From conception, not the immaculate kind, to the drawing board took Lois all morning. Merritt coaxed her to get out of the office for lunch. She splashed out on a sandwich from Betty's Milk Bar, and sat with Merritt on the high stools at the Formica counter, trying to hide the large ladder in her stocking.

'I love a good milk shake, how about you?'

'Nice,' Lois sucked on her straw.

Betty had gone all out with fake snow, snowmen on the window and sleigh bells over the door. Lois looked at the tired decorations and sighed.

'Oh, I know just what you mean,' Merritt rolled his eyes and picked at his sandwich. 'It just makes you sick.'

'We use fresh meat,' the woman behind the counter said with some indignation. 'None of your three day old spam here I'll have you know.

'Oh, sorry Luv, I was talking about something else.' Merritt waved his hands in the direction of the Christmas lights. 'It's just so...so...not Australian, that's what it is.' If there was one person who could suck on an idea and then regurgitate it as original it was Merritt. He added, 'What we need is Australian traditions at Christmas.'

'Too right mate.' A burly fellow said as he dolloped tomato sauce on his pie. 'Bloody snow. Who's ever seen the stuff anyway?'

'Not me,' the sandwich maker said.

'Me neither,' said a young lad with a sausage roll.

'Closest I ever got was defrosting the freezer,' a mother added. 'Ridiculous really isn't it,' she wiped her child's face with a hanky and spit.

'Sure is.' Lois fished around for the scoop of ice-cream at the bottom of her metal cup.

They all looked at the small blinking Christmas lights, Rudolf's nose lighting up at every second flash.

'Merritt?' Lois started on her fresh tomato and cheese sandwich.

'Yes?'

'Do you think I'm...sort of...well...intense?'

'Oh, honey, you are very intense.' Merritt ran his fingers through his hair and licked his lips. 'You have intense written all over you.' If there was one thing Merritt was good at it was flattery. It wasn't much to write on his curriculum Vitae, but it was something.

'I just wonder if I'm a bit...you know...too intense.'

'Never!'

Lois ate her lunch mulling over her bright idea, the small Vox poll from Betty's customers and Merritt's unequivocal answer. *Twelve easy steps to success* by Frederik Swan posited one needed to be driven, powerful, passionate to succeed. Lois had read the book several times. She felt this was her time to shine. The Fridge-o-matic was made for her. It was a gift.

The afternoon whizzed by as Lois organised her coloured pencils, rearranged her folders, spilt some ink and lost her mechanical pencil. She made a list;

#find pencil

#slogan, 5 words.

#write report for W & C

#flow chart

#

Then, with determination she took her three deep breaths and drew up a flow chart that might have given her a high credit at university. It had coloured boxes. It actually ticked all the boxes in execution. It was text book correct. Perfect.

'Nice,' Merritt wandered over to take a look.

'Yes, you see with this,' Lois pointed to a green box, you can see how the campaign will develop to week four over here,' she pointed to a yellow box. 'It will flow.' She waved her hand over the sheet and knocked the pencil shavings onto her lap. 'Oh damn.' The colours smeared as she brushed them off. 'Oh hell.'

Norm came over for a look.

'Pretty.'

'Well, it's to show the relationship of the campaign to the...'

Norm shook his head. 'University eh?' He retreated to his illustration corner and clip-on ties.

'Well, I like it.' Merritt said and coloured in an orange box. 'Ol' man Shotley will be impressed.'

'I hope so.' Lois gave a blue pencil to Merritt and pointed to her flow chart. 'This one.'

Having a bright idea is all very well, but it's how you put it across that makes all the difference. Earl knew this. Norm knew this. Lois was about to find out.

✦

At university Lois had given her presentation flawlessly. She followed all the steps from the textbook. She meticulously copied the diagrams and made mock-ups of product lines. It was a wonderful presentation. It couldn't be faulted. It received top marks, although Lois thought her colleagues efforts just as impressive.

'No need to blow your own trumpet young lady,' as her mother often said.

⌘

Alice Lomax appeared at the door of the office and beckoned Earl.

'Hmm?'

'Mr Schuler, Mr Wood is anxious to know if there is any news on the Shotley account?' Earl looked over to Lois who was intent on putting the final touches to her flow chart. They watched her frown and scrub out a word and then replace it.

'Miss Mackenzie?' Alice asked.

'Mmm.' Earl said. He lit a Lucky Strike, blew out the smoke and went back to his pink rubber gloves.

'Er, Miss Mackenzie.'

'Oh. Miss Lomax, Alice.' Lois smiled.

'Mr Wood is anxious to know if there is any news on the Shotley account. He telephoned twice.'

'Well, actually I'm in the process right now of putting a proposal together.' Boy, did it feel good saying that. Lois gave herself a *small* pat on the back. This was what it was all about. The cut and thrust of advertising. Pitching a proposal, making people buy things they don't need...or want, just because you are good at your job. Kudos!

Alice looked startled. 'Oh. Right.'

'Give me one more day Alice.'

'Only one,' Alice looked over to Norm and frowned. In her experience a proposal took a good week, maybe two to fine tune. There was the grind of paperwork, budgets, estimates of radio, paper and magazine space to buy, catalogue space to secure. It was a lot of work.

Norm busied himself with his illustration of a young man, glad to have a clip-on tie for his graduation.

‘Perhaps you need to,’ Alice looked over to Earl, ‘well Mr Schuler might just give you some pointers on what you need.’

Lois looked over to Earl who was keeping his head down from the incoming. ‘I’ll certainly do that.’ Lois grinned. Nothing was going to dampen her enthusiasm. She didn’t get a degree in marketing and commerce just to spell check and edit other’s work for the last five months.

As Alice left, Norm said, ‘you better put the kettle on Mac.’

‘Well, in our book on advertising principles, I remember it said to...’

‘University?’ Norm took a deep breath from his illustrators corner.

‘Well yes, of course. It gives you a step by step guide on making and executing a proposal.’

‘Really.’

‘Oh yes.’ Lois tapped her pencil on her teeth and looked thoughtful.

‘Well, off you go then Lois. By the book,’ Earl said and picked up his calendar to fan himself.

‘Ok.’ Lois said with a modicum of caution.

‘Earl. Come on. Give the girl a break.’ Norm came over to the conversation. ‘Mac, listen,’

‘Yes, I’m listening.’ Lois had the feeling she was the butt of a joke. It wasn’t the first time she’d had this particular sensation. The way she was going it might not be the last.

‘At CWA we do all the work on a proposal. We don’t have a team of accountants, marketing managers and such. We do the budget, the forecasts, the proposed advertising space in radio, newspapers and magazine. All of it.’

‘All of it.’ Lois recalled in the textbook, someone else did all those things. Paragraph 3, section 6a: once your mock-up and proposal of 300 words is ready for presentation the relevant departments will handle the rest.

'And I do the 'eye-catching, mouth-watering, head-turning illustrations.'

'Oh.'

'So, you need to see Miss Lomax. She will have a list.'

'A list.' Things were looking up if she had a list. *The Way to the Top via Lists,* practically said you couldn't go wrong with a list.

'That's right.' Earl said. 'A list.' Earl put down 1948 and fetched his rubber glove cheat sheet. 'See. Costings, illustrations, marketing etc.'

'Oh.'

'Look Mac, I know you are new on the block. I know we should have let you get in on the act a little sooner, but well, we had our own work and,' Norm looked at Lois and smiled, 'sorry Mac, but you were straight out of University. You were, um, a girl, and well...' He parked his pencil behind his ear, 'but look at you now. You have the account. Go get 'em Mac.'

'Yes.' Lois said and nodded in agreement. Norm was such a nice man.

'Go get 'em,' Merritt added and slapped Lois on the back which was a grand gesture in the scheme of things, except his cuff link got caught in her lace collar on her blouse and it ripped right off the neckline.

'Cripes. You ok?' Merritt dangled the bit of lace from his cuff link.

Lois rubbed her neck from the burn, 'Yes, its fine. It wasn't very good anyway. Don't worry Merritt.'

'I'll get you another.' Merritt handed over the lace.

'No honestly it's alright.' She looked at the lace and wondered how chaos could creep into her life, when she was so...well so meticulous in everything she put her mind to.

She followed the rules She lived by the book, so much so it was practically a religious experience.

'I insist.

'No.'

'Well at least let me take you out after work, for a drink or something.' Merritt gave a concerned frown.

'Alright.'

'Anyone else?'

Earl nodded and walked back to his desk.

'Only one,' Norm said, 'because I've got to take my son to his practice.'

'Practice?' Merritt said.

'Yeah. He is in the nativity play at school. A big deal apparently and they are practicing.'

'Rehearsals.'

'Yeah, rehearsals.' Norm said. 'He's Joseph I think.'

'Right then. The Nelson Arms at 5pm. I think they have an air-conditioner.

⌘

Lois packed away her thesaurus, her dictionary, her coloured pencils and put her lace collar in her handbag. She checked the money in her purse and thought she could budget for one round, knowing she still had to get some groceries. Although, finding a shop open after 5pm was nigh on impossible.

She took a look at her flow chart and the list Alice had given her. Alice's words were ringing in her ears. 'Mr Wood is quite enthused about the Shotley account. I think it's his last stab at success. Go get 'em girl.'

Norm's words rattled around. 'just a girl.' Lois clenched her jaw. She looked over her work musing on something she'd read in a motivational book. 'The best revenge is success.'

'Ready?' Merritt sat on her desk corner.

'Mmm.' Lois touched her blouse where her collar might have been.

'We better make tracks. We've only got an hour and it's all over red rover.' Merritt readjusted his cuff links while Lois watched.

'Present from the old man. Sort of a bribe. Get a job and you can have...well these. The Clan of Claremont-Grove don't muck about.'

'I bet you got heaps at school,' Lois said.

'Double barrelled name you mean?'

'No. MCG.'

'MCG. What's that?'

'The Melbourne Cricket Ground Merritt. The MCG.'

'Oh.' He thought for a minute. 'MCG. I get it,' he said, although by the frown Lois wondered if he did.

'Ah, ready for the six o'clock swill?' Norm asked as he rolled down his shirt sleeves.

'Ready.' Earl said, picking up his briefcase. They all looked at the clock. On the dot of five, they were out the door.

If you are not familiar with the licencing laws of Australia in 1950, they are quite an education. The Government in their wisdom decided that if the pubs shut at six then the men would step lively on the path to home and hearth at 6:01, full of money for the kids, kisses for the wife and a pat for the dog. What they didn't count on was the swill from five at knock off to six at closing time. Merritt looked at his fellow drinkers, took a look at the crowd and sallied forth with a 'follow me' and a theatrical wave of his hand in the air. Norm rolled his eyes skyward and said, 'wait here Lois, the front bar's no place for a lady.'

The men pushed, shoved, held up a couple of shillings and squashed their way to the bar. The barmaid spied the money and took it. Merritt pointed to the beer tap and held up four fingers. There was no way anyone could be heard over the ruckus. In due course Merritt was handed four beers and expertly held them over his head to find a place outside. His friends followed the beer, shoving their way to the outside and the large window sill which doubled as a table. Lois stood waiting next to the window and a fellow on the inside threw his cigarette stub out which landed on Lois and made its way down her cleavage. She yelled, 'I'm on fire,' and frantically tried to rescue the stub.

'Cripes,' Merritt took immediate action and chucked a beer in her direction quenching the fire and drenching her in the process.

'You alright?'

Lois gasped as the cold beer hit her chest and she tried to breathe.

'I guess.' She looked at the disaster that was her blouse.

'Close call.' Norm gave up his handkerchief to Lois. 'It's clean.'

'Thanks.' She began the process of mopping up.

'Quick thinking I'd say.' Earl took his beer and offered it to Lois.'

'No, honestly. It's alright Earl. I'll wait for the next one.'

'Drink up.' Merritt said and downed half his drink in one gulp.

'All friends eh.' Norm patted Lois on the arm.

'Yes.' She mopped her blouse.

They looked at Earl, but he was just finishing his glass and looking for another.

'My shout,' Lois offered.

'No Mac. Not this time.'

Earl came to life. He shook his head in accord with Norm and pointed with his cigarette. The beer hit the spot and he smiled.

'Nothing personal Lois, but we weren't expecting someone like you when they advertised for help.' Earl wiped his lips on his sleeve, gave a grin and shrugged. He looked quite human in these surroundings. He looked like a man who still had a little umpph left.

'Like me?' Lois asked.

'Yeah. Like you.' Merritt said and burped.

'A woman?'

'A very attractive young woman.' Norm added.

'Oh.'

'And well, we thought...'

'That I was a dumb blonde?' Lois flicked a stray hair over her ear. Earl took a drag on his ciggie and Norm looked sheepishly over his now empty, beer glasses.

'But we know you're not.'

'We know that now of course.' They tried to dig themselves out of a hole.

'I never thought you were dumb,' Merritt said. 'I even wondered if you were blonde.' That about covered it as far as Merritt was concerned.

'Well, women can do things these days you know.'

'Oh we know Lois, we know,' Norm said.

'Women are quite capable. It's 1950. We are our own masters.'

'Or mistresses,' Earl said.

'Exactly,' Merritt nodded.

'Woman should be equal.'

'Oh absolutely,' Earl smiled and took a new cigarette from his pocket.

'You *are* equal Lois,' Merritt gathered the beer glasses ready for another stab at the bar.

‘Except you thought I wasn’t up to the job. And I suppose you think my campaign idea is dumb too.’

‘I like it.’ Merritt said. ‘It’s...’ he disappeared into the melee.

‘Pitch it to me,’ Earl said.

‘Now?’

‘Why not.’

‘Go on Mac. Give it your best shot.’

And as Lois talked of the guiding light of Christmas being a fridge light, as she painted a picture of families looking for the light to shine, kids faces lighting up at the prospect of the cold ham, lime jelly or an icy pole, she came to life. She threw her arms wide, she threw a word salad at the concept and captured their attention.

‘I’m sick of cotton wool snow. I’m sick of a winter wonderland. This is Australia, it’s 100 bloody degrees in the flippin’ shade.’

The men took their beers from Merritt.

‘Oh, I get it now. MCG,’ he nodded. ‘M.C.G. That’s why they called me silly wicket at school. I always wondered you know.’

They looked at Merritt. Norm opened his mouth to say something, but shut it and pursed his lips. Earl took a draft of his beer and looked at Lois. She really did have a brain, and was terrific to look at into the bargain.

Lois shook her head to once again come back to the topic. She ended with, ‘our guiding light doesn’t have an off switch.’

‘So the light stays on when the fridge is closed. Is that it?’ They looked at Merritt and wondered how he tied his shoe laces.

‘You know I always wondered about that too.’ Merritt drank like a man who’d just discovered alcohol.

✦

At just after six, the train to Cream of Tartar Works stop wasn't the sardine tin it was at five. People had enough room to breathe, to read the paper and stare off into the distance trying to remind themselves that a job was a necessary part of living the Australian dream. Lois found a seat and watched the sun-baked world go by when the woman sitting next to her tisked and gave a loud sniff passing judgement on the lifestyle, morals and mores of Lois Mackenzie.

Lois smiled at the woman and stood up. 'I hope you had a wonderful day Madame. And when you get your new fridge at Christmas, think of me won't you.'

A man hanging onto the pole smirked as the train slowed for Lois's stop.

'Bugger,' she said as she left the station. She had nothing to eat at Flat 4.

The only shop open at this late hour was the small corner store run by Mr Moon. He looked about one hundred years old, but always had a nice word, a small chat or a little whinge to impart for every customer.

Lois entered to the ting of the bell and Mr Moon looked up from his Chinese newspaper.

'Ah. Miss Mackenzie.' Mr Moon never forgot a face.

'Hello. I just need a few bits and pieces.'

'Ah.' Mr Moon nodded. 'We have many special. Electric off. All must go.'

'Again.'

'Again.' Moon nodded some more. 'We have cheese. We have egg. We have bacon. We have pork rib. We have milk. Lois held up her hand.

'I need a potato, and um, one onion. I need some mince. The recipe calls for half a pound. I'll have three rashes of bacon and a dozen eggs.' She thought about the milk. It would just go off if the power went out again. Her recipe in *Good Housekeeping on a budget* suggested savoury mince a staple of any cooks repertoire. It gave step by step instructions that Lois followed to the ounce. It always turned out unappetising, never mind the meticulous instruction.

'Fridge broke.' Mr Moon motioned to the old Kelvinator in the back room. He moved his shoulders up and down like a pump. 'Trouble. All trouble.' Mr Moon's woes elicited a frown and Lois sighed while waiting for him to finish.

'You have pound of potato, is alright by me.'

'Have you got anything nice?' Lois asked. She just needed some comfort food. Her mother's voice appeared out of the ether.

'Lois Mary Mackenzie, you don't need that!'

'Nice for Miss Mackenzie.' Mr Moon went out the back and came back with a tired vanilla slice. 'Free for you.'

'Oh, no. I should pay.'

'Free.' Mr Moon said. 'Take.'

'Ok.' Lois wondered if Mr Moon had even read *The Principles of Commerce*, or *Capital and Profit for the business owner* by Malcolm Trilby.

'You have rough day Miss Mackenzie?'

'Actually,' Lois started to smile. 'I've had a great day.'

'That good.'

'Yes it is actually. Really good.'

'You smile more. It suit nice woman like you.'

'I'll take that into consideration Mr Moon.' Why men thought they needed to pontificate on women, she didn't know. But that wasn't going to spoil her mood. She gathered her groceries, paid and walked home thinking on her day. She would nail this account. She would make this campaign something to talk about for years to come.

And fate watched her fumble with the key. It watched Mrs Provoichkin make a bee line for Lois and look longingly at the vanilla slice. And it watched Lois hand over the slice, parcel out three potatoes before shutting the door.

✦

Lois's to do list was extensive. She looked it over as she ate her meal of mashed potatoes and savoury mince. She wrote up Alice's list and put them side by side. One was wishful thinking, the other about a week's worth of work.

Over her cup of tea she made a further list of things to accomplish on her flow chart. It all looked like a lot of work.

'You can do this Lois Mary Mackenzie,' she said. 'This is why you were the only woman in your year to do commerce. You did three years at university. This is your time to shine.' *The Seven Steps to Success* suggested motivation talks. Lois washed her few dishes and told herself she was a candidate for success. Her ideas would ignite the lacklustre, exhausted, bored and lifeless public.

As she made ready for bed, the heat of the room made her think of a Fridge-o-matic. It's cool, inviting innards would be irresistible. It was a gift. The Fridge-o-matic gave hope. It's clear message of salvation from the fires of hell, which was the Australian summer, was clear.

'Who wouldn't want to be a convert,' she mused as she drifted off to sleep, the tin roof cracking like arthritic knees as it cooled to a manageable eighty degrees Fahrenheit.

✦ CHAPTER 5

Mr Moon watched Lois come in every day for a week before he asked,

'You work hard Miss Mackenzie?'

'Eh?' Lois answered. Her head was full of magazine space, costings, a small(ish) budget and Ol' Man Shotley ringing Mr Wood, who in turn rang Alice, who would come down to her desk and enquire, 'when?'

'Soon,' was the standard reply. She wanted it to be perfect. She wanted it to 'knock their socks off' and 'leave them begging for more,' as her book *Perfect Pitch* by Walter Fry suggested.

'I have dry cleaning back tomorrow maybe.' It was Mr Moon's stock answer to everything. 'Tomorrow maybe.'

'You look tired Miss Mackenzie.'

'Just working, you know,' Lois replied.

'Half pound mince, one onion?'

'Yes please.' There must be more to savoury mince than *Good Housekeeping on a Budget* suggested, but Lois had yet to find it. It still tasted bland, unappetising and dull, no matter she followed the recipe to the letter.

'Big job?'

'Yes.'

'You tired.'

'Oh, no. It's just that I need to...well...'

'Ah.' Mr Moon smiled revealing three teeth all vying for front row seats. The rest of the seats were completely empty.

'Fridge broken.' He shrugged repeatedly and threw up his hands at the disaster. 'I teacher once, no problems like fridge.'

'Oh.' Lois collected her ingredients and put her money on the counter. 'I wish I could help, but I only have a small fridge myself.

'Not your problem Miss Mackenzie.' Mr Moon's shoulders went up and down. 'You have important work to do.'

'Well yes, but if I can help in any way Mr Moon.'

'Nice to know Miss Mackenzie. Nice to know.'

✦

And the day came when Alice popped her head into the office and enquired, 'when.'

'Now.' Lois looked up and smiled.

Norm looked up from his clip-on tie, Earl stopped costing a full page spread in the Woman's World magazine and Merritt folded the tea-towel in the kitchenette and hung it on the rail.

'Oh, right. Give me about an hour. I'll ring around.' Alice looked at Lois, 'you're sure about this?'

'Oh, absolutely.' Lois tapped her folders of information, she patted her drawings on oversized cardboard and took five deep breaths. 'Absolutely.'

✦

The thermometer crept up as the day wore on. The office became so hot, Norm pasted old illustrations on the windows to keep out the sharp, unrelenting sunshine. Earl and Merritt rolled up their sleeves and Norm went to far as to sit around in his Bonds singlet.

'So we have a little time Lois. Run through it with us. Call it a rehearsal.'

The men pulled up their chairs in a row and fanned themselves.

What they heard was a well thought out argument. A cohesive campaign that hit all the right markers for attention, public acceptance, innovation and originality. Lois presented pie charts, graphs and a satisfactory conclusion.

The men sat stunned into silence.

Merritt clapped.

'Well?' she asked.

'Mac, it's brilliant,' Norm said.

'Well done.' Earl began to wonder if he should retire if this was the new standard in the industry.

'Just one thing,' Merritt said.

'Hmm'

'So the light.'

'Yes?' Norm wiped his brow with his handkerchief.

'It stays on then.'

Earl looked at Norm. 'I think the word you're looking for is nonplussed.'

Alice popped into the office and her eyes widened as she saw Norm in his underwear. 'Um, Miss Mackenzie. Mr Wood is busy. You are scheduled for ten tomorrow. In Mr. Wood's office. Mr Shotley will be there.'

'Alright.' Lois began to pack up her paraphernalia.

'Good luck,' Alice crossed her fingers and was gone.

'You really like it?' Lois asked.

'It's great. You'll be great.'

'Hmm.' Earl pursed his lips. The 'hmmm' had an ominous sound to it.

'Earl, give the girl a break. It's absolutely brilliant. Shotley will jump at it.' Norm fanned himself with is clip-on tie illustration. 'Lois, you want me to freshen up your poster?'

'Would you?'

'Sure.'

✦

Lois dressed with her presentation in mind. Her wool skirt was corporate smart, and with a white shirt and her jacket she looked every inch the executive cut. The only down side it was hot as blazes. She looked at her meagre wardrobe. Her linen skirt was still at the dry cleaners, her nice shirt with the once lace collar was still in the laundry basket and the wool skirt her only decent option. There was a sun dress, but it's vivid green and white stripes didn't instil business confidence, more like shopping for sandals and bathing suits.

The train station glimmered in the sun. The dozen travellers stuck to the small sliver of shade from a billboard advertising *All New Westinghouse refrigerator! With ice compartment!!* Lois looked at the sign and dissected its potential. It was run of the mill, dull and only had three exclamation points going for it. She slipped into a small section of shade and smiled at her fellow travellers. No-one smiled back as the temperature scoured every last fibre of good-will out of people.

'Scorcher,' Lois said and took off her jacket. She got a 'hmmph' as a reply.

People on the train tried in vain not to touch one another as the sun beat down on the tin can they stood in to go to work so they could earn enough money to pay for the house that was mortgaged and sleep so they could go to work. Lois jostled with the small floor space and held onto her bag, her jacket and the ape strap from the ceiling. It was then she noticed the hole in the underarm of her blouse.

'Oh hell.' She let go the strap and tried to put her jacket on. It was impossible in the crush. With one arm in and one arm out the train decided to come to an abrupt halt and Lois fell forward grazing her leg against a man with a work bag. She looked down. 'There goes another pair.' The man looked at her leg.

'Nice.'

She righted herself and put her jacket on. 'Yes, prosthetics are pretty amazing these days aren't they.'

The fellow laughed. 'You're the fridge lady. Am I right.' It took a moment but it clicked.

'Yes.' Lois looked out the window. Hers was the next stop.

'What was all that about then?'

'Oh, just talk, that's all.'

'Right.'

'My stop.' Lois pushed past and exited with a crowd of people all intent on getting indoors as fast as possible before their make-up drooped, their underarms began to sweat and their pupils shrink to pin pricks. She walked at a leisurely pace to work, knowing the slightest exertion would see her sweating.

She arrived on the second floor still put together. Next, she went to the loo and took her stocking off, the only downside being the wool skirt had lost its lining ages ago in an accident with cinema seat and a metal hinge, so the skirt pricked like it was made from a blackberry bush. She came back scratching and sat down.

'Wool?' Merritt frowned. 'In this weather?'

'I'm not made of money Merritt Claremont-Grove.' She looked at his tailored suit trousers, his top of the shelf shirt and gold cuff-links. 'We don't all have hyphenated names.'

‘No need to get shirty luvvie.’ Merritt went to his own corner and sat down.

‘It’s just that...’ Lois tried to say, but Merritt was busy turning his back and re-arranging his pencils.

‘Morning Mac.’ Norm came by with a cup of tea.

‘Morning Norm.’

‘All set. Big morning. We’ll all be there you know.’

‘Thanks.’

‘It’s not a favour Lois. It’s our job. We are the advertising team of CWA. We all live or die by each and every account.’

‘Oh.’

‘I have some mock-ups if you want to see.’

‘Yes.’

‘Earl, Merritt?’ He called the ‘team’ over.

They stood at Norm’s drafting desk and looked at the wonderfully executed drawings of a fridge, a boy and a light which captured the essence of the campaign perfectly.

‘Holy Shamoly,’ Merritt said.

‘Hit the nail on the head with this one Norm.’ Earl patted Norm on the back.

‘Brilliant. Absolutely brilliant.’

‘Good eh?’ Norm smiled and sipped his tea.

✦

The sun had yet to reach the board room, but soon enough the earth would turn and the room boil.

‘Mr Brucholtz.’

‘Mr Schuler.’ Earl stubbed out his cigarette and smiled at Miss Lomax.

‘Mr Claremont-Grove.’

‘Miss Mackenzie.’

Alice stood at the door and looked at her watch. She heard the lift at the end of the corridor and looked at the captives in the room.

'Good luck.' She stood back as Mr Wood, Mr Catchpole and Mr Shotley filed into the room.

'Miss Lomax, tea at the half hour,' Mr Wood said.

'Tea,' Mr Catchpole echoed.

'Sir.' Alice shook her head in silence. She was a top flight stenographer, 80 words per minute typist and crack short hand writer. She practically ran CWA. A long sign could be heard as she put the kettle on.

Mr Wood introduced Ol' man Shotley to the team and went over the 'people's dreams' once again so they were all aware of the fact. He looked at Earl and inquired,

'So what have we got Mr Schuler?'

Earl coughed and looked to Norm.'

'Mr Brucholtz?'

'Ah,' Norm passed the buck to Merritt who squeaked,

'Me?' and turned red.

There was something forbidding about Mr Theodore Wood. The really forbidding thing was he paid their wages and could stop doing so with a click of his fingers.

All the men in the room looked at Merritt.

'I...' he croaked.

'Mr Wood,' Lois stood up and smoothed her skirt.

'And you are?'

'Lois Mackenzie Sir. You hired me.'

'Did I?'

'Yes, in August this year.'

'Of course,' Wood said. His eye roved over Lois and he raised an eye brow. Norm shot a look at Lois to hold her indignation. She took a breath and adjusted her jacket.

'I have the...Mr Shotley's account. The Fridge-o-matic.'

‘Oh.’ Wood gave a small indication he might smile, but it faded and he looked at Ol’ man Shotley and shrugged. The inference was clear as a bell on Santa’s sleigh. Now we’ve got young women in the mix. Whatever next.

‘Well, let’s hear it girlie,’ Eugene Shotley said.

Lois saw Norm’s trepidation and took her three deep calming breaths.

‘Mr Shotley, are you sick of cotton wool snow, winter wonderlands and sleigh bells? It was a rhetorical question, but Shotley opened his mouth to answer when Lois continued.

‘We live in Australia. It’s 100 bloody degrees in the flippin’ shade.’ That got their attention. Mr Catchpole actually sat up straight.

‘Isn’t it about time we had an Australian Christmas. A new tradition. An Australian tradition?’

Earl, Norm and Merritt sat mesmerised. Lois had the floor.

‘Mr Shotley, your Fridge-o-matic could be that new tradition.’

‘Could it?’

‘Of course.’ Lois whipped out the terrific poster of the boy looking in the refrigerator. ‘Why don’t we make the light in the Fridge-o-matic the guiding light of Christmas. Follow the light to receive your reward. It is the guiding star.’ She explained the vox pol and the people’s choice for a more Australian flavour of Christmas. She wove a story about a little boy’s first words were ‘fridge mummy’ and a small child’s wish for an icy pole. She explained the wish of a young woman about to embark on married life and the desire not for a hope chest full of tablecloths, not a new radiogram or an Australian wool blanket, no...’

‘What did she wish for?’

Again Shotley went to answer when Lois said, 'A fridge. She just wanted a fridge that worked.' She looked at Shotley. 'She didn't know it, but she wanted a Fridge-o-matic. Can you imagine her first words when she gets it delivered? Shotley kept his mouth shut. 'Thank heavens it's a Fridge-o-matic.' She looked at Shotley who was entranced. And she doesn't need to thank heaven, she needs to thank Shotley's.

And then Lois delivered the killer punch.

'The three wise men knew a thing or two when they chipped in for a Fridge-o-matic for Christmas.'

The room remained silent. Lois held her breath. She began to sweat as the sun streamed into the office. Her team beamed and looked at Wood, Catchpole and Shotley for a sign.

'Blood hell.' Shotley stood up.

'And this was your idea?' Wood asked roving his eye over the men in the room. Earl wished for a cigarette, Norm fiddled with his pencil and Merritt just about swallowed his Adam's apple.

'Yes sir,' Lois piped up. Wood looked at the team and narrowed his eyes. Merritt gave a sympathetic look at Lois.

'I have the costings, the magazine space, a pie chart,' Lois offered her heart to the men.

'Well...' Catchpole started, which had the room staring like baby Jesus was just delivered and needed a nappy change. 'Well...I like it. It's different. It's fresh. It's new.'

'New you say,' Shotley said.

'Different,' Wood said.

'A new tradition.' Lois wiped the sweat from her upper lip and squinted in the sun.

'100 bloody degrees in the flippin' shade,' Ol' man Shotley chortled.

'Shade,' Catchpole said.

‘Keep her Wood, she’s a genius.’ Shotley walked around and shook Lois’s hand. ‘Bloody genius.’

‘Tea sir,’ Alice walked in with a tray.

‘Tea, its 100 bloody degrees in the flippin’ shade,’ Shotley laughed, we want a cold beer. This is Australia.’ He smiled at Alice. He slapped Lois on the back and guffawed.

‘Sir?,’ Alice answered and left. Where would she get a cold beer at 10:30 in the morning. The world had gone completely mad.

✦

‘So they really liked it?’

‘You bet they did,’ Merritt said as he rolled up his sleeves. ‘Mr Wood was all for it.’

‘It got Ol’ Shotley’s attention. I’d say he was a born again convert.’ Norm fanned himself.

‘Impressive Lois, very impressive,’ Earl said, taking up 1948 and fanning.

‘And now the fun begins,’ Norm smiled. ‘Can you see a banner on a bus, billboards, radio, magazines, and posters on every train station.’ Lois closed her eyes. The vision she conjured was not of billboards, banners or posters but the Golden Finger with her name on it.

‘Anyone want a sandwich from Betty’s?’ Merritt asked as the team basked in the glory that was a budget approval, a costings analysis that didn’t make the principles choke on their lunch and a campaign that would eclipse anything else on the Christmas wish list.

‘I think they have turkey.’ Merritt grabbed a pencil and paper for a list.

✦ CHAPTER 6

Taking the train home Lois was oblivious to the people around her. She didn't mind the odour of sweat, the trample of feet, the stale cigarette butts on the floor or the pushing and shoving. Nothing was going to spoil her moment of triumph.

'You look happy,' the fellow with the work bag and cheeky smile said. He swayed as the train crossed a junction.

'Hmm?'

'Happy. You look happy.'

'Yes, I am.'

'Makes all the difference doesn't it.'

'What?'

'A smile.' He smiled. 'Easy when you know how.' The train pulled into a station and he exited without a glance behind.

Yes, she thought. She had every reason to smile.

Mr Moon nodded as she came through the door.

'Ah. You happy Miss Mackenzie?'

'Yes.'

What was it about her that made people comment on her wellbeing? She didn't think she was terribly interesting. She thought she wasn't very pretty and yet they felt it their duty to comment. Amethyst Greenock of *How to Overcome* suggested to rise above the mundane, the everyday. Lois closed her eyes in meditation for a second and then asked for half a pound of mince.

Mrs Provoichkin opened her screen door as Lois scooted over the frying pan front yard and tried to put her key in her lock.

'Yoohoooo.' Mrs Provoichkin called then coughed up her larynx.

'Oh, hello,' Lois waved.

'Good day?' she rasped.

'Brilliant thanks.'

They looked at one another. 'I have a currant bun.'

'A currant bun eh?'

The offering was taken with much thanks and Lois popped inside and shut the door.

Lois lay still trying not to let one part of her body touch another part of her body. She thought on her presentation. Brilliant. She remembered the accolades of her team, fabulous. She remembered Mr Shotley's praise. Genius. Now all she needed was the public to co-operate. If they were convinced to buy Wack-*O* breakfast cereal, then it was in the bag.

The fan took up its ting, ting as it oscillated and Lois went to sleep dreaming of icy poles, banners and the golden finger.

✦

It might have taken Jesus thirty-three years from yay to nay, but CWA, once Alice Lomax was on the case, the budget deposited, the sign writers engaged and the graphic artists briefed, well, the whole thing was on starting blocks within three weeks.

The train was particularly packed as it was the last week of school for some, other more fortunate souls had broken up for the summer holidays and were on the hunt for fun.

Lois shoved her way to a pole and hung on as the train swayed over the junctions.

'Tight today,' the fellow said.

'Pardon?'

'Tight.' He smiled and adjusted his grip on the ape strap above his head.

'School holidays for some,' she said. Lois's eye roved over the pimply youths, the gaggle of giggling girls and those twelve-year-old's who still had to shop with their mothers.

'Wait 'till they need to earn a quid. It'll be different then.' He shuffled his work bag a little closer to his foot.

'Hmm.' The train lurched and Lois was shoved into a young man with slicked hair that looked like a shiny liquorice stick. He smirked and ran his fingers through his hair. The train lurched again and his greasy hand fumbled for a grab at the pole and got Lois's blouse instead. It left a mark a dry cleaner might roll her eyes at in disgust.

'Watch it mate.' The fellow pulled the young man's hand away.

'Sorry Miss.' And the liquorice lad scooted off the train with his friends.

'Will ya look at that,' the fellow said. 'That'll need a bit of work.'

'Oh, yes, I guess.' Lois looked at the grease spot.

'Serg.' He held out his hand.

'Lois,' she extended her free hand.

✦

Ol' man Shotley insisted Lois accompany him to the first billboard pasting. She stood in the one square of shade offered by the eucalyptus tree and sweated in her linen skirt with a silk lining. It clung to her thighs and insisted on riding up at the slightest movement.

‘Looky there,’ Shotley pointed. Norms illustration captured the moment.

‘Bloody marvellous.’ Shotley shaded his eyes and smiled. Lois squinted at the giant billboard as trucks, cars and trains whizzed past.

This is Australia. It’s 100 degrees in the flippin’ shade.
THE GUIDING LIGHT OF CHRISTMAS
IS in A
FRIDGE-O-MATIC

A NEW tradition. *An Australian tradition!*

Shotley read the banner aloud and chuckled.

Lois moaned. ‘They forgot your store.’ She shaded her eyes to the blazing light.

‘Ah.’ Shotley took her elbow. ‘I know a thing or two my dear.’

‘Hmm.’ Lois kept her opinions on endearments to herself.

‘There is only one place that sells ‘em. My place. Word of mouth. Worth more than the advertising budget of the Government.’

‘Oh.’

*

‘Well,’ Merritt asked, ‘Was it good.’

‘Oh yes. Good.’ Lois sat down and tried to adjust her lining.

‘Knew it would be.’ Merritt sat on the edge of Earl’s desk and fiddled with a set square.

‘Shouldn’t you be doing something Merritt?’ Earl took the set square and put it back on his desk.

'Dog biscuits.'

'Yes, dog biscuits.' Norm looked up from his latest drawing.

'But they want it just the same as always.' Merritt pouted. 'I have no artistic outlet with dog biscuits.'

'Perhaps you could have the dog saying he prefers them, rather than the human,' Lois offered.

'Try rubber gloves,' Earl said and sighed.

'And Clip-on ties,' Norm added.

The men looked to Lois. She was their inspiration. New thinking, new blood and she was a woman. They were wired differently, didn't get flustered and took each challenge with measured intelligence.

Lois found her lining and pulled. It ripped and as she stood up it fell to the floor. 'Oh bugger. Shit. Damn and blast.' She turned to her team, 'what I wouldn't give to get into someone's trousers right now.' *Why*, she thought, *did her life contain chaos when she did everything with structure, order and lists. Why?*

Yep, women were made different.

✦

The train ride home took in the delights of the billboard. Lois ducked to see it out of the window and caught her sleeve on a woman's handbag buckle.

'Oh wait a sec luvvie.' The woman tried to unhook Lois from her bag. Lois waited and missed the moment. Her sleeve came away with a pulled thread.

'Sorry about that Luv.'

'Not a problem,' Lois said trying to unruck her pulled thread and hang on as the train swayed.

'Trying to see that new sign, were ya?'

'Yes.'

'I saw it earlier when I went into town. Wouldn't that be a surprise for Christmas. Better than fake snow eh?'

'Wouldn't it.'

'Shotley's I heard.'

'Me too.'

''bout time they had somethin' like that.' The woman left the carriage, but her words lingered.

Lois sprang from the train at *Cream of Tartar* and practically skipped her way to Mr Moon's corner store.

'Happy Miss Mackenzie?'

Lois nodded.

'Mince?'

'No Mr Moon. I'm going all out. A bit of a celebration. I'll have a bit of corned beef please.'

'Celebration?'

'Yes.' Lois might have wanted to blab about her recent triumph, her expectations, and her feeling of pride, but her mother's voice floated in the air.

'Pride comes before a fall Lois Mary Mackenzie. No-one wants to hear your aggrandisement.'

'Is good news?'

'Yes.' Lois paid for her one onion, two potatoes and three slices of corned beef. The recipe called for carrots and peas, but she knew she had a tin of those at home.

'You want something nice?'

'Um.'

'Apple slice maybe?'

The Mackenzie budget might just stretch to an apple slice.

'On house. For celebration.' Mr Moon smiled.

'Right. Well thanks.' She took the dessert. Mr Moon really needed some business acumen. She wondered how he ever made a profit.

Mrs Provoichkin yoohooed as Lois put her key in the lock. 'Saw you.'

'Yes,' the sun scorched concrete threw up its 100 degrees making the women sweat.

'Well, I better get in. Hot out here.'

'Sure is.' Mrs Provoichkin adjusted her grip on her walking stick. 'Your place hot?'

'I guess I'll find that out.' Lois handed over the apple slice with a smile and walked inside then shut the door. Mrs Provoichkin had better radar than the Australian Navy.

The evening temperature remained high. Ray Salter, the radio announcer brought every statistic to bear as he explained the high barometric pressure, the currents, the wind velocity and the cloud over Argentina. All the population needed to know was how hot it was going to be tomorrow. Boiling, a scorcher or something like a lava pit. She was about to turn the radio off and do her dishes when something piqued her interest.

Bishop Niall O'Leary is with us this evening talking on the meaning of Christmas.

Lois wiped her plate and listened.

'What we need is to get away from the commercialism of the season. Why, just today I saw an advertisement on a billboard. Large as life. And this just about makes my blood boil.'

'Hmmm?'

'A Fridge-o-matic.'

'Go on.'

'Using the Star of Christmas as a fridge light.'

'Really.'

'And then...'

'Yes Bishop O'Leary?'

'A new tradition. What is wrong with the bloody old tradition? Sorry. But really, it's too much.'

‘Right.’

‘So people should...’

‘Remember what Christmas is all about. Giving, receiving and goodwill to all men.’ Bishop O’Leary was practically shouting at the microphone.

‘Giving and receiving. But just not a Fridge-o-matic?’

And then the Bishop said the word that would become the flint to start the fire.

‘Sacrilege.’

‘Sacrilege?’

‘Too right.’ O’Leary thumped the desk and the announcer cut to a commercial for Christmas crackers on special at Dunnings.

Lois put her tea-towel down. She sat at the small kitchen table and drummed her fingers on the Formica top. Her tutor at university said all publicity is good publicity. Lois ruminated on the Bishop’s words. If she had pen and paper she might have penned a thank you note to Bishop Niall O’Leary of St Cuthbert’s Waverley.

The meaning of Christmas, it was a gift.

✦ CHAPTER 7

The train pulled into the station and Lois boarded automatically. She was still on a high and full of the Bishop's words, *The Meaning of Christmas.*

It couldn't get any better. Daydreaming of the campaign she missed the glaring headlines of the paper. Thinking on the accolades raining down she didn't see the billboard with scrawled graffiti and as the golden finger came within her grasp she overlooked the growing heat of controversy.

'Nice one,' Norm patted her on the back.

'Huh?'

Earl and Merritt met Lois at the door and Merritt handed her the Sydney morning paper. 'You might want this as a souvenir.'

'Huh?' Lois took the paper conveniently folded to reveal the front page. It hadn't taken long before the morning edition took Bishop O'Leary's words and ran with them in three inch headlines.

'Front page,' Earl tapped the paper.

'But I...'

'Save it for Shotley.' Earl sloped to his desk, tipped out his ash tray and started his day with a clean slate and a Lucky Strike.

'It says it is taking a poll. The winner will get a voucher for a Fridge-o-matic,' Merritt read. 'What's it all about anyway. So what if a fridge light stays on. Earl and Lois looked at Merritt as if he'd just told them his uncle had left everything in the will to his carbuncle on the back of his neck.

'Morning,' Norm came in to see two astonished faces.

'Ah, seen the headlines eh?'

'Um, yes.' Lois laid the paper on her desk. Sacrilege glared at her. Bishop O'Leary's face looked none too pleased.

'Well,' Norm began, 'Wood and Catchpole signed off on it.'

'That's right,' Merritt said. 'That's exactly right.' He did a little hop, skip and jump.

'What should I do?' Lois asked.

'Stick to your guns girlie,' Norm replied then corrected himself. 'I mean Lois. Stick to your guns Mac.'

'You have it all scheduled don't you?' Earl asked.

'Yes.'

'Well, this can only be considered a gift.' Earl fiddled with his fountain pen.

'A gift.' And right then Lois Mary Mackenzie saw the light.

*

Alice fielded telephone calls all morning, then she took the phone off the hook and practically galloped down the corridor to the workroom. The team looked up as she burst in, hunting for someone to listen to her rant.

'Miss Mackenzie.'

'Yes?'

'I...'

'Now Miss Lomax, before you get all huffy,' Norm began, 'stop, take a deep breath and,'

'And what?'

'Listen. Wood signed off on it. Catchpole signed off on it. Shotley paid for it. So, it's not our problem.' He looked at the team.

'Not our problem,' Merritt reiterated and wagged a dog biscuit at Miss Lomax.

'I...' Alice looked at Norm.

'I'd say you wait. Wood will come. Catchpole will come. Shotley will come.'

'Come,' Merritt said sounding more like his uncle William Catchpole by the minute.

'You do know my telephone is ringing constantly.'

'Probably.'

'You know I can't get hold of Wood, Catchpole or Shotley.'

'Most likely.'

'Alice. Who runs this joint?' Earl sat back, took a long drag of his fifth cigarette and gave his two bobs worth.

'Um.'

'You do.'

'Well.'

'Be honest Miss Lomax,' Norm said.

'I try.'

'And do a stirling job of it too.' Norm fanned himself.

'Stirling,' Merritt nodded and began to roll up his sleeves.

'So...' Lois fanned herself with the paper. 'So we stand together. We make this work. Problem? What problem? All publicity is good publicity.'

'That's right,' Merritt forgot where he was and began to chew on his doggy-do biscuit.

'I have a pie chart. A campaign strategy.'

'That's the way.'

'We put it to Shotley,' Alice said. 'Like it's a done deal. He can't have his money back. It's been allocated.' It didn't take much to get the heat going with five people fanning the flames. No-one wants to get the sack three weeks away from Christmas.

As Norm predicted Wood took time out from his heady lifestyle schedule, Catchpole cancelled a luncheon date and Shotley in a wholly unprecedented move took a taxi to CWA and they arrived just after lunch when the thermometer reached 101 degrees. Alice ran down to the workroom to gather the forces.

'They're here.'

Lois grabbed her pie chart. Norm snatched his drawing. Earl whipped his notes up and Merritt straightened his tie.

'Ready?' Alice asked.

They made a united front walking into the boardroom. The three men were beetroot red as the sun was shining mercilessly through the window.

'Ah,' Catchpole said.

'Hmm.' Wood stood and dabbed at the sweat on his face.

'Well, well, well,' said Shotley.

Alice shut the door and listened.

Theodore Wood took a deep breath and they waited.

'So...' Lois jumped and her pie chart slipped from her bundle and slid to the floor.

'Sorry.' She bent down as Merritt came to the rescue and a crack of skulls broke the silence.

'You alright?' Merritt grabbed her elbow and rubbed his head with his other hand.

'I'm fine.' Lois frowned and rubbed the lump.

'Miss?'

'Mackenzie,' Lois offered.

'Sit down.'

'Yes sir.'

They settled in their places around the table which threw up a blinding reflection. Everyone squinted which in turn made everyone look very earnest, even Merritt.

'Now, it seems we have a situation on our hands.'

'Situation,' Catchpole came to life.

'Hmm.' Ol' man Shotley nodded. The team looked at Lois.

'Well I for one never thought it would be like this,' Shotley fiddled with his tie.

'Me neither.' Catchpole raised his eye brows.

'Sir, I...' Lois started, but came up short when Norm gave her the look. They knew enough not to begin to dig a hole. 'Never apologise,' Earl had reiterated the motto right before they faced the firing squad.

'Never,' Catchpole echoed Shotley.

Shotley stood up, took off his jacket, put it on the back of his chair and then came around to Lois.

'I want to shake your hand young lady.'

'Sir?' Lois looked at Mr Wood.

'Unprecedented. We were on the front page. And didn't cost a penny. Am I right Wood?'

'Not a penny Eugene.'

'Not a farthing,' Catchpole caught on.

'Brilliant. We've had orders all morning.'

'Really?' Lois said.

'Flat out.' Shotley was still shaking her hand.

'Flat out,' Catchpole reiterated.

'Marvellous work.' Shotley let go her hand and beamed at the team. 'I want CWA to have all I've got. Everything. Grace and what's his name can go take a running jump.' Now it was Mr Wood's turn to raise an eyebrow. Lois looked at the team. Merritt was lagging behind,

'So you like it?'

‘Like it? Like it? It’s brilliant.’ Shotley slapped the table and dust motes flew around in the sun. ‘I want,’ Shotley looked at Lois, ‘I want this young girlie right on it.’

‘It’s Miss Mackenzie.’

‘On it.’ Shotley nodded. ‘That’s right.’ Shotley pulled out a hanky and wiped his brow. ‘One hundred degrees in the shade,’ he chuckled.

‘Sir,’ Lois smoothed her hair, felt her lump and took a breath. ‘I think we should capitalise on Bishop O’Leary’s prophetic words.’ Wood leaned in and fanned himself with Lois’s pie chart.

‘Go on,’ Catchpole said.

‘Well how about...’ and Lois outlined her ideas, her stratagem and her brain cranked up a notch. This was business. This was cut throat competition. This was the meaning of Christmas.

‘It’s a gift.’ Shotley said.

‘That’s just what I said,’ Earl interjected.

‘So,’ Merritt frowned, ‘are you giving a Fridge-o-matic as a gift?’ Merritt might have thought A.D. stood for after dinosaurs. He might not have grasped the concept of a fridge light, but sometimes, not often, but sometimes he came up with something like a bit of a show stopper.

‘What did you say?’

‘Umm, a gift.’

‘Wood, you have geniuses coming out of the woodwork. A gift. Christmas. Holy Cow,’ Shotley said and then saw the nexus. Merritt missed the nexus and the nexus after that. ‘Sweet Jesus, a gift. To what’s his name.’

‘Who?’ Merritt asked.

‘The fellow.’

‘The Bishop of St Cuthbert’s in Waverly, Niall O’Leary.’ Lois said filling in the blank.

‘A stunt,’ Norm said. ‘We haven’t had one of those for...well for a long time.’

‘I think I did the last one with Wack-*O* ,’ Earl said. ‘The Prime Minister if I recollect caught eating Wack-*O* for breakfast.’

‘Ah.’ Catchpole closed his eyes. ‘They were good times.’

‘Indeed,’ Wood said. ‘You shall have your stunt Eugene.’

‘Right.’

‘Papers, photographers, radio,’ Lois fanned herself with demographic statistics. Wood smiled. Catchpole smiled. Shotley’s face practically split from ear to ear.

‘I want this girlie here.’

‘It’s Lois Mackenzie sir.’

‘Eh?’ Catchpole asked.

‘Lois Mackenzie.’

‘Right.’

‘Well Miss. I want your best efforts, ‘Shotley put his handkerchief away and stood up. ‘The meaning of Christmas,’ he walked to the door, ‘I like it.’

What Bishop O’Leary thought on the turn of events was anyone’s guess—although they wouldn’t need to guess for too long.

✦ CHAPTER 8

Now, in religious circles it's a bit of a given that what one mob do, the other is not far behind. From the Spanish Inquisition to Thomas Becket, there has been a bit of argy-bargy on who did what, who has the most, and who comes first on the reservation book at St Peter's pearly gates. But in quiet moments the Anglicans and the Catholics might agree to disagree. Business is business.

Renwick Auden Bothom Archbishop of St Andrews Waverly, (a coincidence with Bishop O'Leary I know, but there you have it), sat at his breakfast and perused the morning paper. Mildred, his faithful housekeeper put the teapot down on the trivet and adjusted the tea cosy she'd knitted which looked like a bishop's mitre. To the man, or woman in the street. that's a pointy Bishop's hat.

'More toast?'

'No thank you Mrs Brewster.' Renwick looked at the headlines. BISHOP IN FUROR. PRICES UP FOR CHRISTMAS. HEAT WAVE CONTINUES.

'Shocking.'

'Yes. 100 degrees in the shade,' Mildred chuckled. She'd seen the billboard on the way to work.

'What?'

'100 degrees in the flippin' shade.'

'Look,' Bothom pointed to the other headline.

'Oh.'

'O'Leary. That man.'

Bishop Bothom had quite a lot to say about his rival for souls in the diocese of Waverly. Mildred had heard it more than once in her tenure as housekeeper.

'He gets front page.'

'Yes, I see that.'

' And the Anglicans? Where are we?'

'I don't know.'

'Neither do I Mrs Brewster, neither do I.'

✦

Bishop Niall O'Leary ate his Wack-*O* cereal and basked in the Glory, not of his particular God, but the God of good editing and two columns on the front page.

'Ah,' he read the report for the third time. This was sure to get some runs on the board at HQ. Although Rome didn't exactly have its finger on the pulse at St Cuthbert's and the Italians wouldn't know a cricket bat if it hit them for six, but Bishop O'Leary was a cheerful soul and a positive attitude never hurt anyone. He thought of Renwick Bothom and a small smile crept over his face.

'Bothom comes bottom again. No runs for you Renwick Auden Bothom.' Even Bishops can gloat, they are human after all—no matter what they might imagine themselves to be.

'Oh, Mrs Cooper,' Bishop O'Leary waved his spoon at Erma Cooper to emphasise his point. 'I'll be out for lunch. I expect I will be summoned.'

'Right you are Bishop.' Erma made a mental list of the things that might be achieved without a rotund Bishop underfoot. Niall O'Leary's positive attitude rarely extended beyond himself.

'Do you happen to know if my secretary has arrived?'

'Father Aspinall?'

‘Um, yes, that’s the fellow.’ O’Leary only had one secretary. It was a habit, one that even a positive attitude couldn’t gloss over that Erma would always answer with what sounded like a question. The uplilt of her speech at the end left the listener hunting for an answer. It was enough to put a bishop off his breakfast. Just as well O’Leary was made of sterner stuff. Any tailor who had the temerity to inquire of his waist measurements would undoubtedly see Bishop O’Leary was made for the long haul.

‘I’ll see, shall I?’

‘If you would Mrs Cooper.’ The Wack-*O* ’s were given a second go as Erma plodded off to enquire.

Father Jeremy Aspinall—aspiring parish priest, secretary to the Bishop and all round good egg, came through the kitchen door and bumped into Erma.

‘Oh, sorry Mrs Cooper.’

‘He’ll be looking for you I expect.’

‘No doubt.’ Jeremy spied some scones and made a beeline for some nourishment.

‘Don’t feed you at your lodgings then?’

‘Well, not like your cooking Mrs Cooper.’

‘Arrhh, get away with ya,’ Erma pushed a hair back into her hairnet. ‘In the dining room,’ she hoiked her head to indicate down the passage.

‘Now?’

‘Most likely,’ Erma gave Father Jeremy a napkin, indicated a bit of jam on his burgeoning moustache and pushed him out the door.

‘Ah,’ O’Leary looked up from his tea. ‘Good God, what is that?’

‘Bishop?’

‘That,’ O’Leary pointed to the moustache in residence on Jeremy’s upper lip.

'This?' Jeremy patted his new pet. 'Sort of modern, up to the minute. It might give us relevance to the young people.' Jeremy liked the movies. He felt his buddy lip hair gave him a debonair man about town look. He envisaged saving girls tied to railway tracks and that sort of melodramatic flavour. He fiddled with it.

The Bishop looked at it with a critical eye. He couldn't see the correlation of young people, the Catholic Church and a moustache, but he had other battles on his mind.

'It will grow?'

'That's the plan,' Jeremy smoothed out his Clark Gable.

'Well,' O'Leary waved his hand to dismiss the subject. 'Seen this?'

'Um no.' Jeremy peered at the proffered paper.

'Read it,' the Bishop pointed. Jeremy read. He digested the columns and looked up at his superior. 'Good.'

'It is?'

'Obviously it is. Made an impression.'

'It did.' Mrs Coopers inflection and upper lilt was quite catchy.

'Of course it did. I'm on the front page.' And then Jeremy was instructed. He was told to write a letter to make it absolutely clear where the Catholic Church stood on such matters.

'And where exactly is it we stand Bishop?' Jeremy asked, because as far as Father Aspinall, aspiring parish priest could see, Christmas was boom time for the company. People found the church after a long absence. People gave to charity like their souls depended on it and people were full of goodwill to all men, (and women). And if an advert jogged their conscience, their memory of the meaning of the Christmas story, it was a win. A little bit of trickle down never hurt anyone.

'Where we stand?' O'Leary picked a wayward Wack-*O* from the tablecloth. 'Where we stand my boy is on the side of tradition. None of this claptrap. There is only one story at Christmas. Our story. Back to basics.' Jeremy hoped it wasn't too basic. Mrs Cooper did a cracking turkey roast and her mince pies were legendary.

'Basics Bishop?'

'Jesus, Mary and Joseph,' the Bishop said. Jeremy wasn't convinced the Bishop hadn't just blasphemed. 'Basics. A letter to this advertising agency. Someone needs to know.'

'To know Bishop?'

'That, well, that we are...'

'Yes?' Jeremy waited.

'That we are watching with interest.'

'Interest?'

'That's it. Interest. As soon as we get word from the umpire,' and here the Bishop winked, 'well then we will see.' The Bishop finished his tea and looked at Jeremy with a raised eye brow. 'You still here?'

'Your Grace.'

'Wait. On second thoughts, go see these people face to face. That will change their tune. The might of the Catholic Church and all that.' Jeremy walked away thinking on what he might say to the Agency. How to convey the might of the Catholic Church with a few chosen words. The Bishop's thought processes were vague on detail. Still, a day in the city was always welcome, even if it was 95 degrees Fahrenheit and climbing.

⁂

By the time Father Jeremy climbed the stairs from the train stations his suit was uncomfortably warm, his hat felt two sizes too small and his sweat had all but disintegrated the starched collar that defined his calling.

He looked at the incline ahead and began to walk to CWA. Rehearsing his little speech along the walk one might mistake his mutterings for prayer, as did a fellow sitting on the footpath in a small square of shade.

'Say one for me will ya?'

'Jeremy startled from his musing. 'Oh, yes, right,' he said and blushed. Although he wanted his own parish, his flock to guide to righteousness, he didn't have much in the way of people skills as the corporate world defined them. People were unpredictable, apt to dislike you just for breathing and Jeremy found they used your goodwill willy-nilly.

'Goodwill,' he muttered as he hunted for the CWA Building.

Miss Lomax looked up as Jeremy stood and ran his finger around his collar.

'Yes?'

'Er, um, ah.' Jeremy's people skills failed him. Young women often did that to him. They were so confident, so forthright, so womanly, it would unnerve anyone, never mind a new priest.

'Sir?' Alice smiled.

Jeremy sweated. 'Look. Um, I have come here on behalf of Bishop O'Leary of the diocese of Waverly.'

'Oh.' Alice recognised the name.

'Yes. And you see, well, the Bishop has some concerns over your billboard.'

'Does he?' Alice wasn't making it easy for the Father.

'Yes. You see he feels that, well that it's a bit too close to, well too close.'

'To what?' Alice asked trying not to smirk.

'Well,' Jeremy fished about for his handkerchief to wipe the sweat from his brow. 'Well, we, that is, the Bishop, that is, I mean to say the Church, That's the Catholic church will be watching with interest.' Oh how he wished he'd written a letter.

'With interest?'

'Yes, that's it. With interest.'

'Thanks for the information Mr ?'

'Oh, Sorry. Aspinall, Jeremy Aspinall, secretary to Bishop O'Leary.'

'Well thanks `Mr Aspinall.'

'Father actually.'

'Father Aspinall,' Alice corrected.

'That's it.' Jeremy pocketed his hanky and took a breath. 'Hot in here isn't it.'

'Wait until you see our campaign for next week. This place will be on fire.' Alice cracked her knuckles and slotted a piece of paper into her typewriter. Jeremy's Adam's apple bobbled.

'Next week?'

'Uhuh.'

'Right.' They looked at one another.

'Oh, and...'

'Yes?' Jeremy hoped for a slither of good news to take back to HQ. 'Thank the Bishop for giving us our slogan. Much obliged.'

'Slogan?'

'Yes.' Alice dinged her typewriter carriage. 'The meaning of Christmas.' Jeremy felt his name being struck off the Bishop's Christmas list of promotions. He thought he might have dropped off St Peter's reservations and slipped into the book of the damned.

The train ride back to the Bishopric was consumed with Jeremy's moral dilemma. Should he come clean on what was about to transpire? Tricky. After all, he had inside knowledge. The Bishop would be furious. Or, could he act surprised when CWA unveiled their banners on busses, posters and a full one page spread in the paper and perhaps save his future prospects?

'I gave them the full weight of your opinion sir.'

'Hmmm.' Bishop O'Leary ate a mince pie and neglected to catch the crumbs. Somehow he'd missed the vital call from the Cardinal's office and therefore missed lunch.

'They listened with interest sir.'

'With contrition?'

Well, I couldn't say sir. But they said they were grateful to you for your input.'

Well, it wasn't a lie!

Bishop O'Leary finished his bounteous afternoon tea as Jeremy looked longingly at the one mince pie left on the plate. He'd missed lunch at his lodgings and although man can't live by bread alone, it was quite an important part of keeping body and soul together.

'I want a letter Aspinall, to HQ.'

'Sir.'

'Let them know I'm on the case. Doing all I can. Day and night. All that sort of thing.' O'Leary weighed up the mince pie -v- his expanding waistline. He popped the whole thing in his mouth. 'to 'et 'em 'now I 'ave' ever'ing under 'on'ol.' Jeremy's stomach rumbled. If he wasn't feasting on goodwill to all men, including Bishops, he might have had rumblings of discontent.

'Yes sir.'

✦ CHAPTER 9

'I haven't had so much fun since they put pineapple in a tin.' (it was some debacle about with or without a hole apparently). Shotley looked at the headlines, then at the one page spread on page four of the Sydney morning paper. The team sat at the large table and basked in the accolades. Wood and Catchpole sat and smiled as they all looked at Page 4.

THE MEANING OF CHRISTMAS

A
FRIDGE-O-MATIC

The 3 wise men knew a thing or two when they chipped in for a **FRIDGE-O-MATIC.**

'Bloody marvellous,' Shotley said.

Alice scooted from the closed door and rushed to the telephone. It would be either an irate citizen using words like disgusting, disgraceful and disrespectful or someone who thought it was a breath of fresh air, about time and usually ended with, 'its 100 degrees in the flippin' shade,' and chuckled at their own cleverness.

'CWA, good morning.' Alice said.

'CWA, I want the advertising agency, not the Country Women's association.'

'That's us sir.'

'Well put me onto the advertising agency.'

'Speaking.'

'Me? I am,' and Archbishop Renwick Bothom drew himself up in his leather chair, put on his pulpit voice and announced his name, his title, his diocese and his connections in high places. Alice listened, rolled her eyes and waited for the Archbishop's ego to run out of steam.

'And your business Mr Bottoms? We are fully booked until the new year if you want our expert services.'

'Bothom. It's Archbishop Bothom. Services. I don't want your services. I want...'

And Alice listened to Archbishop Bothom not bottoms explain he was disgusted, it was disgraceful and very disrespectful. He went on to say he spoke for every Australian when he condemned this outrage. Alice wondered if the Archbishop had ever been to the pub on a Friday night, because every Australian she had seen there couldn't give two bob about their moral outrage.

'Well, I will certainly let Mr Wood, Mr Catchpole and our expert team know of your concerns.'

Bothom sat back and thought it went quite well. He forgot to add the parable he'd pencilled into his notes, but that woman, he felt, would still be smarting from her dressing down. *The Catholics*, he thought *were not the only ones to corner the market in indignation.*

'One needs to make a stand,' he said to himself. 'If the Catholics can get the front page, the Anglicans can get the job done.'

'Pardon?' Mrs Brewster asked as she came in with morning tea.

'Oh. Just musing Mrs Brewster. When I get going, I'm a power to be reckoned with.'

'Right you are Your Grace.' Mrs Brewster looked to heaven, although she might have been rolling her eyes, one can never tell.

✦

Alice hovered at the door. She didn't want to interrupt the meeting, but they needed to know what was happening in the wide world. She listened for a break in the proceedings and knocked.

'Sir,' she smiled at the attendees.

'Yes?'

'I thought you'd like to know that we've had a visit from the clergy and another on the phone. They are quite put out by...well by this.' Alice pointed to the paper on the table. The Archbishop of Waverly was just on the phone, and a fellow, Father,' she consulted her notes, 'Father Aspinall, secretary to Bishop O'Leary was in.'

'Well, this is something.'

'Yes sir.'

'Any mention of legal proceedings Miss Lomax?'

'No sir.'

'Any talk of slander, libel, or such?'

'No sir.'

'Protest letters, rallies or letters to the editor?'

'Not that I heard.'

'Ah.'

'Ah,' reiterated Catchpole.

'Toothless tigers.' Wood said. 'Bluff and blunder.'

'Wait 'till the bishop gets his Fridge-o-matic.' Wood looked at Shotley. 'I'd like to see the indignation on his face then.'

'Oh, I think he'd be rather pleased,' Merritt said missing the irony. He most likely thought irony was something on a label of a shirt and to do with laundering.

⌘

Lois sat at her desk and tapped her pencil on her teeth. She had a few more themed slogans on her lined paper, but her mind wandered to the opportunity to be had when the Bishop got his comeuppance.

'Did Alice say Father Aspinall?' Norm asked anyone within earshot.

'Yes. That's right.' Merritt arranged his dog biscuits in order of size.

'Aspinall. It rings a bell somehow.'

'Know him Norm?' Earl asked.

'I don't know. But the name rings a bell.' He shook the thought away and continued with his rough sketches for Lois's new catchphrase.

Things were hotting up. Alice took to writing down every indignant phone call, every pat on the back and kept a score board. The bus banners were out and about and getting quite a bit of attention.

SICK OF WINTER WONDERLAND?

Its 100° in the flippin' shade.

An *Australian* tradition ~a~ **FRIDGE-O-MATIC.**

So far, the score was definitely in favour of the new Australian tradition. People were hot. They were bothered and women were fed up to the eye teeth with all this clap-trap of snow, sleighs, and slaving over a roast turkey when all they wanted was a cold drink, a ham salad and jelly and ice-cream. Alice commiserated with her callers. She assured them she would pass on their well wishes to the team and she always, always let them know that the genius who dreamt up the campaign, the absolute mastermind was a young lady with exceptional qualities. 'Bout bloody time,' was the general consensus.

As the afternoon wore on the telephone calls thinned. 'So, the score is 50-50' Alice stood at Lois's desk and fanned herself.

'So that's good is it?' Merritt asked.

'It could go either way,' Norm added. Lois bit her fingernail and worried.

'Miss Mackenzie, don't worry.' Alice blew her hair from her face, 'It'll all blow over after Christmas anyway.'

'Short memories,' Earl said. 'The magic of advertising.' He chuckled at his own joke.

⌘

The debate, or the debacle, whichever side of the fence you were on, had taken over the nation, well Sydney anyway and Sydneysiders thought the rest of the country were inconsequential in the scheme of things.

Lois scooted in front of a bus on her way to the train station and jumped to the footpath just in time to see the banner on the side of the bus. It didn't have tinsel, or the usual decorations that denoted Christmas. A Fridge-o-matic and a promise of something wholly Australian.

'Refreshing, isn't it.' A woman said as Lois stared.

'Hmmm?'

'Refreshing. I for one think it's about time.'

'Yes.' The woman's sentiment made Lois smile. She walked through the throng of workers to her platform thinking on the words and waited in the slant of the afternoon sun. People made for the shade, crowding the small patch, waiting.

'Still smiling I see,' Serg sidled up to Lois and put his bag between his feet.

'Oh, hello.' Lois shaded her eyes and screwed up her face as she looked directly into the sun.

'Good day?'

'Um, yes. I guess you could call it a good day.' People jostled as the train pulled in to disgorge its passengers. Lois made ready to rush for a seat when the door opened. 'My campaign is up and running. You might have seen it, Fridge-o-matic.'

'I think I did.' Serg frowned. 'something to do with Christmas?'

'Yes, that's it.' Lois smiled. 'Yes, a good day,' she said.

'Me too,' Serg said.

The doors opened and humanity surged forward. Lois missed her footing, tripped over Serg's work bag and went sprawling on the dirty platform as people stepped over her.

'Bloody hell,' Serg lifted her up and they sprinted for the carriage door, only to be stopped by the platform conductor.

'Stand back,' the little man said and blew his whistle.

'Damn.' Lois looked at her skinned knees, her filthy skirt and picked grit out of her hands.

'My fault.' Serg shrugged and sucked on his teeth.

'The next one is not for half an hour.' Lois thought on Mr Moon. He shut up shop early on a Thursday. Now she'd need to try to make something at home, or splash out on fish and chips. Brushing herself down she took a deep breath, then another and tried to remain calm, focussed and in control. *The Seven Steps to Success* suggested in through the nose and out through the mouth. Her nostrils flares as she sucked in the train fumes. It was always chaos, no matter how hard she tried.

'Look, I feel bad about it, how about I ring my brother. He'll still be at work, and well, he can collect us, and then we could take you home.'

'A taxi?'

'Nah, he has his own car. He owes me a favour.'

There comes a time in a woman's life when she needs to take a leap of faith.

'Oh, alright. But I live over near the Cream of Tartar works.'

'That's ok.' Serg picked up his bag, picked up Lois's bag and they went in search of a telephone kiosk.

'You got any change Lois,' Serg bit his lip and smiled.

✦

Markos waved from the driver's seat and parked in a bus stop. He beckoned the pair over and revved the Holden in some sort of macho show.

'Thanks,' Lois sat in the front and tried to hide her dirty skirt with her handbag.

'It's ok.' Markos winked and turned to his older brother and gave him the 'so you finally snag yourself a woman' look. He looked over Lois and shook his head at his brother. The way Markos saw it, Serg must have acted like a cave man and chased her down before she bolted.

‘Just drive,’ Serg said and Lois offered her address and some instructions on how to get there from the centre of the business district at peak hour traffic chaos.

Markos was one of those lads who think they can chat, take their hand off the wheel to run their fingers through their hair, light a cigarette and fiddle with the rear-vision mirror while driving. Lois hung on as they weaved, squeezed and tooted their way out of the traffic to relatively calmer roads.

‘Um, I just need to stop and get some shopping for my tea,’ Lois said.

‘What. You got nothing at home?’ Markos asked. The thought of not having food in the house was almost a crisis. Greek households always had something in a jar, on the table, in the cupboard or fridge.

‘No, and I really don’t want to splash on fish and chips.’

Markos looked at his brother in the rear-view mirror. He raised an eyebrow, then the other one.

‘Um Lois,’ Serg coughed.

‘Hmmm.’

‘Well...’ He cleared his throat. ‘If you want, well, only if you want, you could have tea at our place. My mum always makes enough for an army.’

‘She sure does,’ Markos said taking his hands off the wheel.

And that ol’ leap of faith kicked in. Lois weighed up the options. She thought on an evening alone in her hot box with a boiled egg and some stale bread. She wasn’t in the habit of being picked up by strange men, not that any strange men had tried, but a home-cooked meal sounded just the ticket.

‘As long as I get home before 9. I’ve got to go to work tomorrow,’ she looked at her skirt, ‘and do some washing.’

‘Easy.’ Markos leaned out of the driver’s window, did some sort of inventive hand gesture and moved into the right turning lane.

Marrickville was almost a satellite city of mainland Greece. A little enclave of olive oil, BBQs and plenty of children. Markos drove up to the Agridopolous house and revved the Holden to let the world know they were back.

'Ah,' Mrs A came out of the house and waved a tea towel at the car.

'That's my mother,' Serg said. When Mrs A saw a woman she whipped the tea towel behind her back, straightened her hair and smoothed her apron.

'Who is this,' she looked Lois over like she was picking fruit at a green grocers.

'Mum, this is Lois.'

'Lois eh.'

'Yep.' Serg put his bag down. She's had a fall and...' he didn't get any further as Mrs A took Lois by the arm, tisked at her sons, worried about Lois's knees, her skirt and her wellbeing and ushered her into the kitchen.

'Really, I'm, alright Mrs Adopolishus.'

''S'all right. A-gri-dop-o-l-ous.'

'Sorry A-gri-dop-o-l-ous,' Lois said as Mrs A plopped her into a chair and went for a basin and some hot water.

'Mum, Lois is staying for tea.' Serg came into the kitchen and began to wash his hands in the sink.

''S'all right. Bathroom Serg. I-yah.' Mrs A shooed her son out. 'Crazy boy,' she said to Lois who watched all the action with a mixture of delight and wonder.

'Now, I-yah, I fix.'

Lois sat in a garden chair with patches of mercurochrome on her knees, a towel around her waist as her skirt was being washed, and a cold drink at the ready.

Serg emerged in shorts and a clean shirt and sat down next to her.

'Alright?'

‘Yes thanks,’ Lois inspected her red knees, her band-aid on her hand and looked at her drink. ‘You really didn’t need to go to all this trouble. Tell your mother she doesn’t need to coddle me.’

‘You tell her.’ Serg smiled and they laughed.

‘Eh,’ Mrs A interrupted their laugh. ‘You want to see Serg photographie?’

‘Mum.’

‘I-yah. I can’t be proud of my son. Come.’

Lois was given the grand tour of the photographic evidence that Serg had grown up. She was also given a tour of the trophies for football, tennis and then his electrical licence.

‘So you’re an electrician?’

‘That’s right,’ Mrs A said and wiped the diploma with her tea towel. ‘And you?’

‘Um, I’m in advertising.’ Mrs A nodded and flicked a tea towel over an icon on the wall.

‘What sort?’ Mrs A asked. She picked up a crucifix and gave it the once over with her spit and tea towel.

‘Um,’ Lois looked at the religious paraphernalia. She took in the nativity scene, the icons, the glowing picture of Mary and the three wise men painted on black velvet. ‘Um,’

Some people are tone deaf. Some are colour blind. Lois was afflicted with that disease known as foot in mouth, or as the French call it faux pas.

‘Well actually,’ Lois began, I’m working on the new campaign for Fridge-o-matic right now.’

‘What? This advertising eh?’ Mrs A picked up a paster statue of the Church of the Holy Sepulchre and rubbed the cupola.

‘Have you seen it, the Fridge-o-matic?’

Serg's eyes opened wide. He gave Lois a look that only a blind man would miss. Mrs A picked up her nativity scene and adjusted the little lamb in the stable.

'And other things. You do other things Lois. Lots of other things don't you?' Serg threw a lifeline. Lois missed it.

'Well, yes other things, but the Fridge-o-matic is sort of, well...' She didn't want to blow her own trumpet, but... 'sort of.' She looked at Serg, and although her tutor often said that some might not understand the subtleties, the nuances, the fineness of advertising, it was an art form to be proud of, Lois stopped short. She looked at Jesus on the wall, with a sacred heart picked out in red light bulbs. She smiled at Serg. She kinda knew which 50% Mrs A might stand with on the issue of the Fridge-o-matic.

'Sort of dog biscuits, men's ties, and oh,' she stood a little taller, 'Wack-*O* .'

'Wack-*O* ?' Mrs A came back into the conversation. 'My Serg, he love the Wack-*O* .'

'Do you?'

'Mum, I was twelve.'

'I-yah, a mother can't remember her own son?'

'Mum.'

As the evening wore on the house filled with people, all talking, all doing things and all controlled to some degree by Mrs A. When Mr A came home there was beer, more shouting, more talking, more shooing out of the kitchen. Serg introduced his family one at a time, and each raised an eye brow at the thought of Serg snaffling a girl.

'First time for everything,' his father said and gave Lois a beer.

'What do you do Miss?' Mr A looked Lois over and gave a nod of approval.

‘She’s in advertising dad. You know, Wack-*O* cereal, all that type of thing.’

‘Wack-*O* ’ Mr nodded in approval once again.

Mrs A invited Lois into the kitchen as the men sat under a gum tree in the yard.

‘You like the lamb?’

‘Oh, yes.’

‘You like the veg?’

‘Uhuh.’

‘Salad.’

‘Hmmm.’ Lois watched Mrs A prepare the meal and not a cook book in sight.

‘What recipe is this?’ Lois asked.

‘Is what?’

‘Recipe. What recipe are you following?’

‘I don’t do recipe. It is food, it is cooking.’ Mrs A took a good look at Lois. ‘You cook?’ It was one of those questions that could have myriad of ramifications the way Mrs A waited for the definitive answer.

‘Um yes. Mostly savoury mince.’

‘Ah.’

‘With Good housekeeping.’

‘Ah.’ Mrs A narrowed her eyes at this young woman who didn’t cook. She crossed herself and looked to heaven in silent prayer that Serg wasn’t making a terrible mistake. She knew her son couldn’t live on savoury mince.

‘You come. I show you. Saturday yes? Seg likes meat pie. You could tell Mrs A until you were blue in the face, but she insisted the meat pie came from Greece. ‘His favourite. You come Saturday.’

‘Um, well, if you’re sure.’

‘I’m sure.’ As a mother she wasn’t about to release her son into the clutches of a woman who couldn’t cook. Her duty was clear.

Without so much as a dinner bell the family began to congregate around the large kitchen table for their evening meal. Nine people, including Lois, who had been reunited with her skirt as it dried in about twenty minutes in the evening heat. There was enough food to feed...well feed a family of eight Greeks, plus one. Serg sat next to Lois and plied her with food as the family watch.

'What do you do Miss?' Daphnie, the youngest asked.

'She's into advertising. Wack-*O* and stuff like that,' Serg said while scooping more beans on Lois's plate.

'Oh. I guess you started off as a secretary,' Daphnie said. 'Dad wants me to be a secretary.'

'Is a good job for a lady.' Mr A said between a mouthful of potato.

'I went to university.'

That made the table wake up. They'd never met a university person before. They had the idea university people were oozing brains, wore glasses and only drank tea.

'University,' Daphnie's eyes blazed in admiration. Adele, Helen and Christina smiled and raised their eyebrows to their father. Markos whistled.

'Eh,' Mrs A waved a tea towel at a fly. She was the only one unimpressed by a degree. If a woman couldn't cook, in her estimation, she was sorely in need of an education.

'What did you do?' Adele asked.

'Marketing and commerce, with a side of sociology.' The Agridopolous family stopped chewing.

Dessert came with ice-cream that melted as quick as you spooned it in your mouth.

'And what about your parents?' Helen asked as she scraped her bowl clean.

'Well, my mother and father live in Queensland.'

‘Ah,’ Mr A said with a sigh. He one day dreamed of moving to sunny climes. Pineapples as big as your head, bananas for everyone and swimming all year round. Of course he conveniently forgot about the mosquitoes, sandflies, stinging jellyfish and flying foxes. Queensland was heaven if the brochures were to be believed.

‘You live alone?’ Daphnie said.

‘Yes. A small flat.’ The Agridopolous girls looked at their mother and father.

‘Your own place?’

‘Yes.’

‘You don’t share at all?’

‘No, just me.’

Oh, this was just about as good as it gets on the female side of the family. Here was living proof that women could go out in the world and make something of themselves. The name of Lois Mackenzie might live forever as a beacon of hope in the Agridopolous family.

‘And your mother, she cooks?’ Mrs A wiped some pear juice from the plastic table cloth with the tea towel.

‘Oh, yes.’ Lois said and finished her pear and icecream.

Coffee was served in the lounge room as the family crowded around the radio. The paper served up the programme for the evening and the family marked what they would like, but Mr A had the dial, although he usually fell asleep and then it was a free for all. Lois sat between the sisters and was bombarded with questions about her flat, her furniture, her prospects and her future. She’d never had a sibling and quite enjoyed the atmosphere when, on the radio the dulcet tones of Ray Salter came over the speaker talking about the latest news around Sydney. He began with Bishop O’Leary.

Lois took in the icons, the baby Jesus, the paster caste of the church and swallowed. The 50% symbol stuck in her throat like a chicken bone.

'Sshhh.' Mrs A said and flapped her tea towel at the girls.

'Bishop O'Leary,' Ray Salter said, and didn't get any further when Lois jumped up, looked at her watch and said,

'Goodness, is that the time.'

Even a woman with a tendency for a faux pas can have a moment of clarity.

She left with a slice of apple cake, a promise to visit again on the Saturday and a bottle of mercurochrome, oh, and the undying admiration of four Agridopolous girls who dreamed of a place of their own, a university education and a decent wage.

'See you tomorrow Lois,' Serg walked her over the concrete front yard as Markos waited in his car.

'Tomorrow,' Lois put the troublesome key in her lock on the first go, saw Mrs Provoichkin's curtains twitch and went inside to her 85° hot box.

✦ CHAPTER 10

A night tossing and turning, your conscience pricking you like a penitence undershirt and your bed feeling like a furnace isn't conducive to a good night's sleep and fresh as a daisy on the morrow.

Lois flopped over on a cool side of the sheet and opened one eye. That's all it took. The clock showed 8:30. She usually caught the 8:33 into work.

'Damn.' Stumbling out of bed she stubbed her toe. Recovering she stood on her shoe and the heel snapped under the weight. Then her nighty caught on the door knob and in frustration she ripped it in two. Things weren't going well.

Any sane person might call it a day at this point, feign a sore throat and call in sick. Lois didn't have a phone in the flat. She'd never been sick enough to take a day off and really didn't relish the prospect of walking to Mr Moon's to call in sick. Her toe throbbed. She looked at her shoe.

'Deep breath,' she said as she waited for the air in the pipes to burp their way to the tap and the water to start flowing.

The shower did nothing to relieve her toe, and while she dressed she thought on the Agridopolous family. Their dinner was obviously the culprit. A full stomach, beer. Yep, that's what it was. She was accustomed to a small serving of mince, not the whopping great big dinner she'd packed away the night before. Mrs A marvelled at the woman and the way she could eat.

The only shoes left in her wardrobe were sandals. They looked flimsy, but... She sighed, beggars can't be choosers.

The apple cake was consumed at the station and fell on her shirt.

'Oh, shit,' she said. An old man looked on.

'Here,' he offered a clean, laundered, ironed handkerchief.

'Oh, I'm alright. It's alright.' Lois said.

'Go on, take it.'

'Thanks,' Lois said. 'How will I get it back to you?'

'Don't worry about it Miss. I got plenty more. I get 'em every Father's Day, Christmas and Birthday. Should be getting some quite soon.' He pointed to a poster of the Fridge-o-matic on the railway platform.

'I guess you'd prefer a Fridge-o-matic,' she pointed.

'Well...' the man began, 'it's like this. I got three sons, three grandchildren, and three great grandchildren. If I get nine hankies well, that'll do me. What do I want with one of them,' he pointed to the poster. 'Every time I blow the ol' hooter I'll know I was in their thoughts. Every time I sneeze I will remember who was thinkin' of me. That's what counts. Not the hankie, but the thought.'

'The thought.'

'That's right Miss. It's not about getting somethin'. It's about givin' somethin'.'

Lois wiped the grease spot on her blouse and looked at the man. 'Thanks Mr...?'

'Eric Miller.'

'Thank you Mr Miller.'

The train arrived and they parted company. Lois narrowly avoided a woman with sharp pointy high heels and found a seat. She looked at her wrist watch and then gazed out at the day. She'd be late, but she'd get there in the end.

✦

Alice looked up from the telephone and rolled her eyes as Lois walked in. She pointed to the workroom and then held up her hand, fingers extended and mouthed five minutes. Lois nodded and made her way to her desk.

'Trouble at mill?' Norm said in a Yorkshire accent as Lois walked through the door.

'Heaven's above Lois, what are you wearing?' Merritt frowned and roved his eye over Lois and her hastily thrown together ensemble.

'I...' Lois looked at the mishmash of clothes she'd flung on.

'Wait there,' Merritt ran out of the office. Lois looked at Earl and shrugged.

'Don't look at me?' Earl said. 'I've been wearing the same thing for twenty years.' Norm stifled a laugh.

'Mac listen,' Norm said, 'Ol' man Shotley is on his way with some lawyers.' He looked at Lois. 'Now don't get your knickers in a twist, yet.'

'Lawyers?'

'Well, it's just to cover us. You know, sometimes these things can blow up.'

'I think this one is about to blow,' Earl chimed in. 'But listen Lois, we are all in this together eh. Teamwork eh?'

'Together,' Norm added.

Merritt rushed in with a skirt, blouse and some heels. He mopped the sweat from his brow and handed the goods over.

'I didn't know your size, but...well, I have an eye.' He winked. 'Get changed. You need to be presentable, smart, and ooze confidence.'

'Where did....?'

'Oh, I have friends in the district.' Lois looked at the labels on the clothes. 'Mrs Rene Larrouche, Haute Couture. These aren't just something off the peg,' Lois said.

‘Oh, alright. She’s my aunt. I made a call or two.’ Merritt smiled. ‘I have a hyphen in my name you know,’ he wiggled his little finger and pranced around the office. ‘Come to lunch on the week-end Lois and you will meet her.’

‘To say thank you?’

‘If you like.’ Merritt blew her a kiss as she scooted into the toilet to change.

Alice shot into the workroom and made a bee line for Lois.

‘Miss Mackenzie,’ she started, ‘Broadacre and Lombardi are coming at eleven o’clock. Mr Wood, Mr Catchpole and Mr Shotley will be attending.’

Lois nodded.

‘You need to be ready.’

‘Right.’

Alice looked at the consternation on Lois’s face. ‘You need your facts, your statistics, your pie chart. You need to face them down Miss Mackenzie. They will want you to take the...’ Alice looked at Norm, Earl and Merritt, ‘the...’

Panic makes some people faint, others freeze in the headlights. Lois swallowed her epiglottis and coughed it up again. She looked at her team. They stared back.

‘Well, I liked it,’ Merritt broke the moment. ‘It was good.’ He picked a thread off Lois and said, ‘they won’t fire you Lois, I’m sure of it.’ The epiglottis disappeared for a second time.

Several deep breaths later Lois walked towards the boardroom, her team giving her the thumbs up. Trying to remain cool, calm and collected she opened the door . The first one on the list *cool, was an impossibility as the sun beat down with a ferocity only matched by the perceived wrath of the principles. The *calm was anything but and the *collected came via a favour Lois wondered how she was going to pay back. All in all it wasn't an illustrious start.

'Ah, here she is,' Shotley stood up and ushered Lois to a chair. He was smiling which put some of the calm back into Lois. 'That's the way.' Shotley took her pie chart bundle and deposited them on the table. 'This is the young genius,' he beamed at the other men in the room. They didn't share Shotley's enthusiasm and refused to beam. 'This 'ere is Georgio Lombardi and that one is Wilson Broadacre.' Shotley pointed to the men who looked like they had been resurrected from the morgue and left out in the sun for a bit. Lombardi wiped his face with a florid handkerchief and Broadacre fanned himself with a manila folder.

'Good morning gentlemen,' Lois nodded in their direction. 'Mr Wood, Mr Catchpole, Mr Shotley,'

'Right then,' Shotley took a seat and undid his tie, popped the first button on his shirt and silently wished for a cold one, or two.

'It seems,' Mr Wood started, 'we have a situation.'

'Bloody understatement if you ask me,' Shotley said, then apologised for the 'bloody'.

'Yes, well, it seems,' and here Wood narrowed his eyes at Lois as if he was picking from a *most wanted* line-up at the police station, 'it seems there is some concern that your campaign has touch a raw nerve.'

'Raw,' Catchpole found his pulse.

'There is some concern that CWA will need to gird it's loins for some sort of legal wrangle.'

'Wrangle.'

'And,'

'Wrangle sir?' Lois frowned at the suggestion. She, for a millisecond thought of Amethyst Greenock and plucked up courage. People pleasers have a backbone, they just need to be reminded of the fact sometimes.

'The last I heard the Christmas story wasn't copyrighted.'

Shotley shook his head. He would have slapped Lois on the back if he'd been closer. 'She's right ya know. I told ya she was smart.'

'Be that as it may,' Broadacre said between flapping his folder, 'we think there might be some sort of...for a better word, libel, vilification, slander, denigration, defamation brought to bear.' Lombardi nodded and mopped his neck.

'By whom?' Lois asked.

'Well, the church of course.'

'Not very Christian of them is it?'

'I like this girl,' Shotley said and beamed a bit more.

'And can you defame a dead person?'

'Ah,' Lombardi said.

'Hmmm,' Broadacre added for emphasis.

'Smart,' Shotley said.

'I wonder if we should stick with jingle bells,' Wood mused.

'I like jingle bells,' Catchpole added and started to hum.

'Sir.' Lois stood up. She felt a million dollars in her Haute Couture. She just knew Amethyst wouldn't take it lying down. She took three deep breaths, pushed back a wayward hair, took another breath just for good measure and looked at the men. 'People want something Australian. We are unique, different, iconic. Australians have, I have observed, a somewhat shocking sense of humour. This campaign is all of these things. It is shockingly good fun, it is iconic, it is different and it is above all Australian. We may sing God Save the Queen, but heaven help the Church when the ordinary man or woman just wants a bit of Christmas that doesn't bend the knee. I say let the Church defend its position. I for one want to see the Bishop wriggle out of his free Fridge-o-matic.'

The men sat and stared. Catchpole's mouth dropped open. The lawyers wondered how they would squeeze their fee from CWA now Lois had laid it on the line. Shotley was beside himself with pride as if he'd given birth to Lois and just discovered the fact.

'What did I tell ya?'

✦

Iconoclast. The word had a nasty ring to it. It was a moniker that many a person in the spotlight tried to shuck off. Mr Wood ran his finger around his collar and wished he'd never heard of the word. But it flapped around on the boardroom table, put there by Mr Lombardi and remained.

'You don't want that distinction, do you?' It wasn't a rhetorical question.

'Well, I...' Wood said and snatched the manila folder from Broadacre to fan himself.

'What's that then?' Shotley asked. He, being a man more accustomed to 'what'll it be then?' than high falutin' jingo, casually raised his eye brow.

'Ah,' Catchpole wagged a finger, 'I know this one.' As a crossword aficionado, iconoclast was one of those words that compositors often use to try to bamboozle (another favourite) the public. 'It is,' Catchpole looked around the room as they waited, 'ungodly, blasphemer, desecrater, free thinker, profaner, agnostic, irreligionist, secular humanist,' and then he ended with 'pagan.'

Shotley lost the will to speak for a moment. Lois pursed her lips lest she say something that would see her unemployed right before Christmas.

'Ah,' Lombardi nodded and laced his fingers together over his file.

'Hmmm.' Broadacre concurred.

The men looked at Lois. The air crackled with anticipation. Mr Wood blinked.

'Oh, and heathen,' Catchpole said.

Lois sucked in air through her nostrils as if it was on a two for one special. They waited.

'Pfft.'

It took a second or two. Shotley came to life. 'That's my girl.'

✦ CHAPTER 11

The train ride home was a blur. The walk to Mr Moon was on automatic, and Mrs Provoichkin a phantom as Lois sat at her kitchenette table and mulled over the word. It wounded. It stung. It hurt, but she didn't quite know why.

'Rise above,' Amethyst Greenock had written. 'Everything is an opportunity,' Walter Fry suggested. Frederik Swan was once called a charlatan, and he was still selling books.

'Iconoclastic.' Lois said the word, rolled it around, repeated it. 'Just a word. Stick and stones may break my bones, but words will never hurt me.' But what did the man in the street think. Would Lois Mary Mackenzie forever be branded a pagan, a heathen? Her brain ruminated on the implications of the slur, for that's what it was, a slur, and all because she was trying her best, doing her darnest to succeed in a world where there were few opportunities to excel for a young woman with brains, daring and dash.

'Well Mr Shotley likes me,' she said to her minced beef. 'Norm likes me. Merritt likes me and Earl. Alice,' and she sat over her grey meat poking it trying to think of anyone else who quite liked a young woman with brains, daring and dash, and a big dollop of blasphemy. No-one came to mind.

⁂

Alice greeted Lois with a smile. Norm stopped on his way from the kettle and said a cheery 'morin''. Earl grinned from ear to ear as he greeted her and Merritt came in with an armful of papers and winked.

They stood and looked at her.

'What?'

'You tell her Earl,' Norm offered.

'What?'

'Lois, sit down.' She sat.

'Word is, you are nominated,' and Earl held up his finger in a pointed manner mimicking the Golden Finger.

'Go girl,' Merritt plonked his papers on her desk and patted her on the back.

'Me?'

'Word is,' Norm nodded.

'Me?' Lois reiterated.

'Only a rumour, but still...' Earl said.

'Oh.'

'Oh boy,' Merritt rubbed his hands together.

'But they called me a pagan, a heathen.'

'What do they know?' Merritt dismissed the legal team with a flick of the wrist. If only it was that easy.

'Anyway, my aunt wants to meet you Lois. Madame Rene Larrouche. Her birthday this Saturday. At the big house. My mother's sister, and, well, she wants to meet you.'

'Me?'

''Course you'll need something, but we can go shopping.' Merritt did a little twirl holding his coat tails out like a frock.

'Oh, and the radio chap rang while you were in the meeting yesterday,' Alice came into the workroom. 'That Salter chap. He wants to meet the bright spark,' Alice pointed with her stenographer's pencil at Lois.

'Me?'

'Said he wanted to have a bit of a chat. Mr Wood approved. Of course Ol' man Shotley was all for it. Free air time you see.' Alice thumbed through the papers. 'Here it is.' She pulled out a full spread on page five. The Fridge-o-matic was emblazoned across the page without a word of explanation, just one headline, but it was a doozy. *The meaning of Christmas.* It was quite a difference from the old, worn style of advertising where the unsuspecting reader was bombarded with prices, deals, and the ol' don't miss out, stocks won't last!!! ploy.

Norm looked at the drawing. He stood back and squinted. 'Pretty good if I do say so myself.'

'It's brilliant.' Earl took the paper, folded it and popped it in his briefcase next to his sandwich. 'A souvenir.'

And in the moment of adulation Lois forgot about the word, the slur, the feeling that something wasn't quite right.

Lois basked in her glory. She worked furiously at her flow chart, pie chart and next attack on the institution which had just over one thousand years of history behind it and a man at the top who had his finger on the pulse of humanity.

'God Almighty,' Norm said as he looked over Lois's shoulder.

The **Fridge-o-matic** A clear message of salvation from the fires of hell, the Australian summer.

Who wouldn't want to be a convert?

'Is it...?' Lois look at Norm.

'Just enough.' Norm answered. 'You know, I did wonder at the beginning that...well that...well you know, but I was at rehearsals the other night, for the nativity play, and well, people are sick and tired of all the other stuff. Everyone was talking about it. We are Australian for God's sake.'

'So that's a yes?'

'Yep.'

‘And it’s not too iconoclastic?’

Norm rubbed the back of his neck and squished his lips into a mangle.

‘Norm?’

‘Close, but look at it this way. In three weeks Christmas will be over. We will have other things to worry about. People will have their fridges, we will have work, a living wage and life goes on.’

Earl shimmied over to the conversation. ‘Do you remember Whatley & Dunne?’

‘Whatley & Dunne?’

‘Yeah, The Gen-u-flex’

‘Ah,’ Norm said, ‘I remember.’

‘Do tell Earl,’ Merritt coaxed.

‘Well, they had this arthritic cream. S’posed to cure or something. The slogan was,’ and here Earl chuckled, ‘don’t thank God, thank Gen-u-flex How to get down on your knees without them cracking like popcorn.’

‘Kicked up a stink if I recall,’ Norm mused.

‘1931. Times were different. Still, it did well for a bit, but was all bull dust in the end. The bloke made the powder out of old plaster and icing sugar or something. Got three years I recall.’

‘Three years,’ Lois wondered if there was a law for iconoclasts.

‘But the slogan stuck. One of those things. People still remember it ‘cause it was funny, different and a little bit irreverent.’

‘So you think ‘the meaning of Christmas’ will stick.’

‘I’d put money on it Lois.’

‘But what will the man in the street think?’

‘Ah,’ Earl waved his hand at the window and the street beyond,’ There you have the wrong end of the stick Lois. He doesn’t think.’

Merritt nodded in agreement. First-hand experience of not thinking just about made him an expert.

✦

'Drinks?' Merritt folded the tea towel, emptied the kettle and reached for his jacket.

The crew looked at the clock. In three minutes they would be free for two whole days. Norm took his pay packet and shoved it in his pocket.

Earl snapped shut his briefcase. 'Just one wouldn't hurt.'

'Not me. Wife wants to go to her mother's for something, so I'm on kitchen duty.'

'Lois?' Merritt asked.

'Well, just one.' She thought of her pay packet and how much she could spend. If Merritt was taking her shopping there was train fare, tea and scones, a frock and stockings, it all added up to more mince and onion during the week.

'Right, that makes three.'

The clock's second hand just touched the top of the hour and the door closed on CWA for the weekend, although advertising works 24/7 if the stakes are high enough.

The pub crowd had busted out of the bar and lolled over the footpath, the gutter and the cobblers next door.

'Up for a challenge?' Merritt said as he buttoned his coat and made for the bar. Earl followed trying to avoid the beers being handed over his head, the feet trying to step on his and the cigarettes dangling from lips while Lois waited outside, the front bar a man's preserve in 1950 Australia.

Merritt appeared with three cold beers and they stood in the scrum shouting over the noise.

'OOOooo that hit the spot,' Earl shouted.

'What?'

'Hit the spot,' he tried again.

‘Hot, yes very,’ Lois shouted back.

‘And I tell ya, it’s about time we had something different. Bloody snowballs and jingle bells. Makes ya sick I tell ya.’

‘Too right mate.’

Lois turned to see the speaker. He was a burly chap lolling on the footpath. He stood over six foot with a large moustache and hands like plates of meat.

‘Rudolph the red nose reindeer. Never seen a reindeer in me bloody life.’

‘Too right Bob.’

‘Flippin’ sleighbells.’

‘Yeah.’

‘Excuse me,’ Lois turned and smiled at the men.

‘G’day Luv.’ Mr Flippin’ sleighbells winked at his companion.

‘I heard you just then, talking about Christmas.’

‘Yeah Luv. You ever seen snow Luv?’

‘No,’ Lois said and grinned.

‘Me neither. You Reg?’

‘Nope.’

Merritt leaned in, ‘Nor me.’

‘Ya seen that advert. The one for the Fridge-o-matic Reg? Bloody about bloody time.’

‘Really?’

‘Too right,’ Reg said and finished his beer.

‘Well you know gentlemen, you are standing next to the genius who...’ Merritt looked at Lois... ‘Who dreamt up the campaign.’ He pointed to Lois. ‘The meaning of Christmas.’

‘Too right,’ Reg looked Lois up and down.

‘It’s 100 bloody degrees in the flippin’ shade!’ Merritt added.

‘Bloody oath it is,’ Mr flippin’ sleighbells said, adding, ‘well I for one want to buy you a drink young lady.’

‘Me?’

‘Eh, this ‘ere lass is the one what made that Fridge-o-matic,’ Mr flippin sleighbells yelled above the din.

‘What?’

‘This girl wants a true blue Aussie Christmas. None of ya snow and stuff,’ and then he went all out with a shout that only a foreman on a building site could muster, ‘It’s 100 bloody degrees in the flippin’ shade.’

Donald Bradman, that famous cricketer couldn’t have had a bigger cheer. The bar erupted and it wasn’t long before pints were lined up at the bar for Lois and company.

‘The wife’ll be beside herself.’

‘Me ol’ mum thought Christmas came early when I showed her the receipt.’

‘My kids are happy as pigs in mud. Cold jelly you see.’

The stories, the accoladed, the man in the street had spoken.

You can’t be the flavour of the month and not feel your ego inflate, just a little. Lois drank three pints and three more appeared. Reg and Mr Flippin’ took over as men and a few hardy women regaled anyone who’d listen that they’d never seen snow, a sleighbell, a reindeer, but only a ridiculous fat man who sweated in fake beard and black boots when it was,

‘100 bloody degrees in the flippin’ shade!’

By the time last orders were called Earl had been lost, Merritt had been trodden on and Lois had lost her hair clip, drunk way too much beer and been patted on the back so many times with grubby workman’s hands she looked like she’d been in a fight, in the gutter.

People drifted out muttering 100 degrees in the bloody shade and chuckling at the thought.

‘Oh, there you are,’ Merritt found Earl, grabbed Lois and they headed for the train.

‘100 bloody degrees in the flippin’ shade,’ Earl said and giggled. ‘What’dItellya Lois. It’s gonna be a stinker...I mean stickler.’

‘Hmm,’ Lois loped along feeling happy, relaxed. The chaos retreated and she giggled. ‘100 degrees.’

Merritt chortled, ‘100 bloody degrees in the flippin’ shade,’ and all of a sudden it was hilarious. Beer has powers beyond normal comprehension. Everything was side-splitting hysterical.

‘Look, Lois luvvie,’ Merritt grabbed her arm. ‘I will meet you under the clock at 10 tomorrow. The party doesn’t start until 5, but no-on gets there at 5.’ He looked at Lois a little worse for wear. ‘tomorrow,’ he blew a kiss and skipped down the road to hail a taxi.

‘He may be a dumb as a bag of hammers, but ya know, I like him.’ Earl peeled off to catch a bus, and Lois floated on cloud nine all the way home.

✦

Mr Moon gave Lois a hot pie that had sat for too long and a currant bun which looked like it had been run over by a bus and pointed to page 5 of the evening paper.

‘Nice eh?’

‘Yes.’ Lois smiled at the advert and picked up her small offerings. ‘Thanks so much.’

‘Is ok Miss Mackenzie.’ Mr Moon smiled showing the full frontal of his gums and tombstone teeth.

Mrs Provoichkin twitched her curtains as Lois put the key in the door. She turned to the curtain and gave the old woman a friendly toodle-loo and a wave, before stepping into her little two room oven.

‘People,’ she said to the empty room. They were quite nice, as long as they were with ya rather an ag’in ya. ‘A hundred degrees in the bloody shade,’ she said and chuckled. The ego, that bit in the brain that runs on not much more than vanity can instil an overinflated sense of self. It has the knack. Lois thought she was rather clever, rather special and rather indispensable. A heady brew, as a psychologist might say.

As the tin roof ticked down the day and the temperature in her flat settled into a sleep inducing 85 degrees, Lois drifted off thinking of accolades, awards and Shotley's last word, Genius. Her mother's words didn't get a look in, although they might have been a small echo around 3am when she woke with a tongue as dry as the Gobi desert. 'Lois Mary Mackenzie, who do you think you are?'

✦ CHAPTER 12

Beer is a great leveller. It can slay a plumber just as easily as a King. It can also give a young woman a whopping headache no amount of lukewarm water, Asprin or orange juice will fix. But that was a minor inconvenience, because it was Saturday. A day for rest and relaxation.

Lois thought it a day for uninterrupted brainstorming until she quite inexplicably remembered she was to meet Merritt under the clock at ten.

Shopping on a Saturday in the city was the one idea everyone had at the same time. Add Christmas into the mix and it is a recipe for frayed tempers, bad manners and every man, (or woman) for himself, (or herself), never mind goodwill to all men (well...you know!). The footpaths were crowded, the traffic was bumper to bumper and the sun unforgiving.

'Watch it,' a man shoved Lois into the road as he tried to hustle his way through the foot traffic. She narrowly missed a car which made a mother with child in tow, gasp.

'You ok?'

'I'm alright. I'm fine.' Lois joined the crowd and was swept along to the Town Hall to arrive with five minutes to spare.

Seeking the one bit of shade she stood and watched the Christmas shoppers all keen to spend money they didn't have, or couldn't afford under the eye of an enormous

Christmas tree and baubles, glass ice crystals, fake snow and dangling ice skates.

'Enough to make you move to the north pole, in' it?' an old woman said as she squeezed into the shade next to Lois.

'Yes. It's hot alright.'

'Still, they got the manger over there, so that's alright in' it?'

The women took in the Christmas manger with three wise men, a donkey and the three main players surrounded by straw.

'Traditional in' it?'

'Yes.'

'I mean, take away the baubles and that right there is the meaning of Christmas, in' it?'

Lois pursed her lips lest her ego say something she might regret. She checked the clock and scanned the crowd for Merritt. She looked at her watch and fiddled with her handbag.

It just popped out. 'But wouldn't you rather have a cold ham, jelly and icream and less of a Christmas from somewhere you've never been?'

'What?'

'An Australian Christmas. Not so much jingle bells and all that?' Lois waved her hand in the direction of the Nativity scene, the Christmas tree and the baubles.

The woman looked at Lois like she'd just said the three wise men were sorry, sent their apologies but couldn't make it to the birth.

'Not 'ave Christmas then?'

'Oh, yes, but an Australian Christmas.' And then Lois delivered the Christmas cracker, 'It's 100 bloody degrees in the flippin' shade.'

The woman looked at the winter scene. Lois saw the wheels turning, albeit slowly. 'And baby Jesus?'

'He was born in Jerusalem,' Lois was thinking on her feet, brainstorming as her ego took over her mouth. 'Jerusalem is practically desert. I don't think he'd want ice skates or a pair of mittens for Christmas.'

'Maud!' an old woman shouted and waved. 'Youhooo.'

'There's me sister in' it. Youhoooo.' Maud waved and turned to Lois. 'Never mind all that, I still like baby Jesus. It's a lovely story in' it?' and Maud walked to meet her sister, disappearing in the crowd.

'Lois,' Merritt scooted up and thread his arm through hers. 'Been waiting long?'

'Hmmm?'

'I said, been waiting long?'

'Oh, not long.' Lois looked at the nativity scene as Maud's words echoed. 'It's a lovely story in' it.'

'Merritt,'

'Yes.'

'Do you think I'm a pagan?'

'Aren't we all darling, just a little bit pagan.' He laughed and they pushed their way into the throng.

✦

'Too expensive.' It was said more than once as Merritt went from boutique to boutique looking for something in Lois's price range.

'Don't be ridiculous,' Lois looked at the price tag. I don't make that in a year.

'Oh.'

'Well what do you make?' Merritt asked.

'That's not the sort of question you ask Merritt.'

And when he divulged his take home pay each week Lois dropped the frock from the hanger in surprise.

'Really?'

'Really.'

'But I thought we were about the same. Granted you have a few years, but I have a degree.'

'But Lois,' Merritt stood back and looked at her. 'You girl, me boy. That's just the way it is.'

'Hmmm.'

'Now, as you are on the poverty line, I think we need to be inventive or very sneaky,' he tapped his nose.

'What are you suggesting?'

'Well, my mother has some frocks...'

'No.'

'You are the same size I think.' He took a good look at her figure. 'Don't worry Lois, she gives away to charity more than she ever wears.'

'No really I couldn't.'

'Don't be silly.'

'Merritt. Do I really need to go to this party?'

'Miss Mackenzie, this isn't just a party. This is an event.' Merritt threw his arms wide and just about knocked Lois's hat off. 'Taxi. We need a taxi.'

✦

Once again Lois missed the shops opening hours and Mr Moon greeted her with his usual smile.

'Hot.'

'Hmmm.'

'You shopping for Christmas?'

'Hmmm?'

Mr Moon pointed to the large Haute Couture bag on Lois's arm.

'Oh, no. Yes. Maybe.' She looked at the small Chinese man behind the counter and came back down to the land of the living, mince and old currant buns. 'You know Mr Moon, I thought I knew posh people, but turns out I only knew people who eat olives.'

'Huh?'

'My mother has soirees. Cheese on sticks. Olives.'

'Olives.'

'Yes.' Lois sighed and relived the last three hours at Mrs Yvonne Claremont-Grove's mansion overlooking Sydney harbour with air-conditioning and white rugs on the marble floors.

'I don't have olives.'

'Oh.' Lois blinked and shook her head. 'I need some nice shampoo. I'm going to a party...an event.'

Mr Moon winked.

'Society event actually,' her ego added, 'in a taxi.'

✦

Wearing someone else's frock and sling back sandals, holding someone else's handbag can be a frightening prospect for a girl who is accident prone. Lois tucked her handkerchief, (just about the only thing that was her own in the ensemble) into her little handbag, checked her few bits of money and the thought struck her like a sledge-hammer. Birthday. She needed a present. What do you get a woman whom you have never met and who probably has everything? A toot from the taxi interrupted the thought and Lois sashayed across the concrete to be greeted by Merritt in a smart lawn suit and tie.

'Nice,' he opened the door and they scooted inside the taxi, Lois protecting her dress and shoes from the filthy floor.

'I thought it was an afternoon party?'

'Lois, no-one ever arrives on time.' Merritt looked at his watch and tisked. 'We'll be early, but I can introduce you without her little tribe of toadies dancing to her tune.'

'So how old is Mrs Larrouche?

'I wouldn't know, and I'm not about to ask. Old enough to have been instrumental in the war...don't ask me which one.'

'And I haven't got a present.'

'Oh, darling. We don't give presents.'

'But it's her birthday Merritt.'

'I know. Well, I have an idea.' There is a first for everything. Merritt tapped the taxi driver on the shoulder and they pulled in next to a milk bar. 'Go get her a mixed bag of lollies. She'll love it. She's got a wicked sweet tooth.'

'Really? Lollies?'

'Go.'

Lois gathered up her frock and tottered in her sling-backs to the lollie counter. 'Sixpence of mixed.'

✦

The green wrought iron gates had pink bows on them and were swung open. Lois gawked at the long, very long sandy driveway to a large, well situated,- within spitting distance of the Harbour Bridge, mansion. She shaded her eyes to look up at the portico with cherubs over the columns and enough windows to keep a cleaner busy until retirement.

'Oh, Merritt I'll pay half,' she offered as the taxi driver pulled away. 'Don't be silly Lois, I invited you, my shout.'

'Thanks.' She gave a sigh of relief.

They were ushered into a grand entrance hall full of flowers and dachshunds.

'Where is my aunt?' Merritt asked the fellow who followed them.

'On the terrace.'

'Right.' Merritt grabbed Lois by the hand and they trekked through the library (grand), skipped through the music room (palatial), scooted past the study (studious. Well it was a small room!) and then filtered through the formal lounge (stuffy) to finally end up on the terrace through the double French doors (original apparently).

'Aunty Rene,' Merritt theatrically held out his arms and embraced a woman who looked every inch an aristocrat.

'Mew Mew,' She said and pecked him on the cheek while looking Lois over with a critical eye.

'Happy birthday,' Merritt gave her a kiss on each cheek. 'Looking wonderful I see,' he touched the diamonds at her throat.

'From Sherman.'

'Nice.'

'And who have we here?' Mrs Larrouche swung around to take Lois's sweaty hand.

'This is the young woman I told you about. The skirt etc,' Merritt waved his hands in the air.'

'Oh.' Mrs Larrouche smiled and winked.

'Um, Mrs Larrouche, Happy Birthday. And um thank you so much for the clothes. They were a very welcome surprise.'

'Glad to be of assistance dear.'

Lois handed over the present, all crumpled and sweating through the little white bag. She wiped her hand on her dress and instantly realised her mistake. Jelly bean colours smeared a rainbow.

'Bloody hell.' She looked up, 'sorry, I'm, so sorry.'

'And what have we here?' Aunty Rene opened the bag and her face lit up. 'Freckles, milk bottles and jubes. Wonderful. The best present ever. Thank you Miss...?'

'Lois. Lois Mackenzie.'

'So thoughtful,' Aunt Rene popped a chocolate freckle in her mouth and chewed.

'Lois, do you want to freshen up?' Merritt threaded his arm through hers and pulled. When they were once again in the house Lois slumped.

‘I made a right fool of myself didn’t I?’

‘Aunty would never say anything. Breeding you know.’

‘But your mother’s dress. How can I ever get this out,’ she pointed to the rainbow of smear.

‘Don’t worry about it. We’ll go to the kitchen and someone will sponge it off. It will dry in minutes in this heat. I’d put money on it.’

One thing that might have been a long shot or 100 to 1 was seeing Serg in a waiter’s uniform picking up trays.

‘Serg?’ Lois did a double take.

‘Lois?’ Serg put down his tray and smiled. ‘Bit of money on the side,’ he shrugged.

‘Look Mr Serg,’ Merritt came into the mix, ‘We need to get this off,’ he pointed to Lois’s frock.

‘Well,’ Serg smiled and raised his eyebrow. I’ve only just met the woman.’

The double entente went straight over Merritt’s head and headed for the door.

‘Have you got a wash cloth or something?’ Lois asked.

‘I’ll get one of the girls, they should be able to do something.’ Serg loped off in the direction of the kitchen and came back with an older woman who had common sense in spades. Crisis averted.

‘Thank you so much.’ Lois shook the woman’s hand.

‘Not a problem.’

‘No really, I’m so grateful. I didn’t want to look a bit of a...well you know, in front of all these sort of people.’

‘Lovvie, if I can give you one bit of advice.’

‘Yes?’ Lois thought she might get a pearl of wisdom from this woman who seemed to have her life together.

‘They all sit down to shit.’

‘OH.’

‘She’s right you know.’ Merritt said while nodding. The subtleties of the pronouncement were a bit too subtle for Merritt Claremont-Grove.

At a birthday bash of this nature, one must mingle. Merritt left Lois on a seat with some words of wisdom of his own,

'We don't generally go into long discussions on our health with people we've just met, so the correct response when one does say to you. 'oh how are you?' The correct and only response is 'yes I'm very well thank you', even if you only have a few days left to live.' He floated away to swan about and mingle with wild hand gestures, raucous laughter and an endless glass of champagne.

Lois hunted for some shade to watch the cream of society at play when there was a frission in the air and heads turned. A man of indeterminate age (when seen from afar) had entered the mix and stood centre stage until every eye had taken in his presence.

Alistair Ulysses Putt waved to Aunt Rene and casually strolled down the stairs.

'Who is he?' Serg asked as he passed Lois on his way back to the kitchen.

'He is Alistair Ulysses Putt,' a woman standing behind Lois answered. 'Darling of the theatre, recipient of the Limelight award, twice and in the hit show of the season, Rocks, Darling, Rocks!'

'Never heard of him,' Serg said and continued on his way.

'The woman asked Lois, What about you?'

'A bit, not really, just a bit in the paper, and on the radio.'

'Want me to introduce you?'

'Oh, no, I couldn't.'

'Why ever not?'

The words of common sense echoed in Lois's mind. Everyone sits down to shit. She repeated it like a mantra.

'Come on.'

Putt was holding court with a champagne glass in one hand and a cigarette in the other. A natural raconteur he had his audience spellbound.

'Hey Putt, I'd like you to meet...'

'Lois Mackenzie.' Lois smiled while repeating her mantra. *Everyone sits down to shit. Everyone sits down to shit. Everyone sits down to shit.*

'Well Miss Mackenzie, and what do you do?' Putt flared his nostrils and played to his audience.

'Shit.' It just popped out.

If silence was golden this break in the proceedings was 24 carat. You could have heard the screams of delight over the harbour at Luna Fun Park.

'Don't we all.' Putt said and the in-crowd erupted in laughter.

'I'll dine out on this one,' someone said and then the crowd was in hysterics.

'That was a beauty Miss Lois Mackenzie. A real rippa. I'm Kelly, Erin Kelly, society reporter for the Morning Echo.'

'Oh.' Lois could envisage the headlines. WOMAN MAKES SOCIETY FAUX PAS OF THE SEASON.

'So, Miss Lois Mackenzie, what do you do besides shit?' Miss Kelly pulled out a pencil and a small notebook.

Of course everyone has come up against the, will I or won't I dilemma in their lives. On the one hand Lois could let her ego take over, and it was on starters orders just itching to tell all. On the other hand dragging her name and that of CWA into the hideous social gaff might lose her the only job she'd ever had.

'Um, well, I work in advertising.'

'I see. Anything I might have seen or are you just hired help aka secretary?'

'Um, well...'

‘Lois,’ Merritt bounded up with two champagne glasses and it didn’t take two seconds for a whip smart society reporter to put two and two together to come up with who was related to whom, who had connections in advertising via an uncle and Catchpole & Wood popped into the conversation.

‘You anything to do with the Fridge-o-matic by any chance?’ Miss Kelly winked.

‘Oh, yes,’ Merritt butted in,’ Lois is the genius. It’s her account.’

‘Is that so.’

‘Oh yes,’ Merritt nodded and passed a glass of champagne to Lois. ‘Miss Mackenzie dreamed up the whole thing.’

‘Merritt.’

‘Don’t hide your light Miss Mackenzie. Tell me everything?’

Now when a reporter asks you to tell them everything, any sane person might step back a bit and reflect on what that reporter would do with the ‘everything’. Any person who had read Amethyst Greenock, *How to overcome* might view it as an opportunity, an occasion to showcase their talents, their drive, their will to succeed. And a people pleaser, well they just can’t help themselves. Want my life story, not a problem, want my mother’s maiden name, my favourite jigsaw puzzle, my left kidney? Lois couldn’t stop herself even if she wanted to, the odds were stacked against her.

‘Merritt is quite correct. It is my account.’ The ego took a deep breath and by the time Miss ego drew a second breath Lois had managed to let off some steam. She ended with,

‘And someone always wants me to put the kettle on.’

Miss Kelly nodded in solidarity. ‘Or take notes,’ she added. They thought about the implications for a moment.

'Or buy a birthday card,' Miss Kelly gave a small hurrump. 'A cake, organise a raffle, collect tea cups, nip out for a packet of cigarettes,' she waved her hand in the air. The et al encompassing the lot of women in the office workforce in the 1950 Australia. 'I did English literature.'

'Marketing and commerce.'

The women looked at the upper echelon of society enjoying themselves.

'Have you read Amethyst Greenock?'

'Read it. I sleep with it under my pillow,' Miss Kelly said, then added, 'This,' she pointed to the stenographers pad, 'This is my chance.'

Lois sighed. 'Me too.' There was more than a mince pie riding on the subsequent story, much more.

Miss Kelly of the Morning Echo had a piece her editor couldn't pass up...although Miss Kelly wasn't strictly allowed to do pieces, and the paper thought women more suited to society, cooking and homemaker advice.

'Well, I'm all for it Lois. About bloody time women made a mark. You know it's the woman who makes the decisions in the house. What to buy, what to eat, where the money goes.'

'Yes. We did a small module of buying power at University.'

'And yet...' Miss Kelly turned her eye to the crowd enjoying the free food, drink and surroundings. 'Men.' It was all she needed to say. Lois understood the word and all it stood for in this modern day.

'And I'm going on the radio. Ray Salter has asked you know.'

Miss Kelly whistled. 'Watch him. He's a wolf.'

'I'll keep that in mind,' Lois finished her drink and then nearly choked on it.

'You ok?' Miss Kelly followed Lois's gaze and their eyes fell on a rotund man in a black suit looking like he was boiling from the inside.

'That's Bishop O'Leary.'

Lois stared.

'Ah.' Miss Kelly once again put two and twenty two together.

'Hmmm.' Lois looked at her nemesis.

Bishop's often look larger in person, it's all that black offset by a personality that dominates a room, a garden party, or anywhere really. Bishop O'Leary dominated the buffet table, a plate in each hand.

'Why don't you just pop over and say howdy?' Miss Kelly nudged Lois.

'Me?'

'You know, just break the ice.' Miss Kelly said.

'I couldn't.'

'Of course you could. He's only a man, albeit with a large waist and an inflated ego.' It might only have been a reporter from the paper, but it sounded like the devil prodding Lois. She'd already put her foot in it with Putt.

'Over inflated.'

'Yes.'

'Ego.'

'That's right.'

Lois took in the measure of the man of the cloth. There was a lot to measure. He stood in the shade and surveyed his surroundings like he was waiting for a round of applause. He was actually waiting to collar a waiter with a champagne glass or two. Serg flitted by and the Bishop took a glass.

Miss Kelly raised her eye brow and smirked, 'It's 100 degrees in the flippin' shade.'

Lois squared her shoulders. She thought on all the times at university she'd been relegated, denigrated and dumped because of men. She thought on Amethyst Greenock and *How to overcome*. Just a man with an overinflated ego.

She took the required three deep breaths.

'Oh, here you are,' Mrs Rene Larrouche linked arms with Lois, 'I want you to meet someone.' She pulled Lois from her decision and steered her towards an old man sitting on a bench with a young fellow at his side.

'Douglas darling,' this is the young lady.' Mrs Larrouche deposited Lois on the seat and patted her hand. 'He's a lamb really, so just,' she waved her manicured nails in the air, 'well, you know darling,' and she floated away.

'I'm fine thank you,' Lois blurted, although she felt at that moment she had about three days left to live.

'Eh?' Douglas looked at her with a critical eye.

'My father is a little hard of hearing.' The man seated on the other side of Douglas leaned over, 'She said she's fine.'

'Who?'

The young man looked inquiringly at Lois.

'Oh, Lois Mackenzie,' she said in a rather loud voice.

The three looked at the scene before them, the silence stretching into eternity.

'Um, and you?' Lois asked after about a minute.

'Douglas Craven and this is my father, Douglas Craven senior.'

'Friend of the family are you?'

'Not really. Neighbours actually.' Douglas pointed to a mansion glistening white through the trees. It cascaded down to the harbour with gradual steps, each one bigger than the last.

Lois squinted to take it all in. She pointed. 'That?'

'That.' Douglas nodded.

'Eh.' Craven Snr looked at Lois. 'You that smart cookie that dreamt up that campaign?'

'Sir?'

'The what-cha-ma-call-it.'

'He means the Fridge-o-matic.'

'Oh.' Lois looked at the house, the man, the son and in a lightbulb moment she realised she was sitting next to the man who owned Cravens Department Store, the only store with its own credit card, car park and air conditioning on all floors.

'The Fridge-o-matic?'

'That's the one.' Old man Craven slapped his thigh and chuckled. '100 bloody degrees in the flippin' shade,' he laughed.

'Dad likes it.'

'Oh.'

'Boy do I like it. It's different.' Craven Snr took Lois's hand. 'When you get another idea, you let me know young lady, you let me know.'

'I will.' Lois smiled. Somehow a bit of old money, new money and hob nobbing with the rich and very rich gave her an air of invincibility. She felt practically bullet proof with Mr Craven Snr on her side. So much so that spying the Bishop eating a bit of birthday cake she thought she'd take a shot at an introduction.

Douglas jnr saw her glance and smiled a knowing smile. 'Your adversary.'

'Sort of.'

'Want an introduction?'

Oh those words yet again. She took her three deep breaths.

'Why not.'

✦ CHAPTER 13

The doctor who attended to the Bishop in the pink bedroom upstairs said he should be alright if he just stopped swallowing strawberries whole.

'It's lucky that waiter knew the Heimlich manoeuvre otherwise you'd be..gkeeeekk,' he drew his finger across his throat.

Bishop O'Leary lay still and closed his eyes. 'Gkeeeekk,' the young doctor said again just for the hell of it. The Bishop opened one eye and made a mental note to strike his doctor off his Christmas Card list. The thought of Christmas brought back the incident and he shuddered.

'Delayed shock,' the doctor said. 'Want something?'

'A whisky?' Niall O'Leary asked knowing Mrs Larrouche kept a well-stocked drinks cabinet.

'I was thinking a pill actually.'

'Oh.'

A timid knock on the door distracted the two and the doctor said, 'Come in.'

Father Aspinall crept into the room and fidgeted with his collar.

'You?'

'Your Grace. I was summoned by a telephone call. I have the car waiting outside. Can he be moved Doctor?'

'Oh, yes, I think so.'

It was later, as the Bishop languished in his bed with a cup of tea and a couple of biscuits that the thought hit him like a hung Christmas pudding thrown at fifty paces to land in his solar plexis. He would be front page news...and all for the wrong reasons.

'A woman,' he said to his chintz curtains. 'A young woman,' he scowled to his Wedgewood tea cup. 'What is the younger generations coming to when someone can cajole the public, make outlandish promises and wring money from them for some sort of salvation.'

Hypocrisy wasn't something Bishop O'Leary thought much about.

His teacup was deposited on the nightstand, the button adjusted on his pyjamas and the sheet stretched over his large corpus. Tomorrow was hours away. It was just a society do, nothing special. It was probably not remarked upon at all. A small column in the women's pages. A slight hiccup. People hardly read the paper at all these days. Who would be interested a little incident on what the Bishop said to the young lady.

These thoughts swirled around the Bishopric all night as Niall O'Leary, Bishop of St Cuthbert's Waverly tossed and turned like a rotisserie chicken flamed from the fires of hell...a particularly vivid dream and three helpings of strawberry flan might have had something to do with his restless night, besides public ridicule, but public ridicule was top of the list.

✦

Father Aspinall lay the morning papers on the table for the Bishop. He tried to hide the headlines under a few letters found on the desk. Then, Jeremy Aspinall silently prayed that the Bishop had eaten a decent breakfast, had a good nights sleep and a bracing bath. His life would be purgatory-

or his day anyway until his superior had his whisky at five o'clock.

A door slammed, a plug was thrown out the window with some force, and a bellow sounding like the souls of the damned issued from the upstairs bathroom. Jeremy tiptoed out of the office, grabbed his hat and a small click could be heard as he exited through the side garden gate. Even priests can have a sick day.

✦

On the other side of Waverly Archbishop Renwick Auden Bothom was having a cracking morning. His eggs went down a treat. His soldier toast done to perfection and all washed down with two cups of tea and bit of gloating on the side.

He spread the morning papers out on the dining table and chuckled once again.

BISHOP SMITES IN SPITE

It was a catchy headline. Renwick wasn't sure it should be smite or smote, either way his rival for the souls of the nation didn't look good. The accompanying picture of O'Leary prone on a garden bench added just the right amount of ridicule to the scene.

The reporter, Miss M Kelly, had a good story. She excelled at setting the scene, the mood, and placing all the players on the board before delivering the coup de grâce.

"It's Christmas, the spirit of good will, it's also 100 bloody degrees in the flippin' shade".

Renwick read once again the bit about O'Leary choking on his indignation only to be saved by a Greek waiter and smiled. Not prone to excesses, Renwick threw caution to the wind.

'I'll have a second egg Mrs Brewster,' Yes, it was turning out to be a cracking morning. He felt a sermon coming on, something along the lines of invoking the Lord on your behalf to do your dirty work, and the perils therein. Although there might have been something in the good book about 'vengeance is mine, sayth the Lord,' which sounded like someone at the top of the corporate ladder was willing to go the extra mile, but Bothom still thought his sermon topical, on point and a salutary lesson.

✦ CHAPTER 14

Things were hotting up at CWA. By 9:30 Alice had fended off what seemed like a dozen queries regarding their stance on the smiting. There were three picketers out the front of the building with home-made placards extolling the occupants to REPENT NOW!! There was also the bible basher, as he was affectionately known, and a bloke who was sure the end of the world was nigh. She took the phone off the cradle.

'It seems to me,' she said to Norm as he stopped to say 'mornin', 'It seems to me the world has gone completely mad.'

'Probably always was, we just didn't notice.'

'Watch this,' Alice put the telephone handpiece on its cradle and it immediately rang. 'Like that since I opened the door.' She picked up the receiver, 'CWA, how can I help?'

Norm winked and went to make a cup of tea.

Earl pulled out the paper from his briefcase and laid it on his desk. He then took a pair of scissors and carefully cut the front page article from the paper and taking a picture of the Queen off the wall, inserted the headline in its place and hung it once again. He stood back and admired his handy-work.

'Nice,' Merritt stood next to Earl.

'That's the way,' Norm entered with a cup of tea. 'She'll get a kick outta that.'

✦

When you've been smote by a bishop and it's on the front page, there is bound to be a bit of finger pointing, pats on the back and a general, 'Ooooo that's her,' the minute you step out in public. Lois, not being accustomed to the hullaballoo turned a deep shade of crimson at every finger, every coo-ee, every nudge with an elbow to their neighbour.

'I've got one luv,' a woman grabbed Lois's arm and smiled. Her sweaty hand patted and gripped. Lois smiled back and wished for her stop. She was already late because of several people stopping her to talk, someone wanting an autograph and another a photograph. Her watch showed 9:45 and Lois pursed her lips. 'People,' she sighed.

The picket line had grown to a crowd of around twelve with picnic chairs, sun umbrellas and a festive air. The bible basher had a dog attached to his sandwich board and it wore a collar of tinsel and a red Father Christmas hat.

Slipping past the gaggle, Lois made her way to the second floor, only to be stopped by a reporter on the landing.

'Miss Mackenzie?'

'Yes,' Lois couldn't help but be polite.

''From the Mirror, for the afternoon edition. Anything to say?'

'Um, well, um.'

'Just a word Miss.'

'Um,'

They looked at one another for a good full minute. 'Um, I'm late, sorry, got to run.' Taking the stairs two at a time, her handbag caught on the banister and clattered to the bottom of the stairwell.

'Here, I'll help.' The man scooted down and retrieved the lipstick, the compact, the notebook which was open at Lois's list of things to achieve before thirty, and her sandwich.

‘Golden Finger eh?’

‘Please.’ She held out her hand for the bag.

‘A word Miss,’ the fellow kept the bag out of reach. It was now nearing ten o’clock.

‘If giving people some hope, something to look forward to and a bit of cheer is a sin, I wonder what the Church has to offer.’

‘Salvation?’

‘Pfft.’

‘Thanks Miss.’ The reporter handed over the bag and took the steps at a gallop. Any editor or reporter of a daily knew a slanging match was a money spinner. This was like printing money.

✦

Alice smiled when Lois appeared. There was a moment where Lois began to apologise for her tardiness, but Alice winked, held up her hand and picked up the telephone. She shooed Lois out with a wave of her hand.

‘Ah,’ Merritt linked arms with his protégé and escorted her to her desk.

‘And here she is,’ Earl beamed.

‘Morning Mac,’ Norm sat on the edge of her desk and pointed to the headline newly framed on the wall.

‘Oh,’ Lois licked her lips and sat down.

‘This is...’ Merritt threw his arms wide.

‘It certainly is,’ Earl beamed some more like a father who had realised his offspring were human after all and proud of the fact.

‘Well,’ Norm scratched the back of his neck, ‘it’s not every day you get smote, or is it smited or smitten. Well it’s not every day you get one in the eye from a Bishop.’

‘It was a strawberry,’ Lois said. ‘It...’ she got no further when Merritt took up the story.

'Ol' Bish was in a right state. He choked on a strawberry, the waiter did the Heimlich manoeuvrer and well,' he looked to Lois.

'It landed on my,' she pointed to her front. 'I'll get it dry cleaned,' she said to Merritt.

'Keep it Lois, mother said you look better in it anyway.'

'I couldn't.'

'Oh, don't be silly.'

Alice interrupted the tete-a-tete, 'There's a phone call for you Miss Mackenzie.'

'Me?'

'At my desk.'

'Mum.'

'Lois Mary Mackenzie,' She frowned as her mother let her know that the Mackenzie's had never been smoted before, and she just knew university was a bad idea for a young woman. Shirley Mackenzie had to keep it short as trunk calls were expensive, but she still had time say she was disappointed, a little upset and she was trying to keep the dreadful news from ruining her soirees with or without olives.

Lois hung up and turned to go. Her skirt caught on the arm of Alice's chair and she knocked a pen holder to the floor.

"Sorry.' She bent down to tidy up.

'Alright, don't worry?' Alice picked up the ringing phone, 'Yes Mr Wood. Of course Mr Wood.'

Lois Mary Mackenzie went back to her desk, but not before tripping on a bit of carpet and twisting her ankle.

'Mac, you want a cup of tea?' Norm asked. As far as the team was concerned the Golden Finger was in the bag, the Agency was on the up and up and their jobs were secure until retirement. There is nothing like the *whole* front page.

Alice came in, ‘Three o’clock. Wood, Catchpole, Shotley, Broadacre and Lombardi and a Mr Trent from the Advertising Oversight Board.’ She saw the look on Lois’s face, ‘Don’t worry, I think they just want to look at all our options.’

‘Options,’ Merritt said and nodded.

The one option Lois could see was unemployed by Christmas. She took three deep breaths and wondered how Amethyst Greenock could overcome this one.

✦ CHAPTER 15

A good smiting can put a dampener on anyone's day. Although there was an atmosphere of jubilation in the office, the man at the entrance with his sandwich board was right on the money. Lois felt the end was nigh.

She couldn't shake the feeling that the campaign had gone beyond the initial brief of the virtues of a Fridge-o-matic to something akin to a religious war between the practical and the spiritual. Everyone was taking sides and Lois Mary Mackenzie was now the saviour of every ordinary Australian who had chocked on a sixpence in their Christmas pudding, when they'd rather eat jelly and ice-cream.

The temperature rose all morning and when Earl tuned his radio at lunch the announcer said it was 100 degrees and climbing.

'Another scorcher,' Earl reiterated. They all looked to the window and the unrelenting Australian summer.

'Our grass is crunchy,' Norm lamented. The statement didn't excite anyone—a collective grunt could be heard in answer.

The afternoon paper landed around four p.m on a good day. But with things coming to a boil the press went into overdrive and by 2:30 the streets were being fed the next instalment of what was now described as 'Tinsel-v-tradition'. Newspapers love a bit of alliteration.

At 2:45 Alice appeared with the paper and gently placed it on Lois's desk. The victory of the morning, the feeling of euphoria has all but left the building for the day. Sweltering in a small office will sap anyone's will to live.

At four minutes to three, the team gathered up their courage, strapped on their invincibility, and filed into the board room. How to ride the roller coaster of public abhorrence, approbation, antipathy and adoration could make you sick.

'Mr Schuler.' Alice nodded. 'Mr Brucholtz.' Alice held the door. 'Mr Claremont-Grove,' she smiled. 'Miss Mackenzie,' Alice winked and grinned.

They all heard the lift door open and stood by their chairs. Lois dropped her pen and as the men entered she straightened up to hear Mr Trent say,

'Sit over there and get every word Miss.'

Norm shot Lois a look as if to say, 'Not now Lois, for the love of God, not now,' as she gritted her teeth and smiled.

'Ah, there's me girl,' Shotley came over, patted Lois on the back and then took his seat, which had Mr Trent in quite a tizz.

'A girl?'

'A genius,' Ol' man Shotley beamed at his protégé.

Lois let out a nervous giggle. She took her three deep breaths and sat down as Alice came in with her stenographer's pad and three sharp pencils.

Everyone began to sweat.

Mr Wood coughed. Mr Catchpole brought out his handkerchief and began to mop is brow. The Lawyers, Lombardi and Broadacre sat stony faced while Mr Trent, a weasel of a man with beady eyes plopped his briefcase down on the table and rummaged for some papers. And everyone waited.

'Now,' Trent began in a squeaky voice which made the collective jump. 'Now what we have here are several anomalies.' He spread some papers over the table. Catchpole craned his neck to take a look.

'Anomalies?' Wood said.

'This campaign.' Trent brought out the page spread of the Fridge-o-matic.'

'Bloody brilliant init.' Shotley said.

'Yes, well, we shall see.' Mr Trent narrowed his gaze at Shotley and made the poor man squirm.

'Anomalies?'

'I have a checklist. Standards. Decency,' and then he hit the crowd with the biggie, 'morality.'

Earl looked longingly at the empty ashtray in the middle of the table. What he wouldn't give for a Lucky Strike. Norm studied the end of his pencil as if his life depended on it. Merritt looked at Lois who had gone a shade a painter might call 'perilously pale white'.

One may be able to choke a three year old with a plastic toy, but poking a stick at the mores and values of the everyday consumer, getting the church off-side and igniting a debate about the merits of old traditions -v- new traditions, well it was, immoral and indecent and downright ungodly.

'What we aim for is probity.' Trent squeaked.

Catchpole came to the rescue; doing crosswords is a boon in certain circs.

'Having strong moral principles. Honesty and decency.'

Exactly,' Wilbur Trent spread his fingers on his papers and looked at the assembled crowd.

Mr Wood looked at the team. They looked at Lois. She briefly wondered if she'd ever get another job when Alice clenched her fist in her lap and looked Lois in the eye. Lois licked her lips and her nostrils flared. Alice narrowed her gaze at Lois and mouthed, ‘go get em,’ and she moved her stenographers pad to reveal a book underneath. Lois had seen that book. It’s lurid purple cover was instantly recognisable.

Amethyst Greenock wouldn’t sit back. She would overcome.

Mr Trent cleared his throat in the vain hope of finding a baritone. ‘My office will we watching this very closely. We can advise. We can recommend and well...we’ve yet to get a formal complaint, but, well...’ Trent left the sentence hanging like a criminal.

The lawyers sat back and congratulated themselves to have sidestepped a civil suit, a slanging match in court and the unenviable task of defending the indefensible. No-one has won against the Catholic Church, except a fellow who might have been the King of England, but that was a long time ago and a chap lost his head in the process. No, the lawyers were certain they dodged a bullet, or the chopping block.

Earl watched as the lawyers took out their cigarettes. He inhaled the smoke, his nostrils flaring like the entrance to a Swiss Alpine tunnel.

‘So, it’s a goer?’ Shotley asked.

‘Just remember,’ Trent focussed on Shotley, ‘we have the power to mould the public, to guide them, to educated them. It is a grave responsibility.’

They all thought on their grave responsibility.

‘So it’s a goer then?’ Shotley asked again, not quite up with the philosophy of responsibility when he was trying to shift his stock of the Fridge-o-matic.

Alice caught Lois’s eye.

‘Sir,’ Lois stood up.

‘Hmm.’ Trent had the idea that the female of the species were winsome and a bit wish-washy.

‘We all had the idea you were going to shut us down because we dared.’

Alice smiled.

‘We dared to be different. We dared to buck the trend. We dared to take a leap...of faith...in the general public.’

The men sat spellbound.

‘We have poked at something that has ignited the ordinary man...or woman. We have raised the question of what it mean to have our own new nation’s traditions. And why shouldn’t we have something of our own?’ No-one blinked.

‘Mr Trent, have you ever seen snow?’

‘I...’

‘No. Have you ever seen a reindeer, a sleigh or struggled to cook a turkey with gravy when it’s...’ Lois looked to Shotley.

‘When it’s 100 bloody degrees in the flippin’ shade,’ Shotley said and beamed.

‘Yes, well...no, but...’ Trent started.

‘And what of our competition. The church have the edge. They deal in souls, we deal in peoples dreams.’ Lois shot a look at Mr Wood and sat down.

Mr Wood beamed. Earl and Norm saw the ploy and wondered why the’d never thought of it. Merritt thought he’d heard those words somewhere before.

‘And jelly and ice-cream,’ Merritt piped up.

‘What do you eat for breakfast lassie, because it’s pure dynamite,’ Shotley said.

‘Well gentlemen, and ladies,’ Mr Wood said nodding to Lois. ‘I think that settles it.’

‘Settles it,’ Catchpole added.

Lombardi stubbed out his cigarette and pulled his briefcase to the table. Trent took a long hard look at Lois and resisted the urge to threaten her with an Advertising Oversight Board warning or worse, a sternly worded letter.

'We will be watching with interest.'

'You do that Mr Trent. Watch with interest.' Shotley chuckled at his clever retort.

✶

"Boy oh boy,' Merritt said as the team watched him put the kettle on.

'You said it,' Norm added.

'Not too much?' Lois bit her fingernail.

'I wish I'd said that,' Earl sighed.

'The new generation Earl.' Norm patted Lois on the back.

'We were once the new kids on the block Norm.'

They looked at a poster of Wack-*O* now leaning at an angle propped up on the filing cabinet.

'Remember the calendars?' Earl took his proffered tea and sat down. 'Money in the bank. Every year we'd give em sliced ham, tyres at discounted prices and haberdashery. The golden years eh?' he nodded to Norm.

'Before my time Earl I'm afraid. I came in on cigarettes and sliced meats.'

'Sliced meats?' Lois sipped her tea.

'Big thing back in the day. Sliced meat in a packet. A clear packet that you could see what you were getting.'

'Oh.'

'We had the Hanlon sliced meat campaign. Brilliant work by Earl. Remember Earl?'

'Hmm.' Earl looked off into the distance. 'Freshness you can see!'

'Yep, that was it.'

'So you could see it then?' Merritt asked.

'It was big. Previously the butcher wrapped it in paper, You were never quite sure he gave you the chop you asked for, but with Hanlon, what you see is what you get.'

'Those were the days.' Earl smiled and sighed.

'But, well, look at us now.' Norm lifted his cup of tea in a salute to Lois. 'Back in business.'

'Am I a pagan Norm? Iconoclast? Heathen?'

'If you're a heathen Lois, I'm a Hanlon sausage.'

Alice popped her head around the corner of the door, 'Ray Salter tonight Miss Mackenzie, Lois.'

'Yes, I remember.' Lois looked at Earl, 'can you come?'

'I'd be there is a heartbeat Lois, but I've got to visit me mum. It's her night. Once a week.' Earl puffed out some smoke. 'She'd got something wrong, sick lung the doc said.' He dragged heavily on his Lucky strike. 'Never smoked in her life. Anyway we play cards. Sorry Lois. But I know you will knock 'em dead.'

'Norm?'

'Sorry. My night with kids. Wife going to her knitting club or something. But, hey, after this afternoon, I'm sure you can handle Mr Salter.'

'Merritt?'

'Me?

'For support.' Lois looked at her last resort.

'Well, I could I suppose. What time?'

'Seven, although I will be there half an hour before.'

'I'll try Lois.'

'Thanks, And thanks Alice.'

'Me? What did I do?'

'Amethyst Greenock.' Lois said.

‘Oh, right. Well...go get ‘em Lois. I will be listening.’ She looked at the team.’

There were nods all round.

✦ CHAPTER 16

Bishops are accustomed to getting their own way. They have, what is sometimes described as, an over inflated self-importance for a man whose only job is to torment the living to save their souls for rewards unspecified in the afterlife. Ray Salter had said as much, more than once.

Being on national radio can often feel like you are stepping into the fires of hell and being poked from behind with a sharp stick. Ray Salter, radio announcer worth his salt, as his boss often said, was quite adept at a sharp prod, a quick jab and a prolonged poke. You don't get to be an icon of in-depth interviews by putting the kettle on and sliding your feet under the kitchen table, not by a long shot.

He now stood in the reception room attached to the studio waiting until the Bishop took a breath from his sermon on the state of the world and the perils therein, to brief the Bishop that they were waiting for another guest to arrive.

Niall O'Leary stopped talking when Lois followed the radio station's receptionist into the little room with Merritt bringing up the rear. The sight of the young woman grabbed him by his ecclesiasticals and he swallowed—hard. To his way of thinking this young lady was the trouble with the youth of today, the state of the nation and the world, well his sphere of influence anyway and that encompassed the world as far as he was concerned. Niall O'Leary turned a shade of cardinal red and his nostrils sucked in air akin to the new-fangled vacuum cleaner on special at Craven's Department store.

Ray Salter sized up the combatants in an instant and winked at his producer on the other side of the glass panel. This was going to be good.

Ray Salter was well suited to radio. He had a deep, sincere timbre to his voice, he had a quick wit, a sharp grasp of anything resembling the ridiculous and he had a face like a dropped pie; as mentioned, well suited to radio.

'Good evening Miss Mackenzie.'

Lois had a hard time matching the beautiful voice to the face. It was quite disconcerting. The thought of Mr Salter being a wolf, as Miss Kelly had warned, seemed unlikely.

'Oh, Mr Salter, good evening. This is one of the team of Catchpole & Wood, Mr Merritt Claremont-Grove.

'Evening Mr Claremont-Grove. Related to Larrouche?'

'Aunt.'

'Fancy.' Mr Salter shook hands. 'Well, I think you've met Bishop Niall O'Leary, Miss Mackenzie,' Salter smiled and stepped back to initiate the face to face. He looked at his guests, then his watch. 'We have ten minutes. Anyone for a drink?'

Now, any normal person would assume the host was offering tea, water or perhaps an Italian coffee. Ray Salter produced a bottle of Scotch and a selection of crystal glasses.

'Soothes the throat.'

You didn't need to ask the Bishop twice. He coughed and said, 'well, just to get rid of the frog in my throat.'

'That's the way.' Salter poured a goodly jigger of Ballantine's finest.

'Miss?'

'No thank you.' Lois smiled.

'You?' Salter proffered the bottle and glass to Merritt.

'Thanks.'

'Sure Lois? It's very soothing for the vocal cords. Loosens them from nerves.' Salter looked at Lois with a penetrating stare. 'You're not nervous are you Miss?'

'Um, no. Not nervous. She threw a look at the Bishop, Mr Salter and Merritt.

'Well, maybe just a small one.' She coughed and cleared her throat.

Never having had straight spirits in her life, the drink went down like a fire swallowers circus act. Three deep breaths turned into five as the alcohol settled.

'Well, shall we,' Mr Salter ushered his lambs into the studio, gave them a minute to settle, positioned the microphones and gave his producer the O.K. signal.

He really was a master of the airwaves. The introduction completed, the advertisement playing he leaned in close and patted Lois's hand,

'Just relax.'

Everyone sits down to shit. The words rolled around in her head as Ray introduced his guests.

'We are all familiar with...bla, bla, bla, he began buttering up the Bishop who had his second scotch at the ready.

'And to be impartial, tonight we have the bright spark, the 'dare I say genuis' who forged this campaign, Miss Lois Mackenzie of Catchpole & Wood Advertising.' Mr Salter smiled, winked and although looking like a dropped pie, gave the feeling of friendship, camaraderie and solidarity.

Lois bit her lip and giggled.

'So Miss Mackenzie, Lois, how does it feel to be smote or is it smitten, or smiteth?'

Lois looked to the Bishop who had produced the bottle and was on his third, if anyone was counting.

‘Um, well...um...’ she looked to Merritt who was giving her the thumbs up and smiling.

‘Well, really, I don’t feel any different Mr Salter. I’m just doing my job.

“And doing a fine job I surmise.’

‘Well. I try.’

‘’Come up through the ranks did you?’

‘No, I went to University actually.’

‘Fancy that.’ Ray Salter smirked. Lois had seen that look before. She remembered Miss Kelly with Amethyst Greenock. She saw Alice with Miss Greenock. She took her required three breaths.

‘Women today can achieve things Mr Salter.’

‘Was I suggesting otherwise Miss Mackenzie?’

‘I can read a smirk as well as the next woman Mr Salter.’

‘Point taken. So, Miss Mackenzie, what did you study, English Literature or some such?’

‘Marketing and commerce with a side of sociology.’

‘Fancy.’

‘More like hard work Mr Salter.’

‘Touchè.’ Salter pulled a bottle of whisky from a drawer and poured as Nash & Sons, painting services played their jingle.

‘I underestimated you Miss Mackenzie.’

‘People often do,’ Lois said. The ON AIR flashed.

And Miss Mackenzie, how did this idea, this rare flash of inspiration come about.

‘I did my job to the best of my abilities Mr Salter. I have a first class degree which afforded me a little expertise, a little creativeness and a lot of hard work.

‘And you hit the nail of the head with this one?’

‘And I happen to hit a raw nerve.’ She narrowed her eyes at the Bishop. Niall poured a measure and swilled it around the crystal glass, inhaling the intoxicating fumes. He may have found his calling, have an ego the size of a

Cathedral and aspirations to wear red socks, but his sin was a rather large one. He was a sucker for a good Scotch.

'A raw nerve?' Niall O'Leary put down his glass and rounded on his adversary. Ray Salter sat back and watched the fireworks. The advert for baby powder at Becks could wait.

'Young lady. You seem to think the Church is worried about a small fry like you. You have the impreshshshhionn we give a doodly squat about your pridge ooooooo matic. You come here and fink youze can dic, dic, dictate the story, our story with a pridge oooooo matic.' O'Leary pierced the air in front of Lois's chest with his finger. 'The people, my people aren't buying it.'

And Lois got her second wind.

'They, Bishop O'Leary, are not buying a fridge.'

'No?'

'No. They are buying into a feeling that it would be un-Australian to do otherwise. They are being patriotic. This is Australia. It makes them feel good, virtuous and righteous.'

'And religion can't?' Ray Salter asked, baiting the hook as only he knew how.

'All I'm saying,' Lois got no further as the Bishop launched himself with a trebuchet of indignation.

'Don't talk to me about shistry young lady. The Church is full of shistry.' O'Leary said. 'We have shistry coming out of our ears.' He threw back his Scotch and licked his lips. Salter gently pushed the bottle a little closer to the glass and nodded. 'Don't mind if I do,' O'Leary said, adding, 'bless you my son.'

'And who said we were trying to usurp that history?' Lois leaned in and knocked her head on the microphone. '

'You alright?' Ray Salter grabbed her hand and squeezed.

'It's alright, I'm alright,' Lois blushed and curled her hair behind her ear.

‘Usurp,’ Bishop O’Leary said and burped.

‘Everyone know the story. Everyone recognises the significance. But,’ Lois looked at Ray Salter. He raised an eyebrow and winked.

‘But, for heaven’s sake, this is Australia. We are irreverent, funny, tough, cheeky, hardy and above all different. What’s wrong with a tradition that starts in the fridge. It’s 100 bloody degrees in the flippin’ shade.’

Bishop O’Leary opened his mouth and then shut it.

‘And now a word from our sponsors, Howells stationary, 2B or not 2B.’

‘Sorry, I...’

‘Genius? They should give you a medal Lois Mackenzie.’ Lois turned a shade of crimson and lowered her gaze.

‘You know Lois, I’ve never seen snow.’

‘Me neither.’

And in a turn of events on-one expected Bishop O’Leary sat up and said, ‘where the hell is my bible,’ then slowly slide to the floor.

‘You forgot to tell him the light stays on,’ Merritt said as they stood on the footpath waiting for a taxi.

‘The light. Oh yes, the light,’ Lois answered while thinking Mr Ray Salter was the nicest man she’d ever met.

✦ CHAPTER 17

The population were split. On the one hand people were sick to death of a European Christmas, when they were boiling in the heat, shopping was pure hell and the school holidays were starting. On the other hand you can't thumb your nose at over one thousand nine hundred and fifty years of tradition and get away with it.

Lois opened her door to a basket of flowers with a note from Mr Salter. Just one word, Genius and his signature. That would put a spring in anyone's step. She looked at the bright blue sky, her hot little flat and wondered how long the flowers would last, when Mrs Provoichkin appeared and wheezed her way to Lois's door.

'Nice,' Mrs Provoichkin croaked.

'Yes, lovely aren't they.'

They looked at the bouquet.

'Look, Mrs Provoichkin, could you do me a favour.'

'Anything I can do to help dearie.'

'Could you look after these please. I don't have a vase, my place is hot as blazes and well, I just think...'

'Leave it to me.' Mrs Provoichkin took the bunch and coughed her way back to her flat. Lois walked a little lighter all the way to the train station.

She saw Mr Miller standing in the shade and gave him a wave. He waved back and pulled out a fresh handkerchief with a smile.

Serg greeted her with a grin and moved his hand so they could share the pole.

'Mum heard you.'

'Oh.'

'She wanted to know if you were, well you know,' he pulled out his crucifix from his shirt front.

'Not particularly. But that doesn't stop me from doing unto other,' she waved her hand in the air to indicated the rest of the short parable.

'Mum wanted to know can you cook?'

'Not particularly.' Lois laughed. 'I'm good at toast.'

'Mum thinks you are pretty famous, being on the radio and all that.'

'Not particularly.'

'She wants to know if you want to come to tea on Friday.'

'I'd love to Serg.' The train stopped and Lois made a move to exit.

'Pick you up at 6.'

'Great.' She alighted the carriage and feeling the world was just about the most lovely place, walked with a spring in her step up the hill to CWA.

'There she is,' the man with his sandwich board pointed and hissed, 'Heathen.' His dog barked and strained at the string around his neck.

'Blasphemer.' A woman with a straw hat and a walking stick assailed Lois. She missed as Lois ran into the building and took the stairs two at a time to the second floor.

'Met the neighbours, have you?' Alice asked.

Lois looked at the door and rolled her eyes. 'Sure have.'

'And here she is,' Merritt took Lois's arm and led her to her desk.

'Mornin',' Norm said over his tea cup.

'I heard it,' Earl said as he took a drag on his morning cigarette. 'Nice one Lois.'

‘Was it? Was it good?’ The evangelical brigade downstairs had knocked a bit of the lovely off the world.

‘The wife said it was good. You didn’t say anything we all haven’t been thinking for a long time. That’s what the wife said.’ Norm finished his tea and rolled up his sleeves.

‘My mum said you were a breath of fresh air.’

‘Really?’ Lois began to think the world was lovely again.

‘I think it was great. Especially for a person who’d been smoteth.’ Merritt fiddled with a pencil on Earl’s desk.

Alice came in and beamed. ‘I heard it. He called you a genius.’

‘I know.’

‘Anyway, just to let you know there is a meeting this afternoon.’

‘Another one?’ Earl frowned.

‘Hmm,’ Alice nodded. ‘The stunt apparently.’

‘Ah,’ Norm said. ‘The stunt.’

Renwick Auden Bothom had listened to the radio and thought it was high time the Anglicans stepped up to the mark. O’Leary was all puff, bluff and blunder. He felt the Anglicans could be just as outraged, just as indignant and affronted. He mused on the idea of a letter to the editor. Too third hand. A sermon? Too remote. A visit to the Catholic diocese of St Cuthbert’s Waverly and the Bishopric. Get right to the heart of the matter. Let O’Leary know his stand on the issue. Present a united front, with the Anglicans talking the cudgel, the banner, the lead—naturally.

The telephone was employed and an appointment scheduled with the Bishop’s secretary taking down all the details.

‘So, Archbishop Bothom, that’s Friday at eleven o’clock.’ Jeremy Aspinall wrote it down.

★

The boardroom took the full brunt of the afternoon sun as the team sat and listened to Mr Wood's views on dealing with people's dreams.

Shotley rested his head in his hands, his elbows on the table and waited. Catchpole closed his eyes and tried to remember if he'd had one or two helping for dessert at his club.

'So,' Mr Wood clapped his hands and the audience snapped awake. 'Mr Schuler?'

'Well, we had thought on the stunt sir.'

'Ah.' Catchpole nodded. He remembered he'd had two helpings.

'Just so.' Mr Wood said.

Ol' man Shotley undid his top button on his shirt. 'We're flat out with orders. It's bedlam in the warehouse.'

'Sir,' Lois stood up.

'Heard you on the radio. Good work lassie. Good work.' Shotley winked at Lois.

'Thank you.'

'You were saying,' Wood interrupted.

'I know a reporter. Miss Kelly. I'm sure she would like to be there for the event.

'Right.'

'And of course Mr Shotley.'

'Naturally.' Mr Wood said.

'And a photographer. I'll ask Miss Kelly.' Lois looked at her team. 'This will probably be a peace offering, don't you think?'

'Hmm.' Mr Wood raised his eyebrows, then pursed his lips. 'Hmmm,' he repeated.

'When?' Shotley enquired, ''cause I can get one by Friday.'

‘Friday it is.’ Mr Wood wiped his brow with his handkerchief.

‘Remember the Prime Minister?’ Catchpole came to life.

‘Wack-*O*.’ Earl nodded. ‘What a coup.’

‘I remember that,’ Shotley said. ‘Never liked ‘em meself.’

‘A fine line between endorsement and ambush,’ Earl added.

‘When we could get away with just about anything,’ Norm came into the nostalgia.

‘Was it against the law then. For the PM to eat breakfast or something?’ Merritt asked.

Merritt had the knack of stopping a conversation just by opening his mouth. You could call it a talent.

Shotley shook his head, ‘Friday then.’

‘Did you hear that ‘hmmm’’ Norm said as they sat at their desks.

‘Sure did,’ Earl lit a much needed cigarette.

‘What?’

‘Mac, controversy sells. We don’t want to get too chummy with the Ol’ Bishop’

‘Exactly,’ Earl said.

‘I just thought that he might forget the smiting, let bygones be bygones and he can have his tradition and we can have ours.’

‘Well...’ Earl started.

‘It’s called psychological arbitrage,’ Lois said.

‘Pardon?’ Merritt came into the conversation.

‘It’s the discovery by somebody of psychological value in a place where nobody realised it existed.’

The men looked on in wonder.

‘University eh?’ Norm said.

‘University,’ Lois blushed.

✦ CHAPTER 18

When you get three capable women on the case it doesn't take a jiffy to ascertain the Bishop would be at home, Miss Kelly had found a photographer, the Fridge-o-matic and truck procured and everything set for eleven o'clock.

Alice came over to Lois's desk and wished her good luck. Earl gave Lois a pat on the back. Norm wished her well and Merritt said he'd shout her lunch when she came back.

A stunt takes planning. A thing like this requires a steady hand and nerves of steel. Anything could happen when the recipient is confronted.

On the Thursday they had gone over the likely scenarios concerning the Bishop and what he might or might not say or do.

a. decline and smite them en mass.

b. he could decline and shut the door

c. he could accept and be gracious.

d. he could give it away.

e. he might accept it as reparation for his spiritual discomfort.

f. he might accept as payment for an indulgence. (If it's good enough for the Pope, it's certainly good enough for the Bishop)

g. he might see it as a stunt and not open the door.

The team mulled over the possibilities.

‘We could say it’s for a raffle for the needy, that way he gets off the hook, looks good and what he does with it is none of our business.’ Earl was enjoying himself. ‘It’s just like the good ol’ days.’

‘That sounds like a plan,’ Norm said.

‘We’re going to need more than one fridge then,’ Merritt chimed in.

‘Huh?’

‘Well, there are lots of needy, aren’t there?’

‘Merritt. The fridge is a raffle prize. The money raised goes to the needy.’ Norm squinted at Merritt and shook his head.

‘Oh.’

✶

The Bishopric of St Cuthbert’s, Waverly was a large, stone edifice with dozens of windows, an ivy covered wall, a long driveway and manicured gardens. The gates were black curly affairs with crosses in the design. They now were swung open by Lionel, the gardener, to admit Archbishop Bothom riding in a taxi. He was early, but he had things to do, although if the Bishop invited him to lunch his full social calendar of visiting the local primary school, signing bible study book prizes and deciding what to have for tea could wait. Renwick Bothom knew Mrs Cooper was a cracking cook, and the Bishop had a well-stocked drinks cabinet.

The taxi paid, Renwick brushed himself down, looked up at the ivy, the palatial residence and wondered why the Anglicans couldn’t stump up for something a little grander. He only had a townhouse across from his place of work. He reminded himself why he had come and stepped up to operate the bell, when the door opened and Father Aspinall let out a gasp.

'Gracious, I didn't hear your car,' Jeremy looked down the drive for a vehicle.

'Taxi,' Renwick said, then added, 'my driver is having the car overhauled for service.'

'Oh, right.' Jeremy stepped back. 'Come in Archbishop Bothom.'

Jeremy led the way to the reception room at the front of the house with a view of the topiary garden. 'I'll announce you. Would you like a drink? Tea, coffee?'

Bothom looked at the cabinet with lead glass doors.

'Ah, perhaps I could bring in the tray when you've conducted your business.'

'Excellent.'

'Make yourself comfortable Archbishop, I won't be long.'

Jeremy took the stairs two at a time to the study and knocked on the panel door.

'Come.'

'There...' he advanced no further when he heard the front door bell ring.

'Archbishop is here Your Grace,' and Jeremy bolted out the door and headed for the entrance hall.

'Do I need to do everything myself,' Niall huffed and puffed, brushed some wayward crumbs from his girth, straightened his robes and descended the stairs.

The stairs are a main feature of the Bishopric. They are majestic, marble and sweeping. Niall huffed his way down and was just in time to see 'that woman' as he described Lois Mackenzie look up.

'Good morning Bishop O'Leary,' Lois smiled over Father Aspinall's shoulder.

Miss Kelly pulled Duncan, her photographer into the doorway and poked him to take a snap.

'Saints preserve us, You!' O'Leary bellowed. This brought the Archbishop out into the hall and in the moment he quite forgot why he was there and thought he was in for a good bit of gossip.

The ruckus brought Mrs Cooper from the kitchen, wooded spoon in hand ready to defend her territory to the last utensil.

'What the blue blazers is going on?'

'Mrs Cooper,' Niall looked at the small woman.

'Your Grace?'

'Archbishop,' Father Aspinall turned to see Renwick with a tumbler of scotch in his hand.

'Father.' Renwick lifted his glass, 'just the one, Mrs Cooper,' Renwick bowed to the cook.

'Bothom,' `Niall narrowed his eyes at the tumbler of his finest scotch.

And then Ol' man Shotley pushed forward into the hall and whistled as if he was calling the sheepdogs from the glen to bring the flock home.

'Now, listen up you lot.'

The assembled players all stared at Ol' man Shotley and listened.

'Who's in charge is what I want to know?'

'I am,' Mrs Cooper said.

'I think you will find I am,' O'Leary interjected as Bothom hid his smirk behind his drink.

'Right,' Shotley pointed to the Bishop, 'stay right there. Don't move.'

'This is my house and I'll jolly well move if I want to thank you very much.'

What transpired next might take up a good three columns in the paper.

Ol' man Shotley smiled. The sort of smile that might have a canny shopper narrowing their eyes and muttering, 'and I'm a monkey's uncle.'

Lois Mackenzie took a deep breath and delivered her practiced speech, noting the goodwill at Christmas, the sentiment of benevolence, and the gesture of charity of which the Catholic church was renowned.

Miss Kelly poked her photographer in the ribs so many times he felt he might be better served taking photographs of babies or birdwatching.

No-one in their right mind thought the Bishop would keep it. Renwick went so far as to place a bet with himself on the odds of 100/1. He went back for a refill of scotch and came out just as the strapping lads from Shotley's Emporium hoisted the Fridge-o-matic across the threshold of the Bishopric and placed it with care on the black and white tiled floor, (purported to be imported for Italy).

'For me?'

Father Aspinall crossed his fingers and offered up a prayer as the photographer fiddled with his long lens.

'Yes,' Lois nodded.

Miss Kelly wrote it down. O'l man Shotley stood next to the two lads like a proud father showing off his first born.

'That's right Bishop. For you.' Shotley thumped the Bishop on the back. 'Goodwill and all that.'

'Goodwill.'

Father Aspinall looked to heaven for divine intervention. He knew a set up when he saw one. The stunt had ambush written all over it.

'Well, I...er...'

Mrs Erma Cooper hovered in the background dreaming of a cold cucumber salad, turkey in aspic and lime jelly. She crossed her fingers behind her back.

'Er,' Archbishop Renwick Bothom interjected. All eyes were on the Anglican. (a rare enough event that Renwick took a good dose of the finest Scotch whisky and blinked) 'Er... it looks like..' he began when the Catholics came to the fore.

‘Can you take it around the back,’ Jeremy Aspinall broke the moment. Mrs Cooper beckoned the fridge with her wooded spoon and began to think of home made icecream and cracked chocolate Florentines.

‘Oh, right,’ Bishop O’Leary woke up. ‘Nice,’ he said. ‘Very nice of you.’

Miss Kelly wrote it down and poked the photographer.

‘Just a few words Bishop O’Leary, for the public you know. They’d like to know how you feel, where you stand, just a few words.’

‘Of course.’ Bishop Niall O’Leary took a deep breath. *Here,* he thought, *was the opportunity to showcase his views, his opinions, his knowledge.* He might have 70% capacity every Sunday, but the newspaper was nation-wide.

‘Well, I’d like to say...’ and he might have been talking to the Italian tiles for all the attention he gained in the hallway because...although Archbishop Renwick Bothom was strictly a two tipples on a Friday sort of fellow, this debacle was too good, the finest Scotch whisky was too good and four glassed in quick succession had gone to his head. He let out a guffaw and sat down on the marble staircase only to miss his bottom and slide unceremoniously to the Italian tiles.

You can envisage the headlines, Bothom missed his bottom or similar. It seems the Anglicans had, for once, upstaged the Catholics. A win is a win.

Lois, every helpful, jumped right in to help the helpless Archbishop and it didn’t take a second for her to compound the debacle. She slipped on the spilt whiskey, tried to right herself and fell into the Archbishop’s lap with a whomp. It might have been the opening of a Noel Coward play if it wasn’t real life.

Niall looked around at the prostrate Archbishop and rolled his eyes heavenward, ‘Anglicans.’

Not to be outdone, Renwick parried with,

‘Catholic.’

‘Ah, goodwill all round,’ O’l man Shotley picked up the whisky bottle, plucked the glass from Renwick’s hand and poured himself a decent slug.

✦ CHAPTER 19

A figure like Niall O'Leary, a man who had a highly inflated opinion of himself and where he stood in the world saw nothing untoward in people giving him things. He was the sort of fellow who could be heard saying, 'Don't they know who I am?' It might not get you a good seat at the Melbourne cricket ground, but it did get you a seat.

Now as Jeremy tried to keep the morning paper from gracing the breakfast table Niall recalled he rather fancied a red currant fool for his dessert and fresh whipped cream. His dear mother sometimes made such a treat when he came home for the week-end back when he was slightly smaller and slightly less pompous.

'Ah, Mrs Cooper.'

'Your Grace?'

'Do you happen to know the recipe for red currant fool?'

'I do.'

'And would you be able to make such a thing?'

'I would.'

'Splendid.' The Bishop beamed. 'All good in the scullery Mrs Cooper?'

'Yes, Your Grace.'

'Splendid.'

'Your Grace...?'

'Yes Mrs Cooper?'

'What about the old one?'

'The old one?' It took Niall a moment. 'Ah, I see...well...'

‘The seminary?’ Mrs Cooper offered her solution.

‘Excellent idea Mrs Cooper.’

‘Right you are then.’ Erma slipped a fruit comport in front of Niall with a dollop of cream and bustled out.

‘He said the seminary can have it?’ Jeremy Aspinall and Erma looked at the old Westinghouse. Rusty in spots, dented and wheezing like an asthmatic.

‘I’ll get a truck today Mrs Cooper.’ Jeremy began to think of cold milk, jelly and tomatoes that lasted more than a day. And in the moment when jelly, red currant and whipped cream took centre stage the news item on page one was forgotten. The moral conundrum overtaken by cold ham. The opinion piece about the meaning of Christmas on page three forgotten. Once settles in his office with a cup of tea and fresh scone - with cream, Niall took a quick look at the paper.

‘Pfft. Don’t they know who I am?’ As rhetorical questions go, this one was a banger.

✶

If the Catholics had listened to the man in the street they might have put a bob or two on the odds of ‘keeping it’ or ‘giving it away’. At the moment the book was odds on favourite for keeping it. What the man in the street thought he knew about the church wasn’t a secret.

Bothom looked over the paper with a magnifying glass and a fine toothed comb. The Anglicans might as well have been the Abyssinian Episcopalians for all the coverage they gleaned. Not that an Archbishop with a girl on his lap and the breath of a bar room floor wasn’t newsworthy, but the editor knew where the value lay. Advertising paid the bills.

‘Not a mention. Nothing.’ Renwick sat back and sucked on sour lemons.

‘Pardon,’ Mrs Brewster fiddled with the jam.

‘Once again Mrs Brewster,’ Renwick threw his paper down.

‘Your Grace?’

‘Not a word. Nothing I was there, you know.’

‘Yes, Your Grace.’

‘I could take you to the spot, Right there to give that man a piece of my mind.’

What Mrs Brewster thought of the Archbishop giving away a scant resource like the ol’ grey matter we will never know.

‘I’m sure he might have appreciated it Your Grace.’

‘And a Fridge-o-matic.’

‘Pardon?’

‘A Fridge-o-matic Mrs Brewster. He was given a Fridge-o-matic.’

‘Really.’

‘I had hoped he’d be shamed. But oh no. That man has more gall that a ball bladder. What did he do? Hmmm?’

Mrs Brewster shrugged and folded a napkin.

‘I’ll tell you what he did. He...he...he kept it.’

‘Really.’

‘You may well say really Mrs Brewster. You may well say it with incredulity. Now, if I’d been given one—then, my word you’d see something.’

‘I’m sure Your Grace.’ Mrs Brewster, a staunch Anglican, wondered, just for a moment mind you, but just wondered what it was that gave the Catholics the edge. What wouldn’t she give for a Fridge-o-matic.

But, what struck the reader of the paper was the deft handling of the goodwill of the giver, one Lois Mackenzie of CWA and Ol’ man Shotley. *This woman* the article stated, *despite being smiteth had turned the other cheek. If that wasn't a Christian attitude then this reporter is a monkey's uncle.*

The sentiment, Miss Kelly wrote, *was more than Australian, it was universal.*

It's the giving, not the getting. That was the meaning of Christmas. And if that was an Australian tradition it was a bloody good one!

'Nice one Miss Mackenzie, Lois.' Alice said and pointed to the headlines as Lois walked through the door and wiped her brow of sweat.

'Thanks.'

'Quite a crowd out there.'

'Yes, they seem to think I will rot in hell or save the world.'

Alice smirked, 'not before you get your Christmas bonus I hope.'

Lois entered the office and Earl looked up with scissors in hand, 'another one for the wall.

'Is he going to raffle it?' Merritt asked as he fanned himself.

'I don't think so,' Lois sat at her desk and instead of her practiced routine of dictionary, pencils and three deep breaths she slumped in her chair.

'What up?' Norm came in with his cup of tea.

'Well, I...'

The three men listened.

'It's just that I think it's all a bit...'

'A bit...?' Norm asked.

'A bit...well it smacks of chicanery.'

'Chicanery?' Earl frowned.

'What's that?' Merritt asked.

'Sort of underhandedness. Double dealing,' Earl explained.

Lois took it a step further. 'The use of deception or subterfuge to achieve one's purpose.'

'And you feel?' Norm asked.

'A bit guilty really.' People pleasing comes with quite a bit of psychological baggage.

'Mac. Lois. It's natural to feel a little bit sticky after a big campaign. It's the let down. Psychological.' Norm tapped his head.

'Sticky?' Merritt tried to keep up.

'Sort of like you just want a good bath to feel right again. We deal in making people want things. Probably things they can't afford or need.'

'But people need a fridge, don't they?' Merritt asked.

'Do you think he knew it was a stunt?'

'Um..' Earl twiddled with his pencil.

'Do you?' Lois looked at Earl.

'Probably not by the look at the photos in the paper.'

'Should I just send him a note. For being a good sport about it all. Just to...'

'Well, you could. Or you might...' Norm began.

'You could use his tacit approval for the Fridge-o-matic in your next poster. If it's good enough for a Bishop.' Earl said.

'Two traditions meet, you mean.' Lois perked up. She began to brainstorm. 'Even Bishops like jelly and ice-cream.'

Earl looked at Norm and smiled. Norm raised his eyebrow.

'So the Bishop likes jelly. Is that it?' Merritt asked.

'Sort of.' Norm patted Merritt on the back.

'Did you tell him about the light staying on.' There is only so much you can do with someone like Merritt.

'Merritt.'

'Yes?'

'Put the kettle on.'

Alice shot into the office as Merritt contemplated the kettle.

'Ten minutes, All of them.'

'Bigger than Ben Hur,' Norm said. Earl stubbed his cigarette and put the stub in his pocket. 'It can only be good news.'

The boardroom smelt stale and was warming up to a slow boil. The team stood and waited. Wood and Co, including Mr Trent of the Oversight Board filed in and Alice shut the door, put her ear to the panelling and concentrated.

Naturally the bit about people's dreams was given the once over, then Mr Wood said,

'Without further ado. Miss Mackenzie, I have the pleasure in telling you that you have been nominated for the Golden Finger award 1950.'

'Me?' Lois squeaked. She looked at Earl and he nodded and smiled.

'That's my girl,' Shotley shot up and pumped Lois's arm like it was a car jack lever.

'Er,' Mr Wood interjected, 'a nomination is not a win, yet. We are up against some tough opposition.'

Mr Trent stood up. 'As the AOB representative I have been informed that Firkle Cigarettes are nominated for their campaign of menthol filters. There was a groan. Cigarettes had BIG budgets. Groad, Oswald and Bull Agency lorded it over the competition year after year. Mr Trent continued in his less than baritone voice. 'And Lyle Soap. They won last year with that little baby, now they have twins.' Smith and Sons Advertising had a stock of babies in the family and rumour has it that they didn't pay model rates, but family rates.

'Tough competition,' Norm said to the room.

'Tough,' Catchpole came to life.

‘And we have this genius here,’ Shotley finally let go of Lois’s hand. ‘We need something Miss. Something to knock their bloody socks off.’

‘Well,’ Lois started. Norm urged her on.

‘Well, now we have we have everyone talking about an Australian tradition, perhaps,’

‘Yes.’ Shotley sat on the edge of his seat.

‘Perhaps we should try to marry our tradition with the,’

‘Yes?’

‘With the other tradition, The church.’

‘Hmm.’ Mr Trent frowned. He cleared his throat. I...’ He got no further as Lois was on a roll.

‘Perhaps we use the Bishop as an example. Plant the seed that he should give the Fridge-o-matic away rather than keep it. Something like...Give a Fridge-o-matic. The gift that keeps on giving. (lifetime warranty on door handle).

‘I like it.’ Catchpole said.

‘Pure genius. Worth bottling I tell ya.’ Shotley gave Lois a slap on the back and a look of pure adoration.

Mr Tent cleared his throat once more trying to put a spanner in the works. ‘I should point out the implications of defamation.’

‘Defamation,’ Catchpole frowned.

Miss Mackenzie’s on the case,’ Shotley said, ‘she knows the drill, so put that in ya pipe and smoke it.’ Mr Trent huffed, puffed, closed his brief case and stood up. ‘Well if that is the way you do business...’

‘Oh, go boil a cabbage,’ Shotley shoved him to the door, opened it and pushed. Alice slid out the way just in time.

‘Never liked the weasel.’ Shotley sat down and wiped his face with a handkerchief. ‘Better get crackin’ eh?’

The staff of CWA just saw their chance of the Golden Finger unceremoniously shoved out the door.

'I don't suppose he's one of the judges?' Merritt asked. It didn't happen often, but Merritt hit the nail right on the head.

✸

'Do you think we are sunk?' Lois sat at her desk and fanned herself with a Wack-*O* poster.

'Firkel,' Norm winced.

'Groad, Oswald and Bull Agency. They have the yearly calendar, it's their bread and butter. Every year. Cigarettes are a gravy train. Sporting events, banners, radio time. Its money in the bank.'

'Oh.' Lois fanned harder and poked herself in the eye.

'You alright?' Earl asked.

'I'm fine.'

'Look, all we can do is our best. Trent isn't the only judge.'

'I liked the gift that keeps on giving,' Merritt said.

'So do I,' Earl added. It's cliché, but it's familiar, it's nice.'

Perhaps we just ask one question on the side of a bus,' Lois said.

'What?' Merritt asked.

'What is the meaning of Christmas?'

The men sat and sweated. Merritt frowned and chewed on the end of his pencil. 'What is the meaning of Christmas? What is the meaning of Christmas?' he mused.

'I like it.' Norm wiped the back of his neck with his handkerchief. 'Naturally people will...'

'Naturally,' Earl began to grin.

'And no-one can say we are demeaning you know who.'

'Who?' Merritt asked.

'It's brilliant.' Earl lit a cigarette and sat back. 'Absolutely bloody brilliant. I wish I'd thought of it myself.'

‘I have an idea for a poster,’ Norm went to work.

‘I’ll do the costing for the posters if you like Lois,’ Norm offered.

‘Thanks.’

‘Shall I sharpen your pencil Lois?’

‘That would be great.’

‘You know,’ Earl looked over to Lois at her desk, ‘I had the idea you were just a pretty face. I was wrong.’

It was a backhanded compliment, but the nicest compliment Lois had ever had. She took a deep breath, closed her eyes and thought, *I’ve arrived.*

✦ CHAPTER 20

If there is one thing to spark the public into debate it's a question that might have polar opposite answers.

On billboards, on buses, in the papers and magazines. It divided the nation (well Sydneysiders anyway) on the answer. Everyone had an opinion.

It soon descended into the us and them. One was ruled by someone a little higher up than Shotley's emporium of Homewares. The others were of the opinion that a Fridge-o-matic, a new Australian tradition in keeping with a new country on the other side of the equator was just the ticket.

Goodwill to all men (and women) was squeezed in the middle.

'We hit the front page again,' Merritt slapped the paper on Lois's desk. She was busy sponging her linen skirt.

Norm entered with a cup of tea, 'What happened?'

'Well, that man, the end is nigh, you know, downstairs,' The men nodded and Earl lit his first cigarette.

'Well, he has a dog. You've seen his dog?'

They nodded again.

'Well, his dog, Buster, that's his name, Well Buster jumped up. I've been brining him a few treats. He sits out all day on that hessian bag, I just thought he'd like some treats.'

'Dog biscuits?' Merritt asked. 'Were they Doggy-do dog biscuits?'

'No, I don't think so.'

'And,' Earl asked.

Well, the sandwich board man was painting his board with days to Christmas. Seven days to Christmas and Buster pulled on his lead and the man yanked and the paint...' Lois looked at her skirt with black paint on the front.'

'Hmmm,' Merritt frowned.

'Ruined. My best one too.'

'Hmmm.' Merritt reiterated.

'The man wasn't very nice either. The woman with the bible hit him. She said 'and that's the meaning of Christmas.' I think his ear was quite swollen. Anyway there was a ruckus of sorts and someone went for the police.'

Norm sat on the edge of Lois's desk and exclaimed, 'Cripes.'

'I shot upstairs.' Lois stopped sponging and surveyed the damage. 'Ruined.'

Earl stubbed out his cigarette. 'I saw a fellow shove another bloke on the bus. He shouted. You wouldn't know the meaning of Christmas if you sat on it.'

'Really?'

'Yup. And then a woman with a shopping trolley, you know the ones with wheels, well she shoved it at a fella's legs and told him to put that in his Christmas pipe and smoke it!.'

'No.' The 'no' was of the incredulous type people often utter in astonishment. Merritt was fully invested in the story.

'What did he say?'

'I dunno. I got off.' Earl said.

Norm put his tea down, 'Well my son was going to be Joseph in the play. We had the tea towel for the headdress, the cord and sandals. The wife went to a lot of trouble making a beard. Now they say it's not wise, knowing where his father works. I'm catholic for heaven's sake.' Norm shook his head.

'Can of worms,' Earl sat back and contemplated the crisis they had created.

'What have I done?' Lois sat down.

'More to the point. What do we do?' Earl posited.

Alice popped her head around the door, 'Miss Mackenzie, telephone call.' She smiled.

'Who is it Alice?' Lois didn't fancy another call from Queensland.

"Mr Craven Jr.'

'Who?'

'Mr Douglas Crave jnr.' Alice eyes widened.

'You know Lois. Aunts neighbour.' Merritt jogged her memory.

'Me?'

'At my desk. I can put it through to the boardroom if you prefer.'

'No,' Lois followed Alice out as Earl and Norm looked at Merritt. 'He's the Cravens Department Store fellow. Lives next to my Aunt. White house.' Earl and Norm envisaged the social circle Merritt inhabited and his nonchalant view of that world. 'Harbour view,' Merritt added 'South Head Peninsula.' As if the men needed to pinpoint just where the upper crust might reside with Harbour bridge views.

Lois fumbled with the telephone ear piece and then said, 'Hello?'

'Oh right. Miss Mackenzie?'

'Yes, that's me,' Lois looked at Alice and smiled.

'Ah, right. Well you may not remember me at the birthday party, but we sat on a bench with my father.'

‘Yes I remember.’

‘Right, well, my father would like to see you.’

‘Oh.’

‘Yes, he’d like to, well, he want to have a talk. He’s very taken with your brain.’

‘My brain.’

‘Well your, um, your thinking. Not your brain per se, but your, um, thinking.’

‘Oh.’

‘And well we have dinner around eight. Would tonight be alright?’ I know its very short notice and I completely understand...’

‘Eight?’

‘Yes, eight. If you give me your address I’ll send someone to pick you up.’

‘Alright.’

Lois handed over the details and hung up.

‘And?’ Alice asked.

‘I’m going to dinner. At eight.’

‘Really.’

‘Oh blast.’ Lois sat on Alice’s desk corner.

‘What?’

‘I’ve got nothing to wear.’

There was a lethargy in the office of CWA as the temperature was a constant simmer and it transpired half the population hated them.

‘Should we tell them about the light?’ Merritt said as he rolled up his sleeves.

‘Well, its only 7 days, then...’ Earl emptied his ash tray.

‘Yes, just seven days.’ Norm brushed his rubber crumbs to the floor.

‘So we just let it run.’ Lois said.

Alice shot into the office and grinned. ‘You’ll never guess.’

'What?' the team said in unison.

'Ol man Shotley just rang. He's sold out. Orders right through to February. He's one happy fellow. He said if we don't get the award he will kick up a stink.'

'After he booted out Mr Trent I don't think his word has much sway do you?'

'You never know,' Alice said. 'Wheels within wheels. He might know someone, who knows someone who...well you get the picture.'

The news lightened the mood and Earl began to reminisce about getting the Golden Finger. 'Big do it was. At the Town Hall. We had crab.'

'Do you really think we have a chance?'

'I do.' Earl said.

'Well its all of us. Not just me. We are a team. Alice, Norm, Merritt and you of course. Without you Earl I just don't think...'

'Nonsense. You're the brains of the outfit on this one Lois.'

'Brains.' Lois blurted. 'Oh my Lord. I'm going to dinner at the Craven mansion and I need to find something to wear.'

'Have half a day Lois,' Alice said. 'You deserve it. Go shopping.'

'Craven invited you?' Merritt asked.

'Yes.'

'Stay right there.' Merritt went to make a telephone call. He came back and patted Lois on the back. 'I rang Aunt Rene. She's expecting you.'

'I can't afford Larrouche Merrett.'

'A present. From me. 'Doggy-Do biscuits liked the idea of the dog. It's the meaning of Christmas. It's the giving, not the getting.'

'Really?'

'Go.'

★

With the words 'We all love Merritt,' still ringing in her ears, Lois juggled the dress box, the shoe box, the hat box and her handbag through the shoppers to the train station.

'Oh, it's you,' Serg saw her navigating the stairs. 'Want a hand?'

'Please,' Lois lightened her load. 'You're early Serg. This is the 4:17.' They watched the train pull into the station.

'Boss wanted us to do some shopping before the madness. We need to work to Xmas eve, so here I am.'

'Oh.'

'And you? Doing the shopping too?'

'Um, yes.' They moved to the open train door and alighted.

'Looks like you got a bonus,' Serg clocked the labels on the bags.

'Long story.'

'Well Lois, how about you come to tea and tell me about it?' As pick-up lines it was straight out of the book. Markos had been giving his brother some tips on women.

'Oh, I can't. I'm already going out,' She held her booty high.

'Ah,' Serg nodded. 'Um, mum wants to know how your fixed for Christmas Day?' Any family? Plans?'

Although only seven days away Lois hadn't put her mind to the future. She shrugged.

'Well, if ya want. Only if ya want to, you can come to our place. It's...well it's a bit...well if you want.'

'I...' Lois began.

'Let mum know by Wednesday.'

'Ok.' Sege took the opportunity to grab Lois by the forearm and then shot out the door. It was only when the train moved off he realised he was still holding a shoe box. Lois watched in horror as the train moved. There it was again. Chaos just when she thought she had it all together. What would Amethyst Greenock do? 'Rise above,' Lois said as she began the walk home.

'Mr Moon, do you think I should take something if I was invited to dinner? A bottle of wine? Something?'

Mr Moon shrugged his shoulders like a texan oil rig. 'I dunno.'

'It's posh.'

'Maybe something.' They looked at the shelf behind the counter. It carried Chinese medicine that looked like dried seaweed, Chinese new year lanterns with red knotted cords, a few plastic toys and a little box containing a delicately painted rice paper fan.

'That's nice,' Lois pointed.

'Ah, for lady of the house. Very feminine for woman.' Mr Moon retrieved the gift and put it on the counter. 'Very pretty Miss Mackenzie.'

'Yes, isn't it.'

'And for him?' Mr Moon retried a bottle opener in the shape of a dragon. 'Last one, on special Miss Mackenzie.'

'I'll take them.' Even high fliers like Lois succumbed to the deal now and again.

'I wrap nice,' Mr Moon fetched some tissue paper and practiced the black art of origami on the gifts. Everyone is an expert at something.

'Thank you.'

As Lois neared her flat she heard a car screech to a stop.

'Lois,' Serg jumped out and ran. 'Your shoes.'

'Serg, thanks. I wondered what I'd do. You're a lifesaver.'

'Well,' Serg scuffed his shoe on the footpath. 'You thought about Christmas?'

‘I...I’d love to. Thank your mum. I’ll be there.’ If you could measure a smile Serg might have hit the high percentile. He grinned from ear to ear.

‘We’ll pick you up early.’

‘Oh, ok.’

‘Eight(ish). Mum likes to get a good start on the day. And it’s not fancy. You don’t need to be fancy.’

‘Right. Well thanks again Serg.’

‘They stood like two statures as the sun beat down. Serg’s brother, Markos beeped the horn startling the two into a fumbled touch of the lips. It was more teeth than lips and Lois came away with a burgeoning bruise.

‘Oh well bye, Serg.’

‘Yeah. Bye Lois.’

They stood some more. ‘Oh, here’s your shoes.’

‘Thanks.’ The day ticked on...

Mrs Provoichkin came out at the sound of a horn.

‘Serg, this is Mrs Provoichkin, my neighbour.’

‘Howdy,’

‘Hello young, man,’ Mrs Provoichkin wheezed. They stood like stuffed mullets in the heat. Sometimes you feel like you need to say something, anything to get over an awkward silence. Mrs Provoichkin knew the value of keeping quiet.

‘Um, I was just inviting Lois to Christmas at my place’

‘Yes, Lois added, ‘at his place.’ They looked at Mrs Provoichkin.

‘You got plans Mrs Provoichkin?’ Serg asked trying to be polite. His brother beeped again. ‘Anything?’

Mrs Provoichkin coughed and griped her walker. Lois looked at the old woman, then at Serg, then back to Mrs Provoichkin. Serg shuffled his feet.

‘Look, I ...well.’

'I'd love to,' Mrs Provoichkin gripped Serg's arm. He looked at the arthritic claw. His nona had such a claw when she was alive.

'Sure. I'll let mum know. We start early. Eight. My brother,' Serg pointed to the car, 'he'll pick you up.

Mrs Provoichkin coughed up her lung and smiled.

'That settles it then,' Lois smiled and her lip gave a twitch.

'Bruise dearie. Vicks vapour rub will fix it.'

'Really?'

'Like me life depended on it,' Mrs Provoichkin said, winked and coughed up her other lung.

✷

A plain cream skirt, a wonderfully cut silk blouse with pearl buttons and small short bolero jacket plus sling backs and Lois felt a million dollars. She wondered how she might keep the cream and white pristine. The trick was to be extra careful, stay away from tomato, beetroot, red wine or just not eat anything at all. A bread roll might work.

The car duly arrived. she was ferried to the front door of the craven family home and shown into the library, while trying not to get dirty, fall over, lean on anything or sweat. The stress of it all was a monumental effort. She had imagined a family dinner. Mr Senior, Mr Junior, Mrs C and any siblings. What she saw made her think she needed more than three deeps breaths to overcome. Twelve impeccably dressed, intelligent looking people stood around with drinks and barely glanced in her direction as she followed the doorman into the room.

'Miss Mackenzie,' Douglas jnr came from behind and tapped her on the shoulder.

'Ahhhh,' she jumped. When you are wound up like a clock spring to be on your best behaviour anything can make you jumpy. The fright cut the conversation and twelve sets of eyes clocked on.

'Dad's in the study, you want to say hello?'

'Yes, say hello, Lois echoed as her throat ran dry.

'You will meet everyone at the table. No-one special.' A rather large understatement in the scheme of things. Captain's of industry, Members of Parliament, a sprinkling of newspaper editors and a couple of senior civil servants just about summed up the who's who. *Everyone sits down to shit.*

The study was a mammoth room with huge windows taking in the harbour and all it had to offer.

'Dad, Miss Lois Mackenzie.'

'Mr Craven,' Lois swallowed as the old man came from the window and held out his hand. He shook like had known her all her life, 'Well, well, well.'

'Um, I,' Lois fished in her shopping bag and handed over her presents. 'Um, Thanks for having me Mr Craven.'

'What's this then?'

'Just something for you and your wife.'

'Mum died about five years ago Lois. Sorry.'

'Oh.' Lois blushed.

'Well, will ya look at that,' Mr Craven held up his bottle opener. 'I like it a lot.' He then opened the fan. 'Oh this is lovely. Just lovely,' he fanned himself. 'Those freeloaders,' he pointed in the direction of the library, 'never give me such nice things. And look at the wrapping. Such trouble. So beautiful.'

'My friend, Mr Moon did that. He's Chinese.' It felt good to call Mr Moon a friend. Lois thought it sounded just about right. He'd been there through thick and thin, ever since she moved to Lucknow Close.

'You know, I'd like to meet this Mr Moon.' Mr Craven took another look at the wrapping.

'Dad?'

'Just thinking son, just thinking.'

Douglas jnr laughed. 'Dad gets an idea and well, I'm the one holding the baby.'

'This young lady has taken the time,' Mr Craven fanned himself. 'I'll treasure them Miss Mackenzie. My word I will treasure them.

'Lois beamed.

'Well I want to pick your brain young lady, later.'

'Oh.'

'We should go in,' Douglas ushered his father and Lois into the library and then shepherded the guests into the dining room. And right there Lois could see something of a dilemma. Five wine glasses, more silverware than an antiques market and the opportunity to make a right fool of herself. She sat down, Douglas on her left and a portly man on her right.

What do you say to someone twice your age and probably a captain of industry?

'Hot isn't it?' Lois said as she tried to fit in.

'Hmmm?'

'Hot, I said it's hot,' Lois tried again.

'Yes, well it's summer.' That finished that introduction. She thought of her mantra, *everyone sits down to shit,* but decided to block that particular faux pas from her repertoire.

Appetiser. Delicate shells of lettuce with a prawn in a pink sauce. Lois looked at it, saw it was eaten with a small fork and decided to pass. Soup. Tomato. Lois declined and sipped water. She was starving, but no-one was going for the bread.

A salad with beetroot puree, a boiled egg surrounded by greenery and little tomatoes. It looked delicious, but those tomatoes would roll and ...well err on the side of caution.

Fish. In a sloppy sauce. She ate so slow they took her plate half eaten.

'Not hungry Lois,' Douglas asked. Oh, if only he knew.

The conversation ranged from politics, philosophy and the boxing day cricket match. She thought of things to say, but by the time she'd rehearsed them in her head, the conversation had moved on. She watched the women who didn't defer to the men. They held their own on any subject and even made jokes at the men's expense.

'Oh poppycock,' a woman said as she speared her chicken main course.' The white wine sauce with parsley looked tempting. Lois leaned in and managed to get something to her mouth without incident.

'You alright,' Douglas asked as he watched her eat.

'Yes, fine, I'm, fine,' Lois smoothed down her blouse and checked for spots.

The conversation lulled and the man on her right turned his attention to Lois.

'So, what is it your known for Miss Mackenzie?' Lois finished chewing, thought of Amethyst Greenock and swallowed.

Mr Craven Snr heard the question and tapped one of his wine glasses with his spoon. The table quietened.

'Miss Mackenzie, this bright young woman is behind, 'The meaning of Christmas.'

Sixteen pairs of eyes plus the wait staff looked at Lois like a specimen under glass.

'The meaning of Christmas?' a woman asked.

'Oh where have you been Sylvia? It's everywhere,' a fellow offered.

'I think it is rather clever,' another guest added.

'Clever. It's more than clever, it's brilliant advertising. Brilliant,' Mr Craven said.

'Well. What is the meaning of Christmas then?' Sylvia asked.

Those eyes bore into Lois and she touched her bruised lip.

'Well, I...' They all waited for some pearl of wisdom, some profound nugget. 'It's really just in the giving, not the getting.'

'That's it,' Mr Craven brought out his fan and used it. 'It's in the giving, not the getting.'

'But what about Him,' a man at the end of the table pointed to the ceiling.

'Religion and the Christmas story.'

'Does it need to be this or that?' Douglas asked.

'Profit or Prophet?' Lois said.

'She's on the ball this one,' Mr Craven smiled and winked at Lois. 'This girl invented a new Australian tradition. It's 100 bloody degrees in the flippin' shade.'

'Was that you?' the man on the right asked.

'Yes'

'Well, I for one like the idea. A bit larrikin. A bit irreverent. Definitely Australian. 100 bloody degrees in the flippin' shade.'

Lois smiled.

'Smacks of commercialism if you ask me.' The man at the end said.

'Says the man who is eating at Mr Craven's table,' Sylvia smirked.

'What's wrong with the old tradition?'

'Nothing. Nothing at all. But don't you think we need something that defines us as Australian?' Lois was getting into her stride. Being intense has it's uses. 'I don't think one thousand nine hundred and fifty years of tradition is going anywhere. It won't be knocked off the top spot. But it's about time Australia busted out of the shadow of the Northern Hemisphere. We're different.' She looked at the faces around the table. A clap could be heard from someone in the kitchen.

'You're not for a republic are you?' A woman clutching her pearls asked.

'It's not about politics, it's about identity,' Douglas said. 'Our own identity.'

'Hear, hear,' a woman raised her glass. 'The meaning of Christmas.' The toast was unanimous. 'It's the giving, not the getting.'

✶

What are you doing for Christmas Lois?' Douglas asked as they ate ice-cream (white vanilla, thank heavens) and stewed plums.

'I'm going to my friends with my neighbour.'

'Oh. We'd be glad to have you over if you are free in the evening.'

'Really.'

'Absolutely.' Douglas lashed out on a winning smile and put his hand over hers. Basking in the trappings of wealth Lois missed the subtle clues of flirtatious overtures. She giggled. Wine on a near empty stomach is never a good mix, sitting with people who know which fork to use, the sayings of Socrates and seeing the lights of Sydney Harbour blinds you to the obvious. Lois almost needed a braille book to get the hint.

'We sort of have a tradition. Go down to our little beach and have, well, have fun.'

'You have your own beach?'

'It's small.'

'Oh.'

At the door Douglas gave it one last shot.

'If there is anything I can do Lois, just ask.'

'Well, there is one thing.' Lois bit her bruise and winced.

'Anything.'

'I need to make a trunk call to my mother. She's in Queensland.' I can't go after work, the exchange is closed.'

‘You want me to call her?’

‘Yes, if you could. I don’t know how else to get hold of her. Letters at Christmas take ages.’

‘Telegram?’

‘That’s it. A telegram.’ Lois laughed. ‘Why didn’t I think of that?’

‘We have blanks in the office.’

‘You have an office?’

‘Come with me.’

That out of the way, Lois pushed her luck.

‘Um.’

‘Yes.’ At this stage Douglas would chew on ants and whistle Waltzing Matilda if Lois asked.

‘Well, I wonder if you could just five me a little bag of leftovers. My neighbour, Mrs Provoichkin, well she doesn’t have much, and well, I kind of feed her sometimes. Not like a pet or anything,’ Lois giggled, ‘but neighbourly like.’

‘Sure. Come with me.’

Mrs Kellett, the type of woman who can cook anything as long as you stay out of her kitchen welcomed Lois with a smile. ‘You’re the young lady eh?’

‘Yes.’

‘100 bloody degrees in the flippin’ shade.’ Mrs Kellett laughed.

A basket was produced. Mrs Kellett went to work filling a Christmas hamper that might have come from a Michelin star restaurant.

‘Just a few treats eh?’

‘This is too much. Really.’ Lois dropped a can of pickled walnuts on her toe. ‘Awwwwww.’

‘Let me,’ Douglas sat her down, took off her shoe and looked at the toe while Mrs Kellett looked on.

‘Ice is what you need eh.’

‘Just bruised I think,’ Douglas held onto her foot.

'Oh.'

There was that moment. A girl could just give into the ministrations of an eligible bachelor, a loaded, handsome, intelligent, eligible bachelor and well inevitably A follows B for wedding bells. The thought was fleeting. Lois had a career in mind. She had plans for a bright future where she had her own money, her own ambitions, her own car. Then there was Serg. He was so darn nice.

'Thanks,' Lois retrieved her shoe and put it on.

'Not a problem,' Douglas stood up. 'I guess you need to work tomorrow?'

'Yes.'

'Me too,' he shrugged and gave one of his winning smiles. 'Um well, I'll send the telegram tomorrow.

'Tomorrow,' Lois picked up the hamper. 'You're very kind.'

'I hope she likes it.'

'I'm sure she will,' They stood around. Lois was making a habit of being a stunned mullet.

'So.'

'So.'

'Um, bye then,' Lois made for the door. 'And thank you Mrs Kettle.'

'Kellett.'

'Yes, Kellett.' They walked to the front door and stood on the steps.

'Bye.'

'Bye Lois.'

It was only when outside Lois realised she had no way of getting home.

'Er,'

'Yes,' Douglas stood holding the door.'

'You couldn't, um, sort of...'

'Oh,' he shook his head. 'Of course. I'll get my car.'

‘Thanks Douglas.’ It was a start. She called him by his name.

‘Do you want to meet Mrs Provoichkin? My neighbour.’

‘It’s late.’

‘She’s up.’ Lois pointed to the light and twitch of the curtain.

‘Alright.’

Seeing Mrs Provoichkin after a hard day smoking would take anyone by surprise. Douglas took a step back as the apparition of Mrs Provoichkin opened the door and peered out, cigarette in hand.

“Mrs Provoichkin,’ Lois thrust the hamper at the woman. ‘A few leftovers from the party. I thought you might enjoy them.’

‘For me?’ Mrs Provoichkin coughed.

‘Yes.’

‘Oh that’s nice,’ she wheezed.

‘This is Douglas. He helped me.’

‘Douglas,’ Mrs Provoichkin eyed the young man. ‘Nice,’ she directed the remark to Lois.

‘Anyway, have a nice evening.’

‘I will,’ the old lady parked her cigarette in the corner of her mouth, winked and shut the door.

‘She doesn’t have much,’ Lois said.

‘No.’

‘She’s nice really. I keep an eye on her.’

‘Yes.’

‘That was a nice gesture.’ Douglas jiggled his car keys.’

‘Hmm.’

‘Well I better get back. Let me know about Xmas night. Oysters, champagne and well just a beach party sort of thing.’

‘Right.’ Lois remembered the beach parties of her youth. Tomato sandwiches with sand. Warm pop drink and sunburn.

‘Well, bye Lois.’

‘Bye Douglas. And thanks for the invitation. I had a wonderful time.’ They stood about as the mosquitoes found their nightly feed.

‘Dad likes you.’

‘That’s nice.’

‘Bye then.’

;Bye.’

He walked to his car and whistled Waltzing Matilda while on the drive home.

It’s the giving, not the getting. Lois Mackenzie was the ‘Meaning of Christmas’ as far as Douglas Craven jnr was concerned.

Lois looked at her blouse, skirt and jacket as she hung them up. ‘Not a spot.’ Things were looking up. She thought on the generous hamper. *What a nice gesture*. It’s the giving, not the getting. Douglas Craven jnr was the ‘Meaning of Christmas’ as far as Lois Mary Mackenzie was concerned.

✦ CHAPTER 21

Newspapers can put a spin on anything. They also know which side their bread is buttered. Editors can – and do - make a headline from the smallest of remarks or throw away lines. The *Sydney Bugle* screamed at the morning commuters.

PROFIT OR PROPHET

There was no confusion as to which they referred.

'So, what did you eat?' Alice asked Lois. 'I bet it was exquisite and cost heaps.' Alice listened to the menu when Norm came through the door.

'Seen this,' he showed the women the headline.

'Oh.'

'OH!'

'They're clever. I'll give 'em that.'

'Actually,' Lois began.

'What? You don't mean to say...'

'I might have.' Lois cringed.

'Well, I know who will win this,' Norm said and pointed to the ceiling.

Earl came in and spied the headline. There's police downstairs. The sandwich man. Out cold by the end of the world man – or it might be the other way around. Either way a fracas. Merritt came in with his jacket off and his shirt ripped.

'Only just made it.'

'Sit down,' Alice gave him her chair.

'What's happened to everyone?' Lois bit her nail.

'A hot topic,' Norm said, then added, 'we need to fix it quick.'

They all looked at Lois.

'Me?'

✹

Ol' man Shotley made a bee line to the office of CWA, fought his way through the throng of Bible study, End of the world and Repent now signs and took the stairs two at a time to arrive at Alice's desk hot, bothered and quite out of sorts.

'Please Mr Shotley, sit down. You look quite unwell.' Alice gave the man a glass of water and scooted into the workroom to announce Shotley was in her reception area and didn't look well.

They gathered around the poor man and fanned, offered water, cup of tea or an Aspirin.

'I'm alright. A woman hit me with a placard, but I'm fine now.' They looked at the man who was their bread and butter. They too know which side was buttered.

'We had to call the police at 9 a.m. A man, a woman and a difference of opinion. She fair whacked him with her handbag. He walloped back with a hymn book.'

'And its alright now?' Alice asked.

'Well, the police said they'd do something, but it's...it's...' Shotley didn't have the words to describe the contagion that made the reformation look like a picnic.

'What I want to know is what are we going to do?' Eugene Shotley looked at the faces in front of him.

'Well, we were just discussing it,' Norm offered.

'Yes, we were just talking about it,' Merritt repeated.

'And,' Shotley mopped his brow and spied the paper on Alice's desk. 'Things are hotting up.'

Merritt looked at the paper. 'You mean they predict the hottest Christmas on record?' If there was another word for dumbfounded, no-one had found it. They looked at Merritt like he'd announced he'd found the cure for warts while eating boiled eggs.

'What I want to know...'

'Well Sir. Mr Shotley,' Lois stepped forward. 'I think we should go with something simple. Something people can repeat. A motto of sorts.'

'Motto,' Merritt said and nodded.

'I think it should be...' They all waited.

'It should be, *It's the giving, not the getting.'*

'It's the giving not the getting,' Shotley repeated and closed his eyes to repeat it silently, only his lips moving.

They watched his deliberation.

'We could get it out by tomorrow. I have the printers on stand-by,' Alice added.

'I could have a Fridge-o-matic with a big bow. Then maybe a...' Norm considered the juxtaposition of the composition.

'A set of Ladies handkerchiefs,' Lois said.

'And...' Merritt began. They waited in anticipation of a bright idea.

'And maybe a home-made ash tray. We made them in school for our fathers.

It didn't happen often, but when Merritt's brain functioned it often came up trumps.

'I like it.' Shotley wiped his brow. 'Get on it. Whatever it costs.' Alice nodded and picked up the phone.

The team sprang into action, ringing for newspaper space, bus banners and billboards. By the next day Sydney would be awash with goodwill to all men (and women) and contemplating the Meaning of Christmas.

*

Twenty four hours can be a long time to hold your breath. The team at CWA reconvened on the dot of nine a.m. and plonked the various papers on Alice's desk. The Bugle, the Standard, the Harbour News all carried the message. The Editors had put their spin on it, naturally, but the gist was clear. It was the giving, not the getting. That Shotley was paying through the nose for front page space and that the Fridge-o-matic was the bone of contention was neither here nor there. Good copy sells.

Bishop O'Leary read the paper and pondered on the turn of events. One minute it was the usurping of the church and its time honoured traditions and now it was all about the giving, not the getting. He ate his cold comport of pears and wondered where he went wrong. Of course a man of his stature could shift the blame without too much effort. It was 'that young woman' he thought. It was the crassness of Christmas and the profit margin that fuelled this latest craze. He chewed on his pears and ruminated on his sermon to come.

With six days to Christmas the Bishop had just one more chance to redeem the souls of his diocese. The sermon should reflect, re-evaluate and revere. He wrote a few notes on his napkin.

Archbishop Bothom looked at the papers and decided he would not hold back when it came to the commercialism of Christmas. Anglicans were apt to be a bit weak willed when it came to principles. Even his housekeeper, Mrs Brewster let slip that she could do with a new refrigerator should they be handing them out like lollies to all and sundry.

Sunday would be a cracker whatever flavour you happened to be.

As the headlines hotted up the debate, there was a ready-made theme for the Catholics, the Anglicans and any number of Christian flavours to make their stand. What the general public though didn't quite equate to the religious view. The Sydney Standard had an over subscription for the Fridge-o-matic raffle. The Sydney Bugle were talking a vox-pol from its dedicated readers and the Harbour News was getting into the spirit of things by posing a rather delicate question. A question that parishioners at St Cuthbert's would debate with vigour.

Does Bishop O'Leary know the meaning of Christmas?

Of course anyone with their ear to the ground knew the inference.

Mrs Cooper looked at her prize possession. It held large plates of food. It's freezer worked a treat. It had room on the door for four bottles of milk and a cheese compartment. The Fridge-o-matic stood proud in the bishopric.

Jeremy Aspinall looked at the paper on the kitchen table, then at Mrs Cooper. It was an emphatic 'no.'

Jeremy didn't want the Fridge-o-matic to disappear any time soon either. He was just getting accustomed to having a fridge at the seminary. The other fellows thought it a stroke of good luck and it was bursting with things mothers' and fathers' had posted to their sons for Christmas.

'What's all this then,' Bishop O'Leary pointed to the question on the front page of the Harbour News. 'Do I know the meaning of Christmas. Of course I know the meaning of Christmas. What tosh.'

'Your Grace,' Jeremy cleared his throat. Obviously the Bishop didn't have his ear too close to the ground. He missed the nuance completely.

'Well?'

‘Well, it’s sort of...well it is a reference you see.’

‘A reference. To what?’ For a man with an inflated ego it was hard for Jeremy to pop the balloon. ‘To what? Spit it out?’

‘Well Your Grace. You have been giving an opportunity here.’ Father Aspinall thanked the Lord for a bit of inspiration. He would notch up a couple of extra prayers when the day was over.

‘Opportunity. Someone wants to give me something?’ Niall O’Leary expected nothing less. People were apt to give him things, just for showing up.

‘Well, the headline. The question is in reference to the appliance you received. They want to know if you ...’ Jeremy swallowed. ‘They want to know if you can lead by example.’

‘What are you blathering on about?’

‘They are referring to the new slogan. It’s the giving, not the getting.’

‘And?’

‘Well, you have, that is to say the church has a golden opportunity handed to it on a plate so to speak. P.R.’

‘P.R? What the devil is P.R?’

‘Public relations Your Grace. It’s the thing these days.’

‘And I have been given it?’

‘Well the prospects of coming out of this smelling like roses.’

Father Aspinall sighed. ‘It’s the giving, not the getting. They want to know if you will give your Fridge-o-matic away. To a needy cause. For a raffle for the poor, that sort of thing.’

‘Give it away. I just got it.’ Niall briefly thought of his red currant fool.

‘Yes, but...well that’s what they are asking.’

Somewhere in the kitchen a pan clattered to the floor and although Mrs Cooper a devout stalwart of the Catholic faith, a few less than correct Hail Mary's could be heard.

'And this P.R chap. He wants it does he?'

'No. Your gesture of magnanimity will be great public relations. P.R.' Jeremy felt sure there was a God up there watching him.

'I think the Catholic church can dispense with jargon like P.R. We have been doing this for a long time. We are not an advertising agency. We are not in the business of touting for customers.'

One could quite possibly point out the Catholics and quite a few other denominations often bypassed the soft touch and went straight to armadas and thumb screws, but no-one wants to rake up the past.

'Right,' Jeremy scooped up the papers and headed for the kitchen. Mrs Cooper sat him down and put the kettle on.

'Mince pie, Father?'

'Don't mind if I do.'

*

Mrs Cooper shopped at Lennard and Sons for the choice cuts of meat. She had ordered a ham, but now with the Fridge-o-matic a permanent fixture she went to revise the order to a BIG ham.

Mrs Mildred Brewster also shopped at Lennard and Sons. Although it might be a coincidence only an author could conjure, Mrs Cooper and Mrs Brewster met in the doorway and after a small polite, 'after you,' they stepped onto the sawdust floor and put their baskets on the stainless steel shelf made for such.

'Mrs Cooper.'

'Mrs Brewster.'

The women eye one another.

'Hot isn't it.'

'Yes, hot.' They smiled politely.

'Ladies?' Bruce Lennard put his pencil behind his ear.

It was a delicate manoeuvrer to acquiesce so that one might hear the other's shopping list and know whose Christmas would be superior, whose inferior.

'After you,' Mrs Cooper said.

'No, I insist.' Mrs Brewster answered.

'And what can I do for two young ladies,' Mr Lennard winked and rolled up his sleeve.

'Well I want a bigger ham Mr Lennard. The biggest you have.'

'Right. One ham for the pretty lady on the left.' Mrs Cooper blushed.

'And some of that pork mince.' She turned to Erma, 'the Bishop likes my pork pies with aspic. An old recipe. I'm known for my pork pies.'

'Anything else for the woman who knows her pork from her onions.' Mr Lennard laid it on thick. He knew the value of customer service.

'Well we have the turkey being delivered?'

'Yes.'

'Well, I wonder if you could just throw in some extra chicken giblets. I'm making some potted meat.'

'And?'

'That's all. On the account if you please Mr Lennard.'

'Right you are Mrs Cooper.'

'Now, this lovely young thing here, Mrs Brewster.' Mildred blushed.

There was a smaller ham, a few sausages and a little leg of lamb. 'The Archbishop doesn't do fancy at this time of year.' Mrs Brewster pursed her lips. 'A traditionalist you might say.'

'And?'

'Nothing else. On the account please Mr Lennard.'

‘Right you are Mrs Brewster.’ Mr Lennard winked.

The woman made for the door.

‘And Merry Christmas to the both of you,’ Mr Lennard shouted to the woman as they exited.

‘He’s quite nice isn’t he,’ Erma said.

‘Very charming. Young lady,’ Mildred laughed.

‘As if we are young,’ Erma giggled.

‘And winking too.’

The women looked at one another.

‘Tea?’

‘Why not.’

There is a saying, don’t telegram, don’t telephone, tell a woman.

And that is how Jeremy Aspinall discovered; far from his prayers being answered, he found himself in possession of a dynamite piece of gossip that might blast his Christmas to smithereens.

*

No matter what religion you are, who you worship and where you live, there will be a moment in your life when your faith will be sorely tested. Father Aspinall, a decent short of bloke who wanted a life full of devotion, love for his fellow man (and woman), and an unwavering faith, now came to his Rubicon.

He sat at Mrs Coopers kitchen table and put his head in his hands and looked at the crumbs on his plate.

‘Another?’ Erma Cooper asked.

‘Well, just the one Mrs Cooper. I should watch my weight. The children at St Cuthbert’s...’ he trailed off.

‘Children?’

‘Well I heard them, the other day. They called me Chubby chops.’

‘Chubby chops.’ Erma smirked. ‘Is that all you’ve got to worry about?’

‘Actually, no.’ Jeremy looked at the font of gossip and sighed, one of those sort of sighs that feel like you’ve been summoned to the headmaster’s office and your punishment is a fair cop. His principles pricked him like a horse hair shirt.

‘Ah,’ Erma filled his tea cup and pushed the sugar his way.

‘What should I do Mrs Cooper?’

‘Call me Erma.’

‘Erma,’ he said. ‘He’ll probably...’ well the thought of what the Bishop might do with the information didn’t bear thinking about. Throwing bath plugs out the window, ripping up letters were small fry. He might start smiting willy-nilly. He might want Jeremy to march right over to...well it didn’t look good.

‘I’d say make a clean breast of it. Put it all on the table. What’s the worst he can do?’

‘That’s just it. I don’t know, I cannot imagine the worst he could do. I had hoped to broach the subject of my appointment to a parish after Christmas. ‘I had fancied Coogee.’ Father Aspinall might blanch at chubby chops, but wait ‘till he finds out the Aboriginal world Coogee translates to ‘big stink’. Chubby chops, a mere flippancy in comparison.

‘But now...’ Father Aspinall fiddled with his moustache, and closed his eyes to the growing crisis.

‘I’ll make his favourite little apple turnovers. He likes them. A nice pot of tea and you take it in. He’s just one man after all, and well...’ Erma knew a thing or two about men, those contrary creatures who can write poetry to make you weep and design a gun to kill you, all before lunch.

‘Right, thanks.’ Jeremy looked at the clock. He had an hour up his sleeve. Just time enough to nip across to St

Cuthbert's school for boys and see how the nativity play was progressing. Wendover, Endwell and Wythes pulled the short straw and were having some issues being the women of Bethlehem.

*

The delicious smell of apple turnovers wafted over the Bishopric. O'Leary whet his appetite on the aroma and looked at the clock. A man of regular habits he always had his morning tea at ten o'clock.

As the mantle clock struck the hour, Father Jeremy Aspinall knocked and walked in with a tray.

'Ah.' Niall breathed deeply through his nostrils.

'Your Grace,' Jeremy set the tray down, moved the crossword from the paper to one side and hovered.

'Yes?'

'Apropos our conversation the other day, I have some...well a bit of a development.'

'What conversation?' Niall was particularly good at filtering out extraneous information. Anything that didn't directly involve him or his stomach was filed as extraneous.

Jeremy offered a silent prayer, checked the door to the study was still open for a hasty exit and began.

'It has come to my attention that the Archbishop of St Andrew's,' Jeremy checked the door again, 'the Anglican,' he added for clarification, 'will be delivering his Sunday sermon on the avarice of the ego.' He checked the door one more time. 'And the object he has in mind for example is...' the door was still open, 'you.'

It took a minute. More like fifty five seconds and Bishop Niall O'Leary, keeper of Catholic souls at St Cuthbert's in the diocese of Waverly put down his apple turnover and drew in a breath that stirred the lace curtains.

‘Avarice of the ego. Avarice of the EGO. AVARICE OF THE EGO.’

‘Yes, Your Grace.’ Jeremy took a step to safety.

‘Me!’

‘Yes Your Grace.’

‘Anglican!’

‘Yes Your Grace.’

Niall went red. He then turned a shade of red that a Cardinal hat would have a hard time copying.

‘The gall. The nerve.’

‘Yes, Your Grace.’ Jeremy took another step closer to the door. ‘Oh, is that the telephone, I’ll get it.’ He shot out the door like a greyhound out of the traps and took the stairs two at a time to the kitchen.

‘Thundering blazes. By all that is HOLY! SAINTS PRESERVE US!!’ If he wasn’t a religious man there might have been a few more choice words. As it was he ended with, ‘HOLY MARY MOTHER OF GOD,’ and a door slammed to wake the dead.

‘Not too bad then?’ Erma pushed an apple turnover to the trembling Father and gave him a strong cup of tea.

‘ASPINALL,’ Niall bellowed down the stairs.

‘You better go,’ Erma gave him a napkin to wipe his fingers. ‘Good luck.’

‘Your Grace,’ Jeremy, fortified with two apple turnovers and a strong cup of tea tried to remain calm and collected.

‘It’s that young woman’s doing. It’s all her doing.’

‘I think Archbishop Bothom thought of it himself Your Grace.’

‘Smiting not good enough. Should have...’ the Bishop trailed off.

‘But we can save the situation.’

The once dimmed light shone on Niall’s face.

‘Save. Situation.’ His telegraphic speech happened in moments of crisis.

‘Yes. You could, well you could just give it away.’

‘What?’

‘The Fridge-o-matic.’

‘*My* Fridge-o-matic?’ The Bishop looked like he was imperviously waterproof to a change of heart. His mouth fell open and he forgot to shut it.

‘Yes Your Grace. A gesture. A grand gesture to show it’s in the giving, not the getting.’

‘Away?’

‘Yes, Your Grace.’

‘You mean, give it away?’

‘Yes, Your Grace. It seems to have become a poisoned chalice.’

‘Chalice.’

‘Yes, Your Grace.’

‘Hot potato,’ Jeremy added thinking of the school yard.

‘How?’

‘Well...’ and Father Aspinall outlined a plan as the Bishop climbed down from his high horse to prevent loss of balance.

And somewhere in the Bishopric a pot was launched through the kitchen window and broke a greenhouse pane.

✦ CHAPTER 22

The power of propaganda can never be underestimated. One minute you love your neighbour and the next you hope his dahlias wither and die, then the sun comes up, the papers are full of giving and not getting and you are once again swapping compost advice over the garden fence.

So it was with the combatants in residence on the steps of the offices of CWA. Although the end of the world was nigh, and you should repent your sins, there was tinsel all round, mince pies and good cheer. One bloke had so much Christmas cheer he'd passed out.

'Hot isn't it,' the bandaged sandwich man said to Norm as he picked his way across the footpath to the steps and sat down.

'Yes, scorcher they say.'

'Here, have a drink,' the bible lady offered a drink to the seated figure.

'Thank you. Much obliged.'

Norm shook his head and walked inside.

Lois, Merritt, Earl and Alice all saw the difference from the previous days and were gossiping about the change when Norm arrived.

'Sorry I'm late. Dress rehearsal at school. I had to drop him off.'

'Has he got his star part back?' Alice asked.

'No, but we are going to a higher authority. The Father will be present today. I sent the boy in with a note.'

'Finger's crossed then,' Lois said.

‘Want to come?’ Norm looked at the team. ‘The more support the better. It’s the day after tomorrow. Six o’clock.’

There was a chorus of acceptance, then everyone went about the business of escalating the propaganda to a level of goodwill that a Hallmark card might have a hard time beating.

It was so darn infectious. Never had humanity been so nice to one another. War? Just a slight disagreement, nothing major. Murder? An accident. Pillage and plunder? An offer to mow the lawn and bake a cake would fix any ill feeling.

However good the Halcyon days might be, nothing lasts forever.

‘Only five days to Christmas,’ Merritt counted off the days on the office Wack-*O* calendar. They all knew the portent of the pronouncement. Five more days and the campaign would end. Five days to bask in the glory. Five days to cement the nomination for the Golden Finger Award for Advertising Excellence. That the award ceremony was on the morrow, didn’t figure in Merritt’s arithmetic.

Another day down and Norm came in with good news.

‘The Father looked over the blatant discrimination and decided to go with my boy. I don’t know, but the rumour, my wife said, was that Wilson Pickering has the mumps. Anyway, my son, Anatol Brucholtz, after his grandfather, is going to be Joseph. The wife is pretty pleased.’

‘Good news.’ Lois gave a pencil to Merritt to sharpen.

‘So it’s on tomorrow. At six. Should be early as the hall is small. Seating at a premium.’

‘Where Norm,’ Earl asked.

‘Oh, I forgot. At St Cuthbert’s school for boys. Napier road. On the 65 bus route.’

‘St Cuthbert’s?’ Lois sat back and frowned.

‘Yes, St Cuthbert’s.’

‘Catholic?’

'Yes.'

'Um...' Earl saw which way the conversation was heading. 'You know Norm, St Cuthbert's is...' he hoiked his head in Lois's direction.

'Hmm?'

'You know. Smiteth. Smitten. Smiting.'

It hadn't occurred to Norm. A family, Christmas, presents, car payments, a wife, all these things took up a sizable proportion of his brain.'

'You mean to tell me all this time...? I knew the name was familiar. Father Aspinall.'

'It seems so.' Earl shook his head and laughed. 'You never put two and two?'

'Nup.'

'You never thought...?'

'Nope.'

'What?' Merritt couldn't quite catch on.

'For those in the back,' Earl said. Merritt looked over his shoulder. 'For those in the back. St Cuthbert's is the church of one Bishop O'Leary of smiteth fame. Norm's son, Anatol is a paid up member of St Cuthbert's school for boys. One and the same.'

'Oh.' Merritt said. 'I get it.'

'Should we go?'

'Go where,' Alice came into the room.

Earl went over the logistics one more time.

'Oh.'

The room ticked, the heat intensified as the dilemma was meditated.

'Well, I think we should all go. A united front. A show that goodwill and the Christmas spirit is alive and well at CWA. Half the people there won't know us from Adam anyway. The other half will be watching their children.'

'Miss Lomax, Alice,' he smiled as he corrected himself, 'is right you know.' Norm parked his pencil behind his ear and went to his drawing board.

'United front,' Merritt said.

'All for one,' Earl lit a cigarette.

'You don't think the Bishop will be there do you?' Lois asked. That put a candle snuff on the light that was the power of positive thinking.

*

The social life of the team was like an advent calendar. Every day there was something new.

The Award night for Advertising excellence was billed as exciting, spectacular, and a number of other superlatives befitting the advertising industry. If they could have shoe horned, 'Get yours now' and 'for a limited time only' it would have been on the invitations.

Mr Shotley greeted Catchpole and Wood, then stood.

'Ladies,' he said and fiddled with his tie. The thing looked like it was about to garrotte him.

'Look,' Merritt indicated a table to the left. There sat Groad, Oswald and Bull Agency. The contenders were sitting around smoking cigars like they had it in the bag. One of their number pointed his fat stogie at Lois and the whole of his party laughed. Lois fumbled with her napkin and dropped it.

'Here, let me,' Merritt dived under the table and as the opposition watched Lois blushed and let out a small huff.

'I don't like the way they are acting,' Earl said. 'Too cocky, too sure.'

'Suspicious?' Norm asked.

'Decidedly.'

Ol' man Shotley pulled out a cigar and popped it in his mouth, then nodded to the enemy.

'Two can play at this game,' he said.

Mr Wood and Mr Catchpole sat down and stared ahead at the dais. There was a table with the coveted trophy under a cloth. There was a easel covered with a cloth, and a rostrum with a small light.

'Uncle,' Merritt smiled at William Catchpole.

'Merritt,' Catchpole nodded. It was all rather uncomfortable, having to fraternise with the hoi-polloi. Mr Wood wriggled in his chair and called the waiter over for a drink. The waiter, being an egalitarian sort of fellow started with the ladies.

'Better not,' Lois said, 'just in case.' She stole a glance at the dais.

'Last time we had crab,' Earl said.

'You told us that,' Norm fiddled with his cutlery.

'Psst, over there,' Alice whispered to Lois. They turned to look at Smith and Sons taking their seats. They looked like carbon copies, all six of them. As the agencies filtered in and took their places at the tables, it was obvious one thing was missing.

'Alice, look,' Lois twizzled her eyes around the room.'

'What.'

'No women. We are the only two in a whole room of men.'

'Don't worry luv,' Shotley patted Alice's hand. You're the best looking people here. He winked.

'And the brains,' Earl said out of the corner of his mouth.

With due ceremony the chairman of the Advertising Oversight Board stepped up to the mark and went over the year, the excellence of the Advertising Oversight Board, the sterling work of the Advertising Oversight Board and the diligence of the Advertising Oversight Board. Anyone would think that Sir Walter Arbroath *was* the Advertising Oversight Board.

'At least it's not dealing in people's dreams,' Norm whispered to Earl and Lois. He spoke too soon. And Sir Arbroath launched into a speech not dissimilar to Mr Wood's.

Nerves can make you jittery. Lois tittered. Norm followed suit. Then it turned into a chuckle. Earl pursed his lip so a giggle didn't escape. The three of them tried not to look at one another but every time they thought they had it under control a chortle escaped. Lois put her napkin up to her mouth and took a deep breath, then another.

Mr Wood couldn't understand what was funny. He thought the speech rather stirring. Catchpole wondered if he'd missed a joke somewhere along the line. Earl stifled a laugh and grabbed a bread roll stuffing it in his mouth.

'What's the joke?' Merritt asked under his breath as Sir Arbroath lumbered on.

This only inflamed the situation. Norm wiped the tears from his eyes and squished them tight. Alice, on the other side of the table watch as her team had a hard time controlling themselves.

'And so,' Sir Arbroath ended, 'we gather to celebrate our profession.'

A polite clap followed and the waiters threw themselves into serving a three course meal to about one hundred people in record time.

'It's crab,' Earl said as he got himself under control.

The meal over, the plates whisked away and drinks now on the pay as you go, people chatted and smoked.

'Nice,' Earl said.

'There was a bell and a hush fell over the audience.

Alice crossed her fingers. Lois held her breath. Mr Shotley winked at her and nodded.

Sir Arbroath once again took to the stage and uncovered the coveted statue.

'He cleared his throat and looked over the audience.

'Gentlemen.' He then spied Alice and Lois. 'And Ladies.' Men from all directions turned to look at the women. Alice and Lois felt like they were in a display case.

Sir Arbroath like the sound of his own voice. He prattled on about the Golden Finger held aloft to reach for the stars. He reiterated people's dreams. He told a story so convoluted no-one knew when it finished. He then looked over his captives.

'Advertising comes with its share of controversy. This year we have seen our fair share.' Those at the CWA table shrank from the glare of notoriety. 'But,' Sir Arbroath continued with finger held high, 'every headline is an opportunity.' He looked over the crowd, 'for improvement.'

'And now.'

Everyone sat a little bit straighter.

'I feel we have seen the best this year. All the nominations were innovative, imaginative and original. The crowed hung off Sir Arbroath's every word.

'But one campaign,' he unveiled the easel and a clap went around the room.

'Twins,' Sir Arbroath said. Lyle Soap, Stanley Smith of Smith and Son's for advertising excellence.

It was a hard pill to swallow.

So, we didn't win,' Merritt asked.

'No.' Earl replied.

Wood and Catchpole looked at Shotley. Shotley looked at Lois. Alice frowned and dabbed at her eyes.

'Well,' Lois said to the team, 'I guess that's what comes of being smitten.'

'Smiteth,' Earl added.

'Smote,' Catchpole said, then added, 'verb, past tense.'

Groad, Oswald & Bull didn't hang around. They stood up as one and walked out.

'Well, I guess that's it then,' Merritt folded his napkin.

The team looked to Mr Wood. He looked at Shotley with a withering stare that could curdle milk.

'You don't suppose it had anything to do with that idiot I threw out do you?'

'Me?' Merritt asked.

'Mr Trent,' Alice said.

'Ah,' Catchpole caught on.

And there it was, flapping on the table gasping for air. Shotley shrugged. 'He was still a bloody idiot.'

'Idiot,' Catchpole said and no-one was just quite sure if he meant Mr Trent or Shotley.

✦ CHAPTER 23

No matter the personal cloud that hung over the attendance of the nativity play, the mood was decidedly upbeat. People chatted, hung about in groups, tried to corral wayward children and the mixture of religion and Christmas baubles gave the whole thing a festive air. That Father Christmas was rumoured to visit after the play married the two traditions perfectly. Children on the whole couldn't give doodly-squat about who said what in folk lore or A.D and B.C. As far as they were concerned baby Jesus was alright, but Father Christmas was on another level.

Norm spied Alice, Lois and Merritt and waved them over to meet his wife and children.

'Earl is just having a last gasper,' Merritt said.

'Ticket?' Mrs Cooper thrust a book of raffle tickets at the group. 'My grandson is a shepherd,' she said with a proud air.

'What's it for?'

'The School.' Mrs Cooper said, adding, 'Sixpence for one.'

Everyone rummaged for money.

Earl joined the group and they sat down. The small electric fans had a hard time cooling the hall as the multitude sweated on metal seats, standing room only.

'Hot isn't it,' Mrs Brucholtz said as she fanned her young daughter with the programme.

In due course the lights dimmed, a drum was heard and the herald came on stage to set the scene. As theatrical experiences go, this one was a corker.

A shepherd, who didn't get the opening cue was facing the wrong way and his tea towel head-dress displayed St Leonards Inn, picked out in blue on a white background. There was a little titter from the audience. The wayward shepherd was prodded in the right direction and the herald thus spake.

'Oh shining light of Christmas.' It didn't take a heckler long to add,

'That'd be a Fridge-o-matic then.' This received another small titter.

At this point the other shepherd, Donald Cooper, was to point to the star, but in his enthusiasm poked the light with his crook and shorted the stage.

'Open the fridge door,' the heckler shouted. A quick slap was the rejoinder.

'Ow give over, just a bit o' fun.'

A long intermission ensued as an electrician was called for from the audience. Earl went for a smoko, as did quite a few fathers. Once illumination was restored Father Aspinall came to the stage to assure everyone the play would proceed. He sent Donald Cooper out to round up the smokers and they were herded back inside.

Mary- Denis Wendover, dressed in his mother nylon petticoat was so full of static he collected most of the straw from the manger, created a spark and dropped the baby Jesus doll on its head and then tripped over his dressing gown cord and suffocated the poor infant. But Anatol rose above the chaos and delivered his lines perfectly, his mother mouthing the words as he spoke. She was about to clap, and it was only Norm's hand that stopped her.

The cast assembled for a round of applause which went on for some time.

'And that,' Father Aspinall said as he took centre stage, 'is the meaning of Christmas.'

The jibe wasn't lost on the audience, or the staff of CWA. There was another cheer and Father Aspinall called for quiet.

'And now,' he began, 'I have the pleasure of presenting Bishop O'Leary for a few words. A small, but audible groan went through the crowd. Father Christmas's entrance would be delayed yet again. The Bishop, on hearing the cheer obviously thought it was for him. He walked out, brushed some crumbs from the front of his gown and waved theatrically to his captive audience.

He started by announcing his wish to see everyone at Mass on the Sunday. The audience shrank from his direct gaze.

'Is he Father Christmas,' a small deluded child asked her mother. A small chuckle percolated across the hall.

'I have...' Bishop O'Leary began. The chuckle turned to a titter, then a guffaw, then a laugh and it wasn't long before the contagion caught.

The Bishop, caught in the headlights, looked to Father Aspinall for rescue. He couldn't recollect he'd even got to his one joke he'd rehearsed for the event.

Father Aspinall bounded on stage and motioned to Roger Endwell to wheel out the tombola barrel. Endwell took his duty seriously and pushed the barrel with the lottery tickets to centre stage and bowed. The crowd, now in a festive mood, clapped. Endwell was about to do a little jig when Father Aspinall gave him a look that could not be mistaken for goodwill to all men, (and boys).

'Bishop?' Jeremy pointed to the barrel, but Roger Endwell thought he should give the thing one more spin. He cranked up the handle and set to work. If Mr Ford had seen the effort involved he might not have bothered with an electric starter motor for his cars. Endwell cranked like he was starting a sixteen cylinder combine harvester. The barrel, not accustomed to such velocity flew off its moorings and crashed into the front row. Mayhem ensued as children began to cry, women clutched their handbags and men pushed chairs out the way. And through it all one ticket fluttered to the Bishop and stuck to his lapel where he'd just recently picked off a bit of toffee. Divine intervention.

It took a good few minutes to restore some order, Endwell achieving legendary status amongst his peers.

Father Aspinall called for calm and then turned to the Bishop and noticed the one ticket that had escaped the catastrophe.

'Ah,' he plucked the winning ticket from the Bishop and called it.

'For the grand prize, generously donated by Bishop O'Leary. It's the giving, not the getting eh?' There was a chuckle from the back. 'Yellow 16.'

A scramble for tickets began. People craned their necks to spy the winner.

'Oh, it's me,' Lois held her ticket aloft. 'Yellow 16.'

'The young lady middle row.' Father Aspinall pointed. 'Now the proud possessor of a brand new Fridge-o-matic generously gifted by our Bishop. It's the giving, not the getting.'

'Oh.' Lois sat down.

All eyes were on her. Merritt said, 'lucky eh,' and pattered her on the back. Earl, Alice and Norm closed their eyes as the inevitable happened.

'You!,' Bishop O'Leary said and pointed. People turned their heads to each participant like a tennis match.

'Me?' Lois tried to shrink.

'It was fair,' Aspinall said holding the ticket in his hand. 'Completely above board.' He looked at the crowd who could go from amiable to rabid at the turn of a word. 'Generously donated by the Bishop,' he added, although no-one was listening anymore.

‘She’s that one that got smoteth.’ The audience looked to the Bishop. Father Aspinall looked to heaven. If ever he needed divine guidance it was now.

‘I seen her in the paper,’ a woman pointed.

‘He smote her,’ a fellow wagged an accusing finger at the Bishop.

‘Refreshments in the gym. Hot tea and SCONES!’ Jeremy shouted above the hullaballoo.

And then, as if God himself had ordained it, Father Christmas took the stage with a sack full of gifts. God Almighty may have the upper hand in some circumstances, but you can’t beat Father Christmas.

Jeremy hustled the Bishop from the stage, put him in a taxi and instructed the driver to make haste.

Mrs Cooper could be heard telling anyone who’d listen that her ham had Buckley’s chance of surviving without a Fridge-o-matic and no-one ever asks her how she felt about it.

And the hot potato moved to another hand.

There is a fine, somewhat wobbly line between generosity and a bribe.

Archbishop Bothom thought he knew the difference and pencilled a note in the margins of his sermon. He had been told of the ‘gift’ to restore the Bishops reputation and it had the hallmarks of a bribe to the public.

‘Theatrics,’ Bothom said as he sipped his tea at Sunday breakfast.

‘Anything else Your Grace,’ Mrs Brewster asked. She wanted to get away to dress for the Sunday service and get back in time to put her gravy on.

‘No thank you Mrs Brewster.’ Renwick Bothom was feeling in fine fettle. A sermon, a captive audience and the

St Andrew's acoustics that had some volume were the portent of a grand day. Mrs Brewster's leg of lamb just about topped it off.

The Anglicans, a practical lot who knew what's what and were vocal with the results listened with growing scepticism at the Archbishops final address before Christmas. They heard words like shame, perfidy, deceit, duplicity and the crowning *ego.* They had the idea that Bothom would be preaching about giving not getting, goodwill and all sweetness and light. What they got came from the fires of hell. One woman actually put her hands over her daughter's ears lest she hear something akin to a swear word. Bothom pointed his finger. He accused. He threw out sweetness and light and went for the jugular. It was too much. Anglicans, being practical sort of people rebuffed the affront.

'Sour grapes,' a voice said from the pews. A murmur ran around the stalls.

'Sour grapes,' someone repeated.

'As plain as the nose on me face.'

'It's that Fridge-o-matic. I bet it's that Fridge-o-matic.'

'Jealous he is.'

'So much for goodwill.'

And then, someone stood up and walked out. 'I've got a piece of meat on,' a woman in the front row announced and left.

'I've left the sprinkler on,' a man followed.

It had never happened. Not in living memory. Bothom lost the will to speak. He blustered. He harrumphed. He shut up.

The congregation, what was left, stared at him. He stared back.

'You alright,' a bloke called.

'He's had a turn,' a woman offered.

‘Sit him down, he’s not quite himself,’ a parishioner came to Bothom’s aid and led him from his pulpit to a pew.

‘Someone get a cup of tea.’

‘Cup of tea, he needs a stiff one.’ A fellow produced a flask, his wife narrowed her eyes and tisked, and held the bottle to the Archbishop’s lips. The brandy revived him.

‘Better?’

Renwick nodded.

‘You had a turn Your Grace.’

‘Yes, a turn,’ he grabbed the flask for another snifter.

Glenda looked at her husband and mouthed, *wait till we get home.* Bert said,

‘It’s the giving, not the getting,’ and blew a kiss at his wife.

‘Yes,’ Renwick blinked. ‘It’s the giving, not the getting. That’s the meaning of Christmas.’

The Lord moves in mysterious ways. Advertising does it with a simple catchphrase.

The parishioners at St Cuthbert’s were having none of it. They knew their onions and the ‘gift’ smacked of a hasty re-gifting to assuage rumour, innuendo and malicious gossip. Who wants to be called callous, grasping and pitiless at Christmas. The motive of the Bishop was as clear as the bells of St Cuthbert’s.

Niall had hoped to build on his reputation by alluding to charity, goodwill and generosity at Christmas. At Father Aspinall’s urging he inserted *it’s the giving not the getting.*

‘We weren’t born yesterday,’ a man whispered to his wife. There wasn’t a walkout, the Catholics were still great believers in the fires of hell, but the mood was sour, the eyes were narrowed in disbelief at, not the towering intellect, but the towering stupidity of the man who couldn’t read the room.

✦ CHAPTER 24

Jeremy Aspinall sat at the kitchen table and thought he'd rather like to be a fisherman. They go to sea for extended periods, never need to deal with Bishops, Fridge-o-matics or little boys. Their life must be one of hard toil and plenty of fresh air.

'Tart?' Mrs Cooper offered.

'Thank you Erma.'

They looked at the Fridge-o-matic whirring away in the corner oblivious to the drama.

'When?' Erma gave the door a wipe with a tea towel.

'Well, I did ask that we extend the departure, but the young woman was insistent she had to have it before Christmas.

'I know the feeling,' Erma opened the door and looked at all the food. The ham, a monster of a pig when it was walking around was wrapped in a cloth and took centre stage.

'So I suppose I will need to accede to her wishes. She won fair and square.'

'And she wants it?'

'Yes.'

'And it's the young lady who was smote?'

'Yes. A bit funny really.'

The fridge whirred in indifference.

'And...' Erma threw her eyes to the ceiling and the Bishop's office above the kitchen.

'Well, you can imagine he's none too happy. And after the sermon debacle it's not good.' They listened to pacing in the room above. 'He seems to think it's all my fault. I gave him erroneous information. I led him astray. I told him the congregation would...well you know.'

'He's not an easy man.'

'No.'

'Not by a long shot.' They looked at the Fridge-o-matic.

A cup of tea and scones later the logistics of Christmas once again came up in discussion in the kitchen.

'So what can I do?' Erma asked.

'Know anyone?' Jeremy was loath to offer the cast off back to the Bishopric. It was full of other people's food for the holiday.

Mrs Cooper considered the question. She pondered her acquaintances, her family, her friends, but they all had stockpiled for the holiday and you couldn't squeeze a cherry into their respective fridges.

'Well,' she began, 'I might know someone. He won't like it,' she pointed to the ceiling.

'He might not need to know,' Jeremy said.

'Oh, he'll know alright.' Erma tapped her nose.

'It's not...'

'That's right.'

'You don't mean...'

'I do.'

'Is there no other way?'

'Let me know when you think of someone.' Erma polished the chrome handle on the fridge and smirked.

Jeremy, a man who did have his ear to the ground thought on the problem. He needed something spectacular. Something memorable. Something the papers could capitalise on – with pictures.

Forget fishing, the man really should have been in advertising.

'I have a plan Mrs Cooper. Your aspic is in safe hands.'

The Christians were sent to the lions. The Israelites spent years wandering in the desert. Those trials seemed a walk in the park compared to the task Father Aspinall had been assigned.

Erma suggested the Father plant the seed of an idea. It was a delicate operation, but one that could quite possibly, with some cajoling have the Bishop in the good books once again. He just had to phrase it in such a way that it would be the Bishop's idea in the first place. He had three days to Christmas. The Fridge was leaving the premises on Christmas Eve.

*

The office of CWA was marking time until the holidays. Eight days to enjoy the season, relax, eat and do nothing. Of course, if you were a mother, wife, girlfriend, or any of the female species talking about doing nothing was as far as you got. Women took the brunt and then some.

'I'm getting it tomorrow,' Lois said in answer to Merritt's query on the Fridge-o-matic. 'I've arranged with a friend to pick it up. He has a truck.'

'Well, if you need a hand,' Merritt made a show of flexing his muscles, such as they were.

'Thanks, I think we'll be fine.'

'Are we going for drinks tonight? Last chance.' Merritt looked at his team mates.

'Sounds like a plan,' Earl said as he put away his rubber gloves.

'Just one. The wife wants me to do something.' Norm smiled.

'Lois?'

'I'm in,' she said.

'

'You know Lois, you haven't snapped, dropped, spilt, broken, smudged or dirtied anything for ages.' Earl lit a cigarette and smiled. 'Getting over your nerves eh?'

'I guess.'

'We're not so bad after all eh?'

Lois blushed.

'Lois, telephone call. Mr Craven.' Alice raised her eye brow and whistled. 'At my desk,' she followed Lois out. 'See if he has a brother,' Alice smirked.

Mr Craven Snr had a proposition to put to Lois. Mr Craven Snr knew the value of capitalising on a sure thing.

'Right, five o'clock. And thank you.' She hung up.

'Good news.'

'Oh yes, good news.'

'I can't go for a drink, I am otherwise engaged,' Lois said to the men.

'Your engaged, Congratulations. Who is the lucky man. Oh this is wonderful,' Merritt gushed.

'No Merritt, she means she has something else to do.'

'Oh.'

'All good I hope.'

'Oh yes. Very good. Excellent in fact.'

They watched the clock reach the stroke of five and headed for the door.

'Have one for me,' Lois said miming a drink.

'Sure will,' Merritt made for the stairs with Norm and Earl hot on his heels.

'Have a nice evening,' Alice said and winked.

'It's not like that.'

'Not yet,' Alice showed her wedding ring finger.
'I don't think so.'

The Craven car was waiting at the roadside as Lois walked past the protesters in a festive mood. Someone put tinsel around her neck and someone said 'Merry Christmas'.

Mr Craven Snr was sitting in the back of the car and smiled when the driver opened the door. 'Miss.'

The car, the drive, the luxury was a long way from Markos and his stunt driving, the train and sweaty hands, plus a hot walk home. Lois revelled in the opulence, that some people took for granted.

Mr Moon was on the pavement fanning himself and watched the car pull up. He squinted to see the occupants and opened his eyes wide when Lois exited and smiled.

'Miss Mackenzie, you make Christmas bonus?'

'No, nothing like that.' She turned as Mr Craven came to the pair. 'This is Mr Craven. You remember I bought the presents for him.'

'You like?' Mr Moon asked.

'Yes very much.'

'Nice ok.'

'Yes nice.' Mr Craven looked past Mr Moon at the interior of the shop.

'My shop.'

'I see that.'

'Well, Mr Craven has a little proposition Mr Moon.'

'Prop-sition?'

'It's like this Mr Moon. Shall we go inside.'

'I'd like to offer you a job.'

'I have job.'

'Well, this would be a little different Mr Moon. I was very taken with your wrapping skills. Marvellous, really marvellous.' Mr Craven fiddled with a lollypop on the counter.

'Old skill. I learn from my mother.'

'And I'd like you to teach my staff, my girls to wrap.'

'Teach?'

'Yes, for remuneration naturally.'

'Moonerashon?'

'Pay, he mean pay,' Lois said.

'Yes. I'd like you to show the girls how to do it. I want Craven department store to give, rather than get. I want Craven department store, the only store with credit card, car park and air conditioning on all floors to now have free gift wrapping in the oriental style.'

'Me?'

'Yes Mr Moon, you.'

'Ah.'

'I have the staff staying back as we speak. We are waiting.'

'I have shop.'

'I can stay here Mr Moon. I can take care of it while you go.' Lois nodded.

'Free wrapping all Christmas Eve. It's the giving not the getting.' Mr Moon looked at Mr Craven, then Lois.

'Go for it.' Lois smiled.

'Alright mate. I go for it.' Mr Moon bowed deeply to Lois. 'You are very honoured friend. Thank you.'

'Have fun,' Lois said as the two were ushered into the car. A window opened. 'Key under mat,' Mr Moon waved and they were gone.

'It's the giving not the getting,' she said to the empty shop.

✦ CHAPTER 25

Christmas Eve at the office was a slow day. The temperature was a constant hot and no-one wanted to start anything only to have it languish for the holidays. All the loose ends were tidied, the New year sales adverts were ready and waiting and all that really needed to be done was the handing out of the Christmas cheer, aka pay and bonuses.

Alice came in with four envelopes. She solemnly handed them over and wished everyone a happy Christmas.

'Mr Wood and Mr Catchpole send their festive wishes and gave us a kitty for a drink.'

'I'll go,' Merritt popped up.

The bottle shop, a hutch that opened to the knock and situated at the side of the pub served bottles – cold. Merritt spent the kitty and hurried back to work.

'Bloody hot eh?' The Repent Now fellow spied the brown paper bag.

'Yes, isn't it.' Merritt wanted to get inside before the drinks warmed to ambient temperature which was about boiling point.

'Thirsty work.'

'You bet,' Merritt made for the door.

'It's the giving not the getting,' the man licked his lips.

'There you go,' Merritt handed over a cold bottle. 'Got to go.'

'You're place is reserved in Heaven,' the man said and snapped the cap off the beer with a practiced flick.

'So what are you doing for Christmas Lois?' Alice asked.

'I've been invited to a lunch at a friends place. Big family do.'

'Not going home?'

'No, my parents are in Queensland. And you?'

Alice counted out her siblings, her cousins, her aunts and uncles and several sets of grandparents. 'It's a thing.'

'Sounds great.' Lois turned to Norm.

'Kids, brother, grandparents then tea at my sisters. She's got six. I promised the wife I'd do the washing up and...well all that sort of stuff.' Norm looked to Earl.

'Well, I thought I'd take my mum to a meal at the local. They do a cracking turkey for the price. Pudding and everything.'

'Sounds nice,' Merritt said.

'Merritt?' Earl asked.

'My parents are on a cruise. My sister is in London. Aunt Rene said I was welcome.'

The team contemplated their respective Christmas plans and finished the beer.

'Well, I guess...' Norm came over to the women. 'Merry Christmas Alice,' he gave her a kiss on the cheek. 'Merry Christmas Lois...Mac.' He gave her a peck.

Earl and Merritt followed the lead, and then shook hands with each other in turn. They looked at the clock.

'I guess we could call it a day.' Alice check the clock to her wrist watch.

'Just a minute,' Lois said. She went to her desk and retrieved four small gifts, expertly wrapped and handed them out. 'It's the giving, not the getting eh?'

The presents were examined and opened with care. Each had a small animal inside. 'I remembered all your birthdays and this is the animal from the Chinese calendar. Merritt you are the year of the pig. Earl the dragon. Norm the snake and Alice you are a rabbit. My friend Mr Moon helped me.'

'This is just perfect.' Alice held up her figurine. There were effusive thanks all round and they once again looked at the clock.

'That's it. I'm calling it a day,' Alice said.

The door was shut. The Fridge-o-matic campaign put to bed and they walked single file down the stairs to the hot afternoon sun.

'Merry Christmas,' the Bible lady said and handed out Christmas lollies.

'And to you,' the team chorused.

'Merry Christmas,' the sandwich man said, followed by the fellow who was in need of a bit of repenting himself. He hiccupped and held a brown paper bag aloft. 'Chrissmaaas,' he slurred. The dog barked as the staff sallied forth.

An early minute gave Lois time to get home, change and wait for Serg and the truck. The last person she expected to see walking up to the building was Serg.

He hailed her, 'Lois.'

'Serg?'

'We have a slight problem. I thought I should come around straight away.'

'Problem?'

'Markos can't make it. Can you help with the lift of the fridge?'

'I can try.'

'I can help,' Merritt came into the conversation.

'Really?'

'Sure.'

✦

Father Aspinall opened the back door of the Bishopric and let Lois, Serg and Merritt into the kitchen.

'Look, I know this is a big impost, but could you do us,' he looked at Mrs Cooper, 'a favour.'

How can you resist a man of the cloth.

'Sit down, have a drink first.' Mrs cooper set out some glasses and a jug of cold lemonade. 'Biscuit?' If Mrs Cooper's knowledge was distilled into one nugget it would be the way to a man's brain was through his stomach.

As the three ate their way through Christmas treats, sugared almonds and mince pies they listened to Father Aspinall outline the plan.

'Fait accompli,' he ended.

'Pardon,' Merritt asked.

'An irreversible fact,' Lois said. Serg looked at Lois and wondered how he scored a fabulously looking girl and with brains. *If she could cook*, he thought, she would be the next thing to heaven.

Father looked to the Fridge-o-matic. Mrs Cooper opened the door and there shone the guiding light illuminating the biggest leg of ham in Sydney and all manner of delights.

'The guiding light of Christmas,' Father said. 'I always thought that was rather clever you know. Yes, very clever.'

'Thank you Father.' Lois popped a sugared almond in her mouth and smiled.

It felt like theft.

Mrs Cooper wrapped her dishes, her potted meats, her beast and fowl in tea towels, bath towels and an old alter cloth (necessity is the mother of invention) and passed them along the line to the truck. Serg loaded the booty up as quickly as possible while Jeremy kept a look-out.

Once all was stowed, Lois, Merritt and Jeremy hopped in the back and Mrs Cooper and Serg in the front.

The trip was a short one.

A knock at the back door and a clandestine greeting and the procedure was repeated in reverse.

'Oh dear,' Mrs Brewster looked at the leg of ham. Mrs Cooper poked it, perhaps in the vain hope it would run away.

'Mildred?'

'Erma?'

Merritt stood by with a jelly. Lois held a roulades of duck liver pate and Serg hefted the leg onto his other arm.

'I don't think...' Mildred said

'What if we...?' Erma shuffled a few vol au vents.

'Um,' Jeremy looked at his watch. The Bishop would be back from bible study anytime soon.

'Well,' Serg shifted the weight once again.

'Hmmm?' Erma inquired.

'We have two fridges at home. I reckon we could fit it in. Mum could find room.'

Mrs Cooper looked at Mrs Brewster. Jeremy looked at the Archbishops laden Westinghouse.

'You could come and get it tomorrow.' Serg shifted the pig one more time. 'Put it on the table. Once it's cut, then it's bound to fit.'

'He's right you know,' Lois said.

'I could get it just before lunch, and bring it over.' He turned to Serg, 'where do you live?'

When the whipped cream had settled, the cheese was wrapped and the turkey stuffed, all that was left was a cherry pie the size of a hub cap and a punnet of strawberries.

'Take it,' Mrs Cooper, now back in her kitchen proffered the pie.

'I couldn't.

'Go on, it's the giving, not the getting.'
'Thank you.'
'Now take your fridge.' Erma wiped the handle one more time as Serg unplugged the beast.

'See you tomorrow. And thanks.' Father Aspinall waved them away as he saw the Bishop being driven up to the front door.

A quick prayer, and he gird his loins for the battle to come; or deft sleight of hand, either way, any help he could muster from God was very welcome.

'Ah, Bishop,' Jeremy greeted his superior. 'A drink?'
God was a handy ally, but alcohol was sure to get the job done.

'As he has generously offered the use of his Westinghouse, it seems your wonderful suggestion would work.' Jeremy gave the Bishop's drink a top up, the fourth, but who's counting.
'So what your suggesting Your Grace, and I must say it is splendid suggestion, is that we offer our Christmas bounty to be shared with Archbishop Bothom in a gesture of friendship and Christmas spirit.'
'Yeth.'
'And a picture, for the paper of the two of you in good spirits at the table would be, and here I think your idea absolute genius, Your Grace, would be a yardstick of exemplary example.' The superlatives tripped off the silver tongued Father.

Mrs Brewster went over the same ground as Father Aspinall, only with a slightly inferior Scotch Whisky.

☆

‘The key is under the mat,’ Lois pointed to the shop as they backed up.

‘Not home?’ Merritt asked.

‘No. It’s a long story, but I know he won’t be in.’

Once the door was opened, a box of oranges pushed out of the way, Serg and Merritt manhandled the Fridge-o-matic inside Mr Moon’s shop.

The old Philips refrigerator was thumping away, but once it was unplugged it gave a sigh of relief, rattled in its last death throws and died.

‘May she rest in peace,’ Merritt said. He then plugged in the new replacement and they began to transfer the goods.

‘He’ll be surprised.’

‘I guess so.’ Lois passed Merritt a Peking duck.

‘Shocked more like,’ Serg handed over some spring onions and a bowl of cooked rice.

‘You just need to write a card Lois,’ Serg said.

He found a pen and a bit of paper in his pocket.

‘Thank Mr Moon. Merry Christmas.’ They stuck it to the fridge door and it fell off.

‘I have a magnet,’ Serg fished in his pocket and pulled out a magnet salvaged from an electric motor.

‘Perfect.’

‘You know,’ Merritt looked at the magnet, ‘if you made them in funny shapes. Like stars, or even Wack-*O* cereal shapes and sold them, I reckon you’d be on a winner.’ They looked at the magnet and then at Merritt. It didn’t happen often, but when it did...

‘He’s right you know.’

Merritt might need to wait for a few years, but eventually there would be a patent with his name on it; Merritt Magnets.

The key was placed under the mat, and the co-conspirators sat in the cab and basked in the delight of the giving not the getting.

'Drink?' Merritt asked.

'Sounds good,' Serg said.

'I'm in.' Lois added.

It was only when then had refreshed with the first beer that someone remembered the ham.

'Holy smokes. The pig.' Serg shook his head. It had been a hot day. It had been a few hours.

'Got to go.' He looked at Lois and Merritt. Can you find your own way, I better get cracking.'

'Go.' Lois waved him away. He came back after getting to the door.

'What?'

'Merritt, wanna come tomorrow? I don't know how you're fixed, but there's always room.'

'Sure. Thanks.'

'Go Serg, go.' Lois waved him off.

'He's quite nice, isn't he,' Merritt said as he fiddled with a Chinese fan.

'Yes, quite nice,' Lois grinned. 'He's an electrician,' she said as if that explained just about everything.

'Oh.'

'Um,' Merritt began, 'where does he live?' Now, there was the conundrum. Lois didn't know. She had been driven to the house. She had sat in the back yard and drunk beer, eaten lamb, but as to the address...

'I don't know.'

They looked at one another. 'Anyway, you know where I live. His brother is picking me up. Just come to my place.'

'Right.'

'Early.'

'How early,' Merritt squished his face into something like a windfall peach.

'Before eight o'clock.'

'Before eight o'clock.' Merritt said.

The walk home to Flat 4 Lucknow Close felt like walking with a clear conscience, a perfect score for morality and quite a bit of goodwill to all men (and women) hovering overhead.

'Oh, hello Mrs Provoichkin. Merry Christmas to you.'

'And you dearie.' Mrs Provoichkin parked her cigarette on her lip.

'Lovely evening isn't it.'

'Yep, sure is.' Mrs Provoichkin hovered.

'Remember, early tomorrow.'

'Yep, I remember.' Mrs Provoichkin loitered. 'You expecting something?'

And Lois remembered the telegram. 'Yes, I am.'

'I got it.'

'Thanks. I'll come and get it.'

'It's heavy.'

'I expect it is.' Lois started for flat 3. She'd never been in Mrs Provoichkin's flat. She didn't even know the woman's first name. Now, she was going into the inner sanctum.

'Shall I just pop in and get it?'

Mrs Provoichkin coughed and made her way to her front door.

'Come in dearie.'

Amid the ashtrays, the old photographs and newspapers was a box.

‘Yes, this is it.’ Lois lifted the box and put it on her hip. ‘Thanks for that Mrs Provoichkin.’ She looked around the little flat, identical to hers.

‘That’s Henry,’ Mrs Provoichkin pointed to a framed photograph of a man in uniform. ‘Handsome eh?’ she coughed.

‘Yes, very,’ Lois said.

‘And that’s me mum. In Poland.’ Mrs Provoichkin pointed with a cigarette.

‘’Very pretty isn’t she.’

‘Some say.’ Mrs Provoichkin nodded. ‘We lived in the mountains. Long time ago now.’

‘Really.’

‘War,’ she coughed the word. A word that could explain a lifetime of woe. ‘Came here, and well...’ They looked at the little flat.

‘Poland,’ Lois said and looked at the few mementos scattered throughout the flat.

‘Polska.’ A word that encompassed her history.

Lois smiled at the old woman.

‘Well, see you tomorrow, early.’

‘Yep. Early.’

The women stood on the concrete which threw up the heat of the day and watched a car pull up on the other side of the road.

‘Hi.’

‘Oh, its Douglas Craven Jnr,’ Lois said to Mrs Provoichkin.

‘Nice,’

‘Yes, isn’t he.’ Lois waved as Douglas walked over.

‘Douglas this is Mrs Provoichkin. Mrs Provoichkin, Douglas,’ Lois said.

‘Nice to meet you,’ Douglas smiled his winning smile.

‘Nice,’ Mrs Provoichkin tried to extract her trachea by coughing.

‘Lois, I wondered if you were free this evening.’ Douglas looked at the old woman who was welded to the spot. He smiled.

‘Well, I guess I am,’ Lois said and looked at Mrs Provoichkin. In polite circles the old woman might have made her excuses and shuffled off. She stuck fast, oblivious to polite society.

Lois shifted the box to her other hip and snagged her dress in the process.

‘Oh damn.’

‘Here, let me help,’ Douglas took the box and the pulled thread came with it. The skirt rucked and pulled a hole.

‘Here, just let me untangle it,’ Douglas pulled and the hole grew.

‘Just a minute,’ Lois snapped the thread and sighed. ‘My one good skirt.’

‘Sorry,’

‘Not your fault.’

Mrs Provoichkin lit a cigarette and seemed immovable.

‘Look, come inside,’ Lois pulled him to her front door and instantly regret the invitation. Her flat would be laughable after his mansion on the harbour.

‘It’s small,’ she fiddled with the troublesome key.

‘I don’t care.’

‘I don’t have...well I don’t have,’ she stepped inside the hot box and he followed.

The gasp he let out made Lois shrink.

‘Bloody hell, it’s hot in here, takes your breath away,’ Douglas began to pant.

‘I can’t open the back door. No through breeze.’

‘Want me to take a look?’

‘No, that’s alright Douglas. I’ll just change.’ Lois flitted out and banged into the door frame. ‘It’s alright. I’m alright.

She took three deep breaths. *Everyone sits down to shit,* she repeated.

'Where do you want the box?'

'Just on the table will be fine.' Douglas put it down and looked at the books left open. All motivational, all designed to build a career, get ahead, succeed. He picked up Amethyst Greenock and began to read.

Lois came out of her bedroom and caught her blouse on the door handle. She unhooked herself, 'ready.'

'Does it help?' Douglas held the book.

'Well, yes it does.' Lois took the book and put it on the table. 'It's not an easy road to the top.'

'And that's where you're headed?'

'I am.' Lois stood her ground.'

'I can see that.' Douglas tapped the book. 'Good luck to you Lois Mackenzie.'

'Thanks.'

'You're lucky. My future is mapped out. No choice, no grand plans. From father to son.' Douglas flicked through the book.

'Just a matter of putting your mind to it.' She dropped her handbag and bent to pick it up as Douglas went to retrieve it and they cracked heads.

'Relax, Lois,' Douglas rubbed his head.

Lois rubbed her burgeoning lump.

'Do you want to see the Craven Christmas Lights?'

The lights were quite festive, but it was the view from the roof that took your breath away. The harbour was visible, the bridge was lit up and as the sun cast it's last golden rays across the view Lois thought, at this point in her life anything was possible.

'I like the view.'

'Me too,' she said hanging onto the railing.

'Lois, can I ask you something?'

When a fellow says something like that a girl is bound to think things. Lois was thinking all sorts of things. She held the rail a bit tighter.

'Of course Douglas.'

'Don't ever change. You are the smartest, funniest, nicest person I have had the pleasure to meet. You're kind. You're generous. You're sympathetic.'

'Douglas.'

'I mean it. Can I count you as a friend? I don't have many. People seem to think...well I...' he trailed off.

'Of course you can.'

'And go for it. The top. Go for it Lois Mackenzie,' he picked her up and whirled her around. It was just a pity her handbag flew over the railing and sailed four stories to the footpath below. It was even more distressing that once they were on the ground floor the bag was gone and with it the only front door key she had.

Breaking into your own home can be a bit tricky when you are in the dark, trying not to make too much noise and the front door refuses to yield to any amount of shoving, pushing, jiggling of wire or cursing.

'It's not working,' Lois whispered.

'Try the back door.' Douglas whispered back.

'That's never worked.' Lois groped to the window and felt for a small gap in the flyscreen. 'Damn, I think I'm bleeding.'

Douglas tried the door again to no avail.

'What now?' Lois said to his right ear.

'Stay at my place?'

'I can't. I'm being picked up early. Mrs Provoichkin is coming and so is my friend from work, you know him, Merritt.'

‘I can get you back in time. And I could bring some tools.’

✦ CHAPTER 26

Waking up in someone else's house, in someone else's pyjamas on Christmas morning at around six a.m. can be quite disorientating. Lois looked at the chintz curtains, the large night stand and the luxurious bed and for a fleeting moment thought she could get accustomed to this type of opulence.

'Lois,' a whisper came through the door.

'Douglas?'

'Merry Christmas,' Douglas knocked.

'Come in,' Lois sat up in bed and fussed with her hair.

'It's six. I thought I should wake you.'

'Thanks. For everything,' Lois smoothed the sheets and felt the morning breeze waft through the open window.

'Breakfast is downstairs. I have my tools.'

People may be a rich as the Queen of England. They may have bone china and a possible Renoir on the wall, but they still eat *Wack-Os* for breakfast.

'Merry Christmas Lois,' Douglas put a little box on the table next her *Wack-Os*.

'I didn't expect anything,' Lois looked at the little box which looked suspiciously like a ring box.

'Open it.'

The wrap was exquisitely done in the oriental style. Lois smiled.

'Mr Moon,' Douglas said.

'Yes.' She peeled back the paper and opened the box.

'Oh.'

'It's a keyring, with a torch.'

'A keyring. With a torch.' Not that she was expecting something else...

'Handy.' Douglas pressed the button. 'See.'

'I think it's just perfect. I always have trouble.' Lois clicked the button. 'Just perfect. Thank you,' She stood up and gave him a kiss on the cheek. 'It's just perfect Douglas.'

'I knew you'd like it,' Douglas helped himself to a bowl of *Wack-Os.*

The streets were near empty at 6:30 and the trip was done in double time. Douglas retrieved his tool bag and headed for the front door of Flat 4 with Lois not far behind.

'You sure you can do it?'

'Yep.' He went to work dismantling the lock while Lois watched.

'Have you done this before? Do you make a habit of dismantling locks and breaking into women's flats?'

'I like tools. Always have done.'

'I can see that,' Lois handed him a screwdriver.

The door finally swung open and hot air rushed out.

'Want me to take a look at the back door?'

'Could you?'

'Sure.' Douglas went to work while Lois took a shower, changed, packed her basket, gathered her bits and pieces and assembled everything on the kitchen table.

'It was a cross threaded screw. All done.' Douglas opened the door and the through breeze ruffled the curtains, the table cloth and took about ten degrees from the room.

'Oh, that's wonderful.'

'Nothing really.' He began to re assemble the front door when Markos drove up.

'Merry Christmas.' Markos bounded over the concrete and watched Douglas work.

'You working on Christmas Day. What happened?'

'Lois lost her key. I'm just helping.'

'Good with the tools are you?'

'I guess.'

'We're short-handed at work. You got a good job?' Markos asked, 'only the boss is looking for a bloke whose handy. A five day week and seven pounds a week. Good money.'

'Well...' Douglas carried on with the job.

'Look, think it over. We build houses all over. What are you doing for Christmas dinner?'

'I'm having it at home.'

'Well, come by later. We can talk about it over a beer. I'm Markos Agridopolous.' Markos held out his hand. Douglas shook it. 'Douglas Craven.'

'See ya later then Dougie.' Markos wrote his address down on a bit of paper.

Douglas looked to Lois.

'Go for it,' she said.

'But...'

'Oh he'll work it out. Aim high.' Lois slapped him on the back.

'Best present ever,' Douglas said. 'Ever.'

'I'll just rustle up Mrs Provoichkin,' Lois scooted over to Flat 3 and knocked as Merritt arrived in a taxi.

'Am I early?' he asked.

There was quite a bit of shifting, organising, packing and getting Mrs Provoichkin and her walker in the car was tricky. In the end the walker was strapped to the roof and they were ready.

Markos stood back and surveyed his pride and joy.

Lois locked the back door and came around the side to see Mr Moon hurrying up the street.

'Miss Mackenzie, Miss Mackenzie,' he called and tottered along.

'Mr Moon.'

'Ah,' he stood puffing from the run. 'Happy Christmas,' he handed over a present.

'Oh, thank you. You didn't need to get me anything.'

'Open now,' Mr Moon said as Markos, Douglas and Merritt looked on. They all stood on the concrete as the sun began its duty for the day and the flies woke up.

'A frying pan,' Lois quizzed.

'A wok. For cooking. For Chinese.'

'A wok?' Lois tried out the foreign word. 'Thank you. It's marvellous.'

'I give Miss Mackenzie lessons. For Chinese cooking. No more mince.'

'Really, lessons.'

'You eat good food yes?'

'Yes.' Lois looked at the wok and then at Mr Moon. Thank you.'

'I see Fridge-o-matic Miss Mackenzie. Is most wonderful gift. Li Moon is most honoured.' He bowed deeply as everyone watched.

'It's the giving, not the getting eh,' Merritt nudged Douglas.

'Sure is.' Douglas put away his tools. Mrs Provoichkin coughed in the front seat of the car, turned a shade of purple and broke the moment.

'Better get crackin'. Mum likes an early start.'

✦ CHAPTER 27

They managed to squeeze one more into the car. Mr Moon sat with Mrs Provoichkin in the back and Merritt, Lois and Markos shared the bench seat in front.

Markos showed off his driving skills, such as they were and threw his passengers this way and that as he rounded corners like a formula 1 driver while lighting a cigarette, looking in the rear view mirror and talking non-stop.

'You're gonna love it. Dad's got it all happening in the back yard.

His passengers hung on for dear life when in due course he stopped out the front of the Agridopolous house and tooted his horn.

There were kids in the street with new bicycles, girls with new prams and dolls, boys with balls, yoyos and cricket bats.

'Come on, Mum's gonna love this.' Markos led the way as Merritt helped Mrs Provoichkin up the garden path.

'Ah, hello, hello,' Mrs A came out to greet her guests with a tea towel in her hand. 'Come, come.'

'Lois,' Serg stood with a couple of folding chairs under his arms.

'Serg,' she took a chair and set it on the lawn.

'Lois.' Daphnie smiled. Helen and Adele came in for a friendly continental kiss on each cheek. 'Happy Christmas,' they chorused.

‘And to you,’ Lois looked around at the family atmosphere, the people and thought this just might be the best Christmas she had had in a long time.

‘Ah,’ Mr A slapped her on the back and then linked arms. ‘We was-a waiting for you.’ He led her to a trestle table and sat her down. ‘Ephima, Ephima, you come. éla, éla,’

Mrs A came out of the kitchen and stood next to her husband. All the family gathered around, Merritt bringing Mrs Provoichkin and Mr Moon and sat them down.

‘Now, we have all together.’ Mr A puffed out his chest.

‘Now?’ Serg asked.

‘Now. We give the presents.’ ‘I don’t know much,’ Mr A said, ‘but I know this,’ he spread his hands wide over the assembled family and friends. ‘We all good here. Is good for everybody.’

There was a cheer.

There were cardigans, stockings, socks, handkerchiefs and scarves, car sponges, a new lunch box and Mrs A was given a shopping basket on wheels. She gave it a whirl in the garden to the delight of the audience.

Lois called for quiet.

‘Thank you for inviting me. She looked over the friendly faces. ‘And thank you for welcoming my friends,’ she looked at Mr Moon and Mrs Provoichkin.

‘All welcome here,’ Mr A said and slapped Mr Moon on the back.

‘For you Mr and Mrs A.’ Lois put a box on the table and Mrs A opened it.

‘Mangos?’ Mr A said.

‘From Queensland. My parents sent them. You are welcome to stay at their house any time.

‘Is Queensland.’ Mr A wiped a tear from his eye. He told everyone they had bananas you could eat, straight from the tree. Mrs A picked up a mango and sniffed.

'Like this,' Lois opened one by slitting in lengthwise and then criss-crossing the cheek of the fruit.

'Oh,' Mrs A took a bite. 'Is good.'

'Mrs A,' Lois held an envelope out.

'For me?' She opened the envelope. There was an autographed photo of the Bishop.'

'Oh.' She held it up for all to see.

'Markos.' Lois said.

He held a figurine of a dragon.

'To hang from your rear-view mirror,' Lois explained.

To the sisters she handed each an envelope.

'What it say?' Mrs A asked.

'An invitation to use her flat,' if they wanted a bit of privacy in exchange for cooking lessons. The sisters beamed. Daphnie and Christina gave Lois a kiss. '

'Serg,' Lois gave him an envelope.

'What it say?' Mrs A waved her tea towel at a fly.

'A promise,' Serg read, 'to make a meat pie from scratch.' Mrs A nodded in approval.

'Mrs Provoichkin,' Lois passed over a box.

'Well,' Mrs Provoichkin looked at the wrapping in the Oriental style. 'A cigarette holder,' she coughed and smiled. I had one once, like Bette Davis.

'I know, I saw it in the photo when I was in your flat,' Lois smiled.

'Is all good. Is the giving, not the getting,' Mr A said.

'Dad!' the girls laughed.

'Lois,' Serg stood to attention. 'For you.'

'Mrs A came out with a large box.' 'For you,' she said and kissed Lois on the cheek then shooshed a fly away with her tea towel.

There was a wooden spoon. An egg beater, a chopping board and a sharp knife.

'Mum thinks you can't cook,' Serg said.

'She's right about that.'

The morning progressed with the kitchen taking centre stage as Mrs A flitted in and out with food. Drinks were imbibed, fly swats were put to good use and they listened to Mr A's dream of moving his family to Queensland where the bananas can be picked straight from the tree and they never have a winter.

It was around eleven o'clock when Serg let out a holey shamoley and yelled, 'ham.'

'We have,' Mrs A said.

'The Bishop's ham.'

✦

Bishop O'Leary had some recollection of his bright idea. He recollected he thought it was brilliant. Beyond that it was just a blur.

'Er, just wondering, did I jot anything down yesterday, in the way of jotting down something.' Father Aspinall took a deep breath. He'd been to morning service and fortified his soul. He'd had a beaut breakfast with Mrs Cooper and fortified his stomach, and now he took the leap.

'Your Grace?'

'Just thought I might have put my thoughts on paper.'

'You said that you thought it was a grand idea to show the public your magnanimous nature this Christmas.'

'Did I?'

'Yes Your Grace.'

'And what did I think was a fitting example?'

'You,' Jeremy thought of Mrs Cooper, Mrs Brewster and the photographer that was coming at one o'clock.

'You decided that you would share your gracious bounty with Archbishop Bothom as he has generously loaned his refrigerator.'

'Did I?'

'Yes Your Grace. You said it would show a level of unity and it wouldn't hurt to show the Anglicans the Catholics do things a little...a little differently.'

'Style.'

'That's it. With panache I think you said.'

'Did I?'

'Yes Your Grace.' Jeremy looked at his watch. 'I believe we, that is, you are expected at eleven o'clock.'

'Am I?'

'Mrs Cooper is supervising the lunch as we speak.'

'Is she.'

'Yes Your Grace.'

'Well. I do recollect now. Just the minor details slipped my mind.'

'Oh, and you suggested a photographic souvenir of the moment. I think you suggested a photographer at one o'clock.'

'Yes, I think that was mentioned.' The Bishop looked at the clock in the hall. 'See if you can find those trousers with the expanding gusset will you.'

'Yes Your Grace.'

Archbishop Bothom looked at the contents of the fridge and poked at the red current fool.

'All good Mrs Brewster?'

'Yes Your Grace.'

Mrs Cooper came out from the pantry and curtseyed in deference.

'Mrs Cooper is it?'

'Yes Your Grace. Very kind of you.'

'Well, it's Christmas after all,' Renwick picked a jam tart off the table and popped it in his mouth. 'Wee awwwl got to dooo our parrrrt,' he said. He eyes widened as Mrs Cooper set a bottle of Scotch whisky on the table.

'The Bishop likes a tipple before lunch.'

'I'll take it in shall I,' Renwick wiped the crumbs from his mouth, grabbed the neck of the bottle and strode out of the kitchen like a man who knows his cut glass from his lead crystal.

*

'Ah,' Niall O'Leary spied the bottle of whisky on the sideboard and thought, although Anglican he had good taste in whisky.

'Help yourself,' Renwick said.

'Don't mind if I do.' Niall poured. 'This is my preferred bottle too.'

Decorum prevented Renwick from divulging the nature of the misconception.

'Well, here's to a cracking Christmas.' Niall held his glass aloft.

'Absolutely,' Renwick concurred. And the two men of the cloth got down to business.

'Do you like cricket?' Niall asked as they sat down near the open window to catch what little breeze stirred the air.

'Cricket. Well I did play when I was in college.'

'There is a cricket match on Boxing Day. First one apparently. Some sort of live wire from the Melbourne Cricket Ground. On the radio.'

'Really.'

'Should be good. I have a wireless set. Do you fancy a bit of turkey on Boxing day?'

Renwick thought over the proposal for a second. 'That sounds like a plan.'

'Splendid.' Niall sat back and looked over the room. 'Cosy,' he said.

‘Yes, we like to keep it simple.’ Anglicans can put a spin on almost anything given the right motivation. There was a commonality, after all they had the same CEO, but just work in different departments.

‘Another Your Grace?’

‘Don’t mind if I do Your Grace.’ Ecclesiastical humour can be a bit dry, but there is not much to work with when your stock in trade is saving souls.

The Bishops were interrupted by Mrs Brewster.

‘If you’d be so kind.’ She pointed to the dining room.

‘Splendid.’

‘It was over turkey that Renwick pointed his fork at his guest and said, ‘I though your handling of the ‘affair’ rather good.’

‘Affair,’ Niall asked with a mouth full of roast potato.

‘The, um, the hot potato.’

‘Ah. My idea actually. Went rather well. I have my ear to the ground on these things.’

‘Yes, we need to be right on the ball.’ Renwick said

‘Absolutely otherwise a sticky wicket. Of course, it left us in a bit of a pickle, vis-à-vis the refrigerator, but, well, isn’t this jolly. We can all get along Renwick. What do you say?’

‘A bit of red wine?’

‘Don’t mind if I do. This is all rather nice. We can all get along eh?’

‘Oh, absolutely Niall. Absolutely. I mean we are but one religion under the eye of the Lord. No-one has gone to war over religion.’

Hubris and alcohol are a heady mix. Goodwill to all men (and women) overrides history apparently.

'I don't know why we didn't think of it earlier. Jolly pleasant. Clear the air.' Niall helped himself to more brussels sprouts.

'Correct me if I'm in error Renwick, but I think Mrs Cooper has made a red currant fool. My favourite.'

'A red currant fool,' Renwick repeated.

'After the pudding of course.' Niall said. 'Got to have the pudding first.'

'Absolutely.' Renwick knocked back another glass of red. He would have acceded to a horseradish trifle with onion custard if there was red currant fool for afters washed down with the finest scotch whisky the Bishop Niall O'Leary of St Cuthbert's in the diocese of Waverly could muster.

*

'Another tipple Erma?'

'Don't mind if I do,' Mildred.

The women sat back and put the world to rights, when there was a knock at the door.

'Now who could that be?' Mildred opened the door. 'Oh, Father Aspinall.' She stood back and Jeremy came in and sat down at the kitchen table.

'Sorry, I'm late. I was helping at the Salvation Army kitchen. Bit busy. It's a stinker of a day. Hot as blazes. We had one woman faint on the gravy line.'

'Sit down Father,' I'll get you a plate.' Those words were better than six Hail Mary's

'Thank you Erma.' Jeremy watched as his plate was piled with the trappings of a Christmas dinner. He was just about to get stuck in when he remembered the ham.

'Oh my Lord, the ham.' He might very well said 'the ham' but without transport, (a bicycle just didn't make the grade) the retrieval was nigh on impossible.

'A car?'

The three looked at one another. Jeremy closed his eyes.

'Pray Father, like your life depends upon it.' Erma said.

A knock at the door once again interrupted their lunch.

'Who could it be now?'

And his prayer was answered.

'Sorry,' Serg smiled and deposited the ham on the kitchen table. 'Forgot it.'

'Never mind. You're here now.' The ladies looked at the ginormous leg, then at Father Aspinall. If it was God, he had impeccable timing.

'It'll never fit,' Mrs Brewster looked at the pig then at the fridge.

'Erma?' Mildred said.

'Mildred?' Erma supped her sherry.

'How many have you sitting down at your table?'

'Thirteen I think.'

The women looked at Serg, when there was a knock at the door.

'It's like a train station today,' Mildred opened the door to find Miss Kelly and her photographer standing and smiling.

'From the paper. A picture of the two Bishop's at Christmas.'

'Oh.' Erma looked at Mildred. A photograph of the two gastronomes enjoying festive cheer wouldn't go down particularly well with the man (or woman) on the street, when most people were ... well, it wouldn't exactly look like they had their fingers on the pulse of life in the parish of Waverley.

'Could you wait a bit?' Mildred asked.

'Well...'

'Sit down,'

Jeremy scooted over and Miss Kelly sat and the fellow she was fond of prodding with her finger sat beside her. Two more Christmas dinners were served.

'And the ham?' Serg wanted to get back to his Christmas.

'Keep it, and Happy Christmas to you.'

'What's that then?' Miss Kelly asked.

'The Bishop thought that he would make amends.'

'To who?' Miss Kelly asked. Reporters have the knack of the who, what, where, when and why.

'To Miss Mackenzie,' Serg blurted. 'She's at our Christmas dinner. Smoteth and all that,' he added for flavour.

'Oh, Lois Mackenzie,' Miss Kelly pulled out her pad and wrote it down. 'Where?'

Serg furnished her with the address and Miss Kelly prodded her photographer who was eating his turkey. He stopped long enough to take a photo of the leg of ham.

'Well, thanks, I'll be off now.' Serg hoisted the leg on his shoulder and let himself out.

'Such a nice man, Erma said. 'It's the giving, not the getting,' she chuckled.

'Yes, such a nice man,' Mildred added and poured gravy for Jeremy, Duncan, the photographer and Miss Kelly.

⌘

Mrs A upon seeing the ham and hearing the explanation was under the mistaken impression the Bishop had blessed it. Therefore it was sacred. She said a prayer of thanks and it was put on the table under a fly screen.

✦ CHAPTER 28

A trestle table is a marvellous thing. It can hold the biggest ham this side of the black stump. A turkey cooked to perfection. A salad that could fit in a baby's bath. Bread to feed a multitude and all manner of vegetables, fried, baked, roasted, mashed, boiled and steamed. Then there were the traditional Greek dishes. Mrs A had been busy. Daphnie, Adele, Helen, Christina, Markos, Serg and Christos had mucked in and the Christmas feast was the result.

With her tea towel flicking over the food, Mrs A called everyone to sit.

'Mr Moon,' Mr A said, 'You sit here, I want to talk.' Mr A patted a chair to his right.

'Christos,' Mrs A called and her husband stood up and cleared his throat as people waved the flies away.

'It is,' he began, 'It is good. Ephema is the best cook. My wife.' He pointed to Mrs A and blew her a kiss. 'Is the best Christmas.' He sat down.

A cheer went up and plates were passed around. Lois piled Mrs Provoichkins plate and made sure she had a bit of everything.

'It's very nice, isn't it.' Mrs Provoichkin coughed. 'Wesołych Świąt,' she said in Polish. 'Merry Christmas.'

‘Is good to be Australian.’ Mr Moon said. ‘Shèngdàn kuàilè,’ he added in Chinese. ‘Is happy Christmas.’

‘Is good to be an Australian,’ Mr A said with a mouthful of turkey. ‘Kalá Christoúgenna, is Merry Christmas.’

‘So, you’re not Greek then?’ Merritt asked.

‘Merritt, he means now. It’s good to be an Australian now. He’s still Greek heritage.’

‘Oh.’ Merritt held up his beer. ‘To an Australian tradition.’

A toast went around the table.

‘It’s 100 bloody degrees in the flippin’ shade,’ Markos added and a ripple of good cheer went around the table.

A toot from a car made everyone turn and Miss Kelly waved as Duncan parked.

‘I invited them,’ Serg shrugged to his mother.

‘Get chairs Serg.’

It’s not often you get to eat two Christmas dinners back to back. Duncan was up to the challenge. Erin Kelly took a deep breath and let out her belt.

‘In Ireland we say, Nollaig shona. Merry Christmas everyone.’ Erin poked Duncan to take a photo worthy of the front page.

✦

The first wave of eating was over and bodies lounged around in the shade, replete.

‘Lois,’

‘Hmm?’

‘This is the meaning of Christmas.’ Serg held her hand.

‘QED, Lois said.

‘What’s that,’ Merritt asked.

‘Quod erat demonstrandum,’ Lois said. ‘The proof of the argument is complete.’

She looked around at the family, her friends and said,

‘That you’ve proved something that you wanted to prove.’

‘That the light stays on?’ Merritt asked.

‘The meaning of Christmas,’ Lois said and waved a fly away.

Reviews help authors enormously. If you feel so inclined it would be much appreciated.

My other titles and all the hoo-ha can be found here.

www.linktr.ee/hettieashwin
https://mybook.to/LAUGHOUTLOUD

www.ingramcontent.com/pod-product-compliance
Lightning Source LLC
LaVergne TN
LVHW020708110826
845149LV00012B/2167

* 9 7 8 2 4 9 1 4 9 0 3 4 8 *